You X
Young, Laura.
Killer looks

$ 23.95

W9-CJL-080

Killer Looks

Laura Young

An Imprint of
The Overmountain Press
JOHNSON CITY, TENNESSEE

This book is a work of fiction. All names, characters, places, and events are either the product of the author's imagination or are used fictitiously. Any resemblance to actual events or persons, living or dead, is entirely coincidental and beyond the intent of either the author or the publisher.

For Mom and Aunt Lavin, with love

Acknowledgements

Making a dream come true takes the help of many people. I am forever thankful for the support and friendship of Alison Shaw. Without your enthusiasm, encouragement, and insistence on meeting deadlines, this book would never have happened.

As a freshman author, I am extremely grateful for the support and guidance of those who have gone before me, particularly author Dianne Aprile and the "quad of trios"—authors Julie Wray Herman, Barbara Taylor McCafferty, Beverly Taylor Herald, and Sara Hoskinson Frommer. You showed me how to make it work.

To the entire "crew" who assisted with the 25th-hour "title crisis," my smiling thanks. Toss in a box of chocolates, too, (you know what to do with them) to Bill Workman and Terri and Brian Pulford and their family for the new title.

For going above and beyond the call of friendship, I send big hugs to Chris Vale, Rita Priddy, Elaine Munsch, and Molly Wolfram. And, of course, my love to Mom, who put that first mystery in my hands all those years ago. This one's for you.

And, to the great people at Silver Dagger—Beth, Karin, and Sherry—thanks for making that dream come true.

Chapter 1

THEY SAY you can never go home again. Maybe it's not so much that you can't go home again, but that getting there isn't always easy. I found that out a few weeks ago when I made an unscheduled detour. Initially, I planned on a quiet, relaxing week at my parents' house, but I soon discovered getting there was murder.

My name is Kate Kelly. I'm a writer for a Washington-based travel magazine called, appropriately, *Travel Adventures*. I'm constantly on the go these days, covering all sorts of interesting and sometimes not-so-interesting little towns, restaurants, and tourist stops. My latest adventure found me in the Hoosier state of Indiana, soaking in the sights and sounds of the annual Madison Powerboat Regatta. I spent the weekend crafting "A Reader's Guide to the Regatta," then quickly packed my notebooks and camera and headed for the airport.

I've been working a great deal lately, so I took advantage of a few deserved days off in my hometown of Williamsburg, Virginia. The flight to Richmond was short, rating only a package of stale pretzels and a watered-down Coke. Once safely on the ground, I grabbed the keys to my rental car and hit the highway.

That's where the trouble began.

"She's coming around, Doctor," a voice said.

I was awash in bright lights and lots of hustle and bustle. I blinked my eyes and tried to focus.

"Welcome back to the living," a deep voice said. Either I was having one hell of a dream or I had just awakened to *GQ*'s answer to the medical profession. He was in his mid-thirties, with wavy black hair and huge chocolate-colored eyes that could melt ice. He was tall and ruggedly handsome, with a gleaming Pepsodent smile and the fine angular nose of a Greek god.

My hormonal rages aside, it dawned on me that I was the object of all this attention. A throbbing ache pulsated through my body and landed with a deafening thud in my head. It was not the general feeling I hoped to have as I stared at Dr. Handsome.

"You're going to be just fine," he continued. "These nice people are going to take good care of you."

Perhaps it was a dumb question, but I asked anyway. "What happened?"

Dr. Handsome responded by flashing a penlight in my eyes. "You and your car had a little disagreement." He clicked off the blinding glare. "The car won. Now, what do you say we provide you with a nice room for the night with a lovely oceanfront view?"

"Oh, please," grunted a nurse, who looked like she had eaten one too many Twinkies in her time. "She has a concussion, but she's not delirious."

He shrugged. "Okay, so it's not an oceanfront view. Will you settle for the fountain in the parking lot?" He scribbled some notes. "I'll be up to check on you later. Try to get some rest."

I must have followed his instructions, because I don't remember anything else until I woke up in a small, antiseptic hospital room.

He was right; it wasn't exactly the Ritz-Carlton. It was your basic hospital room, with a lumpy bed, two horribly uncomfortable chairs, walls painted the color of wilted lettuce, and one small window covered in a faded chintz curtain that would surely offend Martha Stewart.

My raging headache was still rapping against my temples, but a quick observation concluded that despite being tethered to an IV drip, I was in one piece. I still had all my fingers and toes, and I didn't have any broken bones.

My personal medical evaluation was interrupted by a tap on my door. It was Dr. Handsome. He wore snug, faded jeans with a jade knit polo shirt under his white lab coat. He peeked into a folder and settled on the corner of my bed.

Now, that's what I call a good bedside manner.

"So, Katherine Kelly, we meet again. How are you feeling?"

With this beautiful specimen of manhood sitting willingly on my bed, I should have spouted something eloquent, but all I managed was a decidedly plebeian "Fine. Kate. Please call me Kate."

He smiled and made another note in his folder. He shoved his pen into the back pocket of his jeans. "Please excuse the way I look. I was on call tonight. I usually look a little better than this. I'm Dr. Donovan—John."

I thought he looked fabulous. "Well, Dr. Donovan—John—I hate to be a pest, but could you please tell me how I got here?"

"You're not a pest. A little memory loss is quite common with a concussion. As I understand it, someone hit your car from behind, and it went off the road and took a bite out of one of Virginia's finer trees. In fact, there's an officer here who would like to ask you a few questions about the accident. Are you up to seeing him for a few minutes?"

Something told me I didn't have much of a choice. Funny how it's like that with the police.

"Sure, send him in."

John walked to the door and turned around. "Is there anyone who should know you're here? A husband? Boyfriend?"

I put on the best smile I could muster. "Unfortunately, no on both accounts."

He smiled. That was encouraging.

"I guess my father should be called. I was on my way to visit him in Williamsburg. He's a professor at William & Mary. His name is Jim Kelly, and he's probably home by now."

John winked and my heart rate fluttered dangerously off course. "I'll see he's notified. I'll get the sheriff."

I watched him walk out of the room and wondered where he'd been all my life. That was a good question, because it dawned on me that I didn't know where I was. I looked around the room unsuccessfully for some clue to my whereabouts. On a hunch, I tugged on the night-stand drawer next to my bed. Inside, I found a colorful brochure welcoming me to Woodbury Memorial Hospital. From what I could recall, Woodbury was about a half-hour drive from Williamsburg.

The door opened, and John returned with the sheriff. He was a tall, rotund, African-American in his late forties, with a presence so imposing that I doubted he needed a gun. From the looks of him, I imagined a growl was the only weapon he carried.

However, from this ferocious-looking lawman came a voice as smooth as whipped cream on a sultry summer night. "Good evening, Miss Kelly. Doc here says you're up to answering some questions." He took off his tan cap. "I'm Sheriff Bowman Thompson."

John leaned against the windowsill and watched as the sheriff pulled a silver pen from his chest pocket and began scribbling on an accident report.

Sheriff Thompson looked down at me. "Miss Kelly, what exactly can you tell me about your accident?"

I shrugged. "Unfortunately, not much. The last thing I remember is driving down the highway, thinking I was almost home. Honestly, I can't recall the actual accident, but—"

The sheriff interrupted. "Miss Kelly, you just said you were 'almost home.' Now, according to your license, you hail from Washington. Woodbury is quite a distance from D.C."

"I do live in D.C., Sheriff. I was on my way to visit my parents' home in Williamsburg. I flew into Richmond this evening."

He nodded and made a note. "You felt the need to fly to Richmond from Washington?"

This was getting tedious. "I was arriving on a flight from Indiana. I'm a writer for a travel magazine based in Washington. If you must know, I was covering hydroplane races in Madison, Indiana. I have a few days left before I'm due back in D.C."

Sheriff Thompson's head bobbed. "Does your magazine have a name?"

What difference did that make? Was he looking for reading suggestions for the next stakeout?

"It's called *Travel Adventures*."

John perked up. "I've read that magazine. Do you write those feature articles? I love those."

I smiled at my dear doctor. There's no better medicine for a writer than to hear someone say he enjoyed a story.

The sheriff looked less than enthralled. He shifted his ample frame onto one foot. "Miss Kelly, does your magazine pay you well?"

"Excuse me?"

"Did you have a reason to be carrying a large amount of cash with you?"

His last question made me chuckle as I thought of the vast reserves of money in my purse. I had maybe $15 in my wallet, an untold amount of change hibernating in the deepest recesses of my purse, and a company credit card that I'd used in Madison. There was also my checkbook, but its contents weren't worth discussing.

"The answer is no," I said, "but I'm afraid I don't see the relevancy of your question."

Thompson apparently found merit in it. He looked at John, then slowly turned his gaze toward me. "What about your luggage? Did you have anything valuable in it?"

"Just some camera equipment," I said, suddenly filled with the sick vision of a week's worth of film destroyed or lost. "Where is my luggage? Did something happen to it?"

Thompson completely ignored me. "Were you traveling alone, Miss Kelly?"

This time John interrupted before I morphed into Kate the Banshee. "Sheriff, is there something we should know? You're asking a lot of questions. Miss Kelly has had a rough evening. I don't think she needs to be upset any further."

The sheriff obviously didn't appreciate our curiosity over his line of questioning. He swept a look from John to me that said it all. It was the same expression you see when you roll down your car window after being pulled over for doing 55 mph in a school zone and say, "Is there a problem, officer?"

The sheriff returned his gaze to John. "I'm merely trying to establish the events of this evening's accident, Doctor. The way it happened just doesn't add up correctly in my mind. It's my job to put together the entire story." He turned back to me. "Being a writer, Miss Kelly, I'm sure you can appreciate that."

I nodded. "I do, Sheriff, but honestly, I've told you everything that I can possibly remember. My flight arrived at 8:30 P.M., and I rented a car at the airport, tossed my luggage in the backseat, and headed for Williamsburg. There wasn't much traffic on the interstate, just a car here and there. It must have happened very quickly, because I can't remember being run off the road. I'm sure I didn't fall asleep at the wheel."

"Oh, you didn't fall asleep," Thompson interjected. "There was enough damage to the back of the car to see very plainly that someone hit you at a fairly high rate of speed." He cocked his head to one side. "You say you tossed your luggage into the backseat?"

There was the question about my luggage again. I was really beginning to worry that something dreadful had happened to the material for my article on Madison. My editor would just love that.

"I only had one suitcase and a carry-on bag filled with camera equipment. I didn't see a need to open the trunk," I explained, "so I just tossed everything in the backseat."

Thompson rested his clipboard on his hip and scratched his chin thoughtfully. After a long silence, he apparently decided that I was telling the truth. He began to speak but, instead, sighed deeply. He paused and said, "Miss Kelly, I'm afraid I've never read your magazine. Have you recently written anything that would upset someone enough that they'd want to hurt you?"

His question stunned me. I'm hardly among the ranks of investigative journalists like Morley Safer or Bob Woodward. The majority of articles I pen for *Travel Adventures* amount to fluff pieces about great resorts, sinfully delicious restaurants, and historical hideaways. Of course, some day I aspire to lock myself away and write the great American novel, but for now, this pays the bills. And let's face it, I travel to dozens of expensive vacation spots and charge everything to my employer. How many people can do that?

I smiled. "Why no, unless I trashed some rule of etiquette on how to serve high tea at the governor's mansion."

John laughed out loud. Even the sheriff cracked a smile, but when I thought about what he was implying, I failed to see what was so funny about being purposely run off the road.

Thompson realized that he was smiling and quickly retreated into his grim lawman stance. "When my officers arrived on the scene, there were no skid marks on the road, just your car resting against a tree at the bottom of a small ravine. However, there were indentations in the grass around the car which could be construed as footprints."

He paused and addressed John. "Now, since they also found Miss Kelly here unconscious and still strapped into her seat belt, that makes it pretty safe to assume that someone else was there first."

Brilliant deduction. I'm sure he'll be heading up the FBI any day now.

"I can assure you that I was alone, Sheriff. Could it have been someone who lived in the area? Maybe they found the car and reported the accident?"

Thompson shook his head. "No, one of my deputies on patrol came across the scene. The area where you landed is part of a state forest. There are no houses or people for miles around." He frowned. "When you look at the scene, the most logical assumption is that you were struck from behind and your car barreled straight off the road and continued until it hit the tree. However, we found your luggage open and strewn about the site some fifteen to twenty feet away from the car."

That news made my head pound harder. Don't get me wrong. Madison, Indiana, is a nice little town, but I'm not exactly a hydroplane enthusiast. The thought that I probably just wasted a week pretending to enjoy earsplitting engines roaring down the Ohio River and interviewing drunken, sunburned spectators wearing nothing but neon shorts and Budweiser baseball caps made me dizzy.

I hated to ask. "Was anything missing or destroyed?"

Thompson sensed my dread. "Well, that's something you'll have to tell us. We found clothes and two cameras with various attachments, all of which seem to be in reasonable shape. However, your trunk was pried open. It was empty with the exception of two $100 bills. We found something else in the grass under the back bumper."

Sheriff Bowman Thompson straightened his bulky, six-foot-three frame and looked directly at me. "We found six wrapped stacks of $100 bills. That's a great deal of money to be hauling around in your car trunk. Can you explain where that came from, Miss Kelly?"

Any medication that was floating around in my veins ceased to work. I was fully awake and alert. "Of course I have no idea where that came from. Like I told you, I never bothered to open the trunk. It was a rental car for a very short trip. Believe me, I don't carry money like that with me. What do you think I did, rob a bank?"

He raised an eyebrow. "I don't know, did you?"

John walked to my bed. "Sheriff, it's late. Can't this wait until morning?" He stood very straight and tried to match Thompson's statuesque height. He missed by a few inches. "As Miss Kelly's physician, I'm asking you to postpone this until she's had the chance to rest."

My hero.

Thompson returned a chilly stare. "All right," he capitulated. "I don't like the way this accident smells. You can be assured that I'll get to the bottom of this."

"I'm sure you will, Sheriff," I said. He promptly put his tan hat on again and stalked out the door without as much as a good-bye.

John watched the door snap shut and shook his head. "I'm sorry about that. I had no idea he'd be that gruff. I'm sure he meant no harm." He rested his hand on my arm. "Don't worry about all that stuff he was implying. There's got to be a logical explanation. Things will be much clearer in the morning."

He smiled and squeezed my hand. "Let's call it a night. I'll be back in the morning to check on you. Sweet dreams." He smiled again, clicked off the light, and slipped out the door. Quite a charmer, my Dr. Donovan.

I stared at the ceiling, trying to remember my drive down the freeway, but came up with nothing out of the ordinary. It had been a long week in the fine state of Indiana, and I was eager to wrap up the story and move on to something more interesting. All I had been concentrating on was reaching Williamsburg, where I could spend the rest of my time off wallowing in the comforts of my childhood home.

Growing up with a history-professor father, as a kid I could spout the saga of the colonies before I could quote Dr. Seuss stories. My mother is a political columnist for the *Virginia Tribune*, so it's pretty obvious I was doomed from the start to combine those influences and become a journalist covering what mostly amounts to historical vacation spots.

It also meant that I grew up in a wonderful Victorian house packed to the rafters with books and antiques and covered on the outside with ivy and climbing wisteria vines. I thought of my comfortable old brass bed there as I shifted in my lumpy hospital bed and tried to avoid a stubborn spring that was intent on poking me in the back. I would have been much happier wrapped in a down comforter at home.

A soft patter of rain tap-danced on the window across the room and helped lull me to sleep. I had been asleep only a short while when I felt something bump my bed. A moment later the plastic cup on the bedside table crashed to the floor with a loud rattle. I rolled over just in time to see the back of a man in a dark suit sprinting out the door.

I glanced at the clock on the wall—2:40 A.M. I've heard of nurses popping in and out of a patient's room during the night, but something told me visiting hours for men in dark suits were over long ago. He must have picked the wrong room.

The rain continued overnight and was occasionally peppered with small rolls of thunder. The storm woke me once, and I opened my eyes to check the time again and found more than just the echoes of thunder occupying my room.

The shadow of a man towered over my bed.

Chapter 2

"WELL, KIDDO, you seem to go to great lengths to get attention around here." It was the unmistakable voice of my dad, Professor Jim Kelly.

"It's not that I'm trying to get attention," I said slowly. "It's just that I like to make dramatic entrances."

Dad made a face and pulled off his glasses. He whipped out a monogrammed white handkerchief, then polished the lenses. "Your flair for the dramatic has outdone itself this time, my dear Katherine. A simple 'Surprise, Dad, I'm home' would have sufficed."

He often comes across as a crusty curmudgeon, but I know that underneath the façade that strikes fear in the hearts of students is a great guy with a wonderful sense of humor. He's also one of the few people who can call me "kiddo" and "Katherine" and live to tell about it.

"I would have been here sooner," he continued, "but I didn't find out about your accident until nearly midnight. I was at my office until after eleven tutoring a few fraternity kids about the French Resistance."

He shook his head and perched his glasses on the bridge of his nose. "Would you believe one of those boys actually asked if Humphrey Bogart was able to keep Rick's Café in Casablanca open after the war? Amazing what an athletic scholarship can produce.

"Anyway, when I got home, there was a message on the answering machine from the hospital. I called and they patched me through to a Dr. Donovan, who said you were doing just fine. I was going to come straight over, but he thought it would be best to let you sleep. So here I am, up with the sun, to see what kind of a scrape you've gotten into this time."

"You haven't told Mom about this, have you? She'll worry herself to death over nothing."

"Well, I had to tell her. She called sometime after midnight, angry that we hadn't called her in Louisiana to say hello." He chuckled. "Her story is going well down there. She's following up on a local council-man who's busying himself with more than local issues." A devilish grin that I knew very well crept across his face. "I told her you should be down there as her partner. You could combine your talents and have quite a story—'Councilman Jenkins was caught explaining matters of state to several eager young women in the depths of the French Quarter last evening. The councilman was deeply under the influence of Jack Daniel's and Cajun shrimp, which was delightfully prepared by master chef Rocco Sleaze at the Hotel de Call Girl. The hostesses are quite friendly and offer room rates at various prices per night.'"

I was recovering from a fit of giggles when John opened the door. "I like to hear laughter when I'm entering a patient's room. That means you're feeling better."

"Much better," I answered.

I hadn't been dreaming, John still looked great. His jeans and polo shirt were replaced by khaki slacks and a pale yellow button-down shirt. A hastily knotted navy tie bunched up under the stethoscope slung around his neck.

He smiled and reached for Dad's hand and said, "You must be Professor Kelly. I'm Dr. Donovan. We spoke last night."

Dad raised an eyebrow and stared quizzically at John. I knew what was coming. "You're Dr. Donovan? You look like one of my students. How long have you been practicing medicine?"

"Long enough." John gently brushed aside an unruly wisp of my bangs and ran his hand across my forehead. "Nice bruise you've got there. I'd say you were conked pretty well in the noggin last night."

Dad raised his voice. "Conked in the noggin?"

"I'm sorry, Professor. Your daughter sustained considerable trauma to the frontal region of her cranium, resulting in a significant hematoma and a mild concussion."

Dad's face screwed up in the expression he usually reserves for conferences with students who average a D or F.

I thought it was best to intervene. "Truce, gentlemen. I am feeling much better this morning. I think the question of the day should be *When can I go home?*"

"Well," John began, "there aren't any complications, so if you can promise me you'll take it easy for the next few days, you can go home today."

"I'll make sure she gets some rest, Doctor," Dad said.

I ignored Dad and tried to flirt with a headache. "No offense," I said to John, "this is a really nice hospital, but what time can I blow this popsicle stand?"

I thought I was being devastatingly clever. Dad thought I was being devastatingly juvenile. "I'm not so sure this concussion didn't interfere with her maturity and vocabulary. Maybe you should do some further tests."

John laughed. "Not necessary. By the time the discharge papers make their rounds through the red-tape department, you're looking at about 11:30 or noon before you can go home."

Dad frowned. "That's not good. I have lecture classes at 10:00 and 11:30, then I have a meeting with the dean about my budget."

That was not what I wanted to hear. "I could take a cab home."

"Oh, no," John said hastily. "I couldn't let you do that." He paused, then tentatively looked at Dad. "If you wouldn't mind, I have this afternoon free anyway. I'd be happy to see that she got home."

Dad's eyes grew larger. He looked ready to comment, but I seized the chance to interrupt. "That would be very nice of you, Dr. Donovan. Isn't that nice of him to offer, Dad?"

He stood there, hands on hips and eyebrows raised, obviously struggling with the fact that I wasn't 19 anymore. Try adding ten years on that. "All right," he said, "but I want you to call my office the minute you get home." Dad looked at John, then trained his fatherly raised eyebrow on me again. "And I expect you to heed the doctor's orders and spend the afternoon resting—alone."

I've always been amazed that despite the fact I've lived on my own for eight years, have a master's degree in journalism, and have spent the last three years traveling the country alone on assignment, I still feel like a teenager when my dad zings that raised eyebrow my way. I guess it's something you never outgrow.

"Don't worry, Professor Kelly," John replied. "Your daughter is in good hands."

I fought a smile as I thought of the prospect of being in his "good hands."

John cleared his throat. "I need to get moving. It was a pleasure to meet you, Professor Kelly. I'm sure we'll see each other soon."

Dad begrudgingly shook John's outstretched hand. "Nice to meet you too, Doctor. Drive safely and have my daughter home at a reasonable hour."

I felt like I was getting ready to leave for the prom. "Dad, please," I groaned.

John grinned and winked as he headed out the door. "I'll be back soon."

Dad stayed with me for another hour, and I told him about my visit with Sheriff Thompson. He didn't like the news. "Why would someone run you off the road? You shouldn't be traveling alone at night."

"Dad, this could have happened in broad daylight," I said. "I'm sure it was just a freak accident."

He shook his head. "I don't know. What about the money in the trunk and the tampered luggage? I don't even want to think what could have happened."

My clumsy overnight visitor popped in my mind. Was he connected to my accident? No, why worry about something that didn't turn ugly? My imagination was working overtime.

"Dad," I said, "don't worry about it so much. I can't spend my life locked away in an ivory tower."

"That might not be a bad idea." He stood and bent over to kiss my forehead. "Whether you like it or not, kiddo, you'll always be my little girl. It's my God-given right as a father to worry as much as I want." He reached for his navy blazer.

Most of my professors in college tended to favor jeans and sloppy sweaters. Dad was from the old school. I can't remember a day when he didn't head off to the university without wearing a coat and tie.

He adjusted his gold initialed cufflinks and said, "I've got to get to work. Rooms of eager young college students await my arrival so I may fill their empty little heads with the wisdom of centuries. Don't forget to call me when your handsome young doctor finally gets you home."

I promised I would obey his instructions, then said good-bye. My poor parents. If Dad wasn't busy fending off the evils of men descending around his only child, my mother was busy trying to marry me off to one of Dad's castaways. It was a game neither had been successful at so far.

I've lived just outside of D.C. for three years now, happily single. I'm much too busy writing for *Travel Adventures* to even contemplate settling down. In fact, I have my mother to thank for my job at the magazine.

After college I got a job at the *Virginia Tribune* as a cub reporter. The only problem was that everyone constantly referred to me as "Helen Kelly's kid," since my mom is practically an institution at the *Tribune*.

Even though she saw herself as a serious journalist, she had been stuck writing society columns until she stumbled upon an illicit affair involving three local judges and their less-than-judicial nocturnal activities. She broke the story and stayed with it through the ensuing scandal, divorces, and disbarment of the judges.

Since that fateful story, she's become somewhat famous at the *Tribune* for her investigation into the torrid tangle of Virginia politics. That often involves quick trips to our nation's capital to sneak around the files of some of our shadier congressmen and senators. I often accompanied Mom on these trips with the hope that some of her investigative talents would rub off on me.

Instead, it led to an introduction to Delmont Patton, the publisher of *Travel Adventures*. We met at a cocktail party while Mom was busy snooping around about a Congressman suspected of skimming funds from charity benefits he hosted. While she was busy with that, I managed to talk my way into a job at *Travel Adventures*. The job paid well, and the idea of traveling around to vacation spots as opposed to covering local lawsuits and ribbon cuttings was too much to pass up.

So here I was, three years later. I twiddled my thumbs until noon, when a young nurse entered my room. She handed me a bag that held exactly what I wanted.

"Afternoon, Miss Kelly, I'm Nurse Webber. Here are the clothes you had on when you were brought in last night," she said through a thick Southern drawl. She nodded a thick mane of bleached blonde hair in my direction. "I heard you really smashed up your car right nicely. And, on top of that, you get Dr. Donovan."

"Is that good?"

She nodded. "Shoot, every woman in this hospital wants to get her hands on Dr. Donovan. Why, I've even heard of women faking illnesses just so they can come to our emergency room and see him."

I thought about my impending ride home and frowned. Maybe it wasn't my looks and charm that attracted the good doctor. Maybe this was just a daily treat for him, the swine. "So, I take it he's quite a Casanova."

I struck a chord in Nurse Webber. She was in the process of removing my IV, but stopped and sank into the chair next to the bed. "That's just it, you see. He's not a Casanova. He never ever goes out or flirts with anyone. He just works, works, works. Every woman here is just dying to snap him up."

She sat up straight and shook her blonde curls fiercely. "Me, I think he's been burned real bad by some girl and is just looking for the right woman to mend his broken heart."

I tugged at my IV. "That's very interesting. Say, could you help me with this? Someone is coming soon to take me home, and I'd like to be ready to leave."

I didn't have the heart to tell her Dr. Donovan was that somebody.

"Oh, sure, honey," she said. "I'm just sitting here rattling on like I don't have good sense."

A few moments later, I was feeling human again, safely back in my jeans and blouse. I rummaged through my purse and retrieved a brush and some lipstick. I figured I might as well try to look appealing to John if his chivalry was such a rarity.

I glanced in the bathroom mirror and grimaced. John was right, I did look like I'd been "conked in the noggin" pretty well. A large, irregularly shaped glob of brown, yellow, and sickly green decorated the left side of my forehead. I gingerly brushed my bangs to cover the bruise and consoled myself that at least I wasn't sporting a black eye.

"You look ready to escape," a voice behind me said. I turned to see John standing in the doorway. "All you need to do is sign these discharge papers I hold in my hand."

"Consider them signed," I said.

He handed over the papers. "I'll be right back." He disappeared into the hall and returned pushing a wheelchair.

"What's that for?"

He held up his hand. "Hospital regulations. Your carriage awaits, madam."

Despite my better judgment, I climbed into the wheelchair. After I bid my hospital room adieu, John wheeled me through the halls and to the elevator, past the envious gazes of stunned nurses who should have been paying attention to their duties. Instead, they seemed mesmerized by the sight of the eminent Dr. John Donovan pushing some slug like me past their jealous eyes.

We made it out to the parking lot and into the September sunshine. We stopped at a shiny, black, late-model Mazda that was eons away from the measly Honda I call mine.

"It's not a Porsche," John apologized. "But you've got to understand I still have student loans to pay off. The Porsche will come in due time."

"Oh, this will do nicely," I assured him.

He was helping me into the front seat when a voice rang out, "Donovan! How's life treating you?"

The voice belonged to a distinguished-looking man in his early fifties. He wore a tailored gray suit and burgundy tie and carried a lab coat. His small, deep-set blue eyes crinkled with a smile as he slapped John on the shoulder and said, "It's good to see you leaving at a decent hour. You give the other doctors here a bad rap with all the OT you put in. How have you been?"

John looked perplexed by his colleague's enthusiasm. "Just fine, Dr. Shelby. It's kind of you to ask."

Dr. Shelby ran his hand through his short, wavy, salt-and-pepper hair and addressed me. "Looks like you had quite a bump on the head. Car accident? Those windshields hurt."

Psychic, was he?

John's eyes narrowed. "Yes, she was in an accident last night."

"I'm sorry," Dr. Shelby said. "Are you a friend of Dr. Donovan's?"

John stumbled for an answer. "Uh, yes. Dr. Mason Shelby, may I introduce Kate Kelly."

Dr. Mason Shelby momentarily lost his stately demeanor. "Kelly? Kate Kelly?" He shot a surprised look at me and said with a slightly raised voice, "Are you from Woodbury? I'm sorry, but your name sounds familiar."

He was staring so intently that I felt uncomfortable. I wasn't sure how to answer. "No, I'm only visiting the area. Are you familiar with the *Virginia Tribune*?"

His eyes darted from John to me before he broke into an insincere smile. "The columnist—Helen Kelly?"

Mom wins again.

"Yes. I'm her daughter."

"She's a good writer. Well, I have patients to see. Have a nice day,

Doctor. Nice to meet you, Miss Kelly." With that he turned on his Italian leather wing-tip shoes and hurried toward the hospital entrance.

John stood at the car door, staring after Dr. Shelby. "That was so strange," he said.

"Why?" I asked. "He seemed nice enough."

"Dr. Shelby has never spoken to me before today. I didn't know he knew my name."

Chapter 3

VINTAGE EAGLES played on John's radio as he turned onto the highway leading out of Woodbury. The day had dawned warm and humid following the previous night's storms. The frenzied chorus of cicadas cut through the misty air, accompanying the soulful refrains of "Hotel California" wafting out the top of John's sunroof. It all transported me back to memories of college and similar rides in the sunshine with Matt Emery. Or was it Brian Jameson? I smiled. Probably both of them.

John interrupted my ruminations. "I can't get over the fact that Dr. Shelby spoke to me in the parking lot."

"Why is that such a major event?"

"Well, you have to know Dr. Shelby. He has quite a history in Woodbury. Let me put it this way: He's Dr. Mason Shelby Jr. His father was Woodbury's premier family doctor years ago, not to mention one of the founding fathers of Woodbury Memorial Hospital."

"A real Marcus Welby, huh?"

"Oh, you could say that. Dr. Shelby Sr. probably knew more about Woodbury's citizens and history than the town librarian. He was a true old-fashioned physician. In fact, his office was in his home on Clover Street. I would imagine most residents over a certain age were probably delivered right there in that house."

"That's quite a legacy to live up to," I said. "Is he still around?"

"No. Dr. Shelby Sr. died about ten or fifteen years ago. A heart attack, I believe. It was a pretty emotional event for Woodbury's inhabitants, almost like a member of their own family had passed on."

John punched a button on the radio, sending the Eagles into flight. They were replaced by the cheery voice of a DJ reading the weather forecast. No surprise for September in Virginia—sunny, hot, and humid. John made a face and clicked the radio off. "That was the point Dr. Shelby Jr. returned and all the whispers began."

That sounded intriguing. So, maybe Woodbury wasn't the sleepy little town I had always envisioned.

"What type of whispers? Did the younger Dr. Shelby have skeletons in his closet?"

John rolled his eyes. "Very funny. Story is, the young Mason was an only child. His mother died when he was just a kid. You'd think that he would've been thrilled to grow up with such a role model as a father, but apparently he was pretty anxious to get out of Woodbury. He went to Harvard, and that was the last Woodbury saw of him until the funeral several years later."

Traffic was heavy as workers hurried back to their offices after lunch. John switched lanes. "In fact, it was the way he returned to Woodbury that started tongues wagging. He missed his father's visitation completely and didn't show up at the funeral until just minutes before it was scheduled to begin. I've even heard rumors that he excused himself from the service itself to make a phone call."

I shook my head. "Not exactly wallowing in grief for his dear old dad, was he?"

"Hardly," John replied. "You have the entire town in mourning, and his only son can't wait to leave. Pretty harsh, if you ask me. He disappeared again, leaving his father's house to sit vacant and decaying. The next anyone saw of him was when he returned a few months later for the settlement of the will. From what I understand, the elder Dr. Shelby may have been an old country physician, but he was far from a financial novice. Rumor has it that he had quite a sum of money stashed away."

"All inherited by the undeserving son," I concluded.

"Not necessarily," John answered. "Most of it, including the house on Clover Street, went to his son. Another portion went to Dr. Shelby's housekeeper."

"So did he settle into his late father's house after the funeral?"

John nodded. "Yes and no. He moved into an apartment while the old Clover Street house was remodeled. That was another controversy. He doesn't exactly have conservative Woodbury tastes. From what I understand, he gutted the inside and created a very modern look. Lots of dark interiors and enough modern art to significantly raise the blood pressure of the ladies in the beauty shop down the street."

"Sounds like a real charming guy. Does he have much of a practice?"

"Oh, sure," John replied. "He snapped up all his father's old patients. Of course, they don't care for his less-than-cheery personality, but old habits die hard. I guess as long as he has the name Mason Shelby, people will hold out the hope that he'll miraculously turn into his father."

"So how did you come upon all this information?"

John glanced at me quickly. "Most of it is common knowledge in Woodbury. News travels quickly around here. I guess I learned a lot of the seamier details from a girl I dated when I first came to town."

I decided to let that one slip past. I didn't really care to hear about any competition.

Apparently John was eager to change the subject also. "I was going to tell you about this earlier, but I rambled on about Dr. Shelby too long. Sheriff Thompson called me this morning. He wanted to talk with you again about the accident. I told him I would bring you by his office on the way home. I hope you don't mind. I thought it might be better if I was with you." We rolled to a stop at a red light.

There wasn't much I could argue with, considering the fact that the sheriff's department sat to our right. We pulled into the lot and parked. The Woodbury Sheriff's Department was housed in a lone, one-story, concrete-block building whose only landscaping consisted of the Virginia state flag flapping lazily over a row of dried-out boxwoods.

The interior of the building was no more inviting. The walls were a musty shade of eggshell and were covered only with faded posters titled MOST WANTED. A large round clock took center stage on the far wall, hovering above another state flag, proudly stretched and framed. It was the only splash of color to be found.

The only color, that is, until we came to the receptionist's desk, which sat in the center of the office. Official forms were piled in neat stacks next to a calendar tended by Mrs. Ripley. I knew Mrs. Ripley's name because it was emblazoned in large letters on a magnetic board which hung over the front of the desk.

Mrs. Ripley commanded the desk with a presence befitting a head-master at a private school. Her orange Clairol #43 hair crowned a face well-worn by several decades. A gingham-checked polyester dress, which draped her reed-straight frame, smartly matched the blue-rimmed half glasses held in place by a beaded chain around her neck.

She lifted her head at an angle, perched her glasses on her nose, and said in a throaty, cigarette-laden voice, "Are you here for an emergency, to report a crime, or are you looking for directions?"

"We're here to see Sheriff Thompson," I answered.

"Is that so?" she hummed. "You must be foreigners. I know most everyone in Woodbury, but I can't say I recall your faces. That's an awfully nasty mark you've got on your forehead. Is someone not treating you sweetly?"

Mrs. Ripley swiveled her head toward John. I wasn't sure if the clicking sound we heard was the chain on her glasses beating against the string of Woolworth's pearls she was wearing or merely the bones in her aging neck getting their daily exercise.

John jumped in. "We're here to speak with the sheriff about a car accident. He's expecting us."

Mrs. Ripley interrupted John by poking her pencil in the air. "Oh, you're the one." Her eyes trained on me. "I heard all about that."

How kind of her.

Sheriff Thompson mercifully appeared in a doorway a few feet behind the desk. "Afternoon, Dr. Donovan, Miss Kelly," he said. "You look in considerably better shape today than you did last night. Won't you please join me in my office?"

Thompson quickly whisked his tan hat off a wooden chair and sat it haphazardly over the top of a large, marble and gold-plated softball trophy sitting on the windowsill. As I settled into the now-vacant chair, I glanced at the trophy. It read, FIRST PLACE CHAMPIONS—VIRGINIA LAW ENFORCEMENT WEEKEND—1998. I heard the sheriff's chair groan as he sank his ample frame onto it, and I couldn't help but think he'd probably be pretty handy with a bat. I certainly wouldn't want to be on the receiving end.

"So, Dr. Donovan," Thompson began. "I didn't know doctors these days made house calls." He rocked back in his chair.

A deep red blotch crept up John's neckline. "She didn't have a way home, so as her physician, I thought it best to make sure she made it there safely."

The sheriff smiled. "Of course. As her physician."

I felt as if I weren't present in the room. "Excuse me, Sheriff," I interrupted. "Is there anything more you can tell us about the accident? I really would like to be on my way home."

Thompson reached for a folder resting on top of a scratched gray file cabinet. "As a matter of fact, I can." He opened the file and shuffled some papers. "Miss Kelly, do you have a sister who lives in the area?"

"No," I answered. "I don't have a sister anywhere. I'm an only child."

He frowned. That was clearly not the answer he wanted to hear. "Are you familiar with a young woman named Karen Kelly?"

"No, that name doesn't ring a bell. Should I know her?"

He stared at me for a moment. "It's all very odd, Miss Kelly, very odd. I dropped by the rental car agency this morning to check the receipts for your car. You signed for it, but the agency log shows the car reserved for a Karen Kelly."

John shrugged. "Karen, Kate, what's the difference? Those places aren't exactly run with military precision. Don't you think they probably just wrote down the wrong first name?"

As an answer, Thompson pulled two xeroxed forms out of the folder. He placed them in front of John and me. "If you look at these rental records, I think you'll see my quandary. A woman by the name of Karen Kelly picked up a blue Ford Taurus last night at 8:45 P.M. If you look closely at the top of this form, you'll see it's reserved under the name of Katherine Kelly."

He paused for effect, then said, "Now, Katherine Kelly picked up an identical blue Ford Taurus at 9:10 P.M. This particular car was reserved under the name Karen Kelly." The sheriff sat back in his chair and folded his arms across his expansive chest.

If he was waiting for a spectacular explanation from me, he would have to age a few years. "I agree it's a very strange coincidence, Sheriff, but how could that possibly be connected to my accident?"

"It could mean a great deal," he said. "Now, remember, they keep records on those things. When the cars were reserved, the rental agent wrote the license numbers on the form, but apparently, you girls were given the wrong cars. The Taurus that was supposed to go to Karen Kelly is now sitting in Cooper's Body Shop on Tyler Street. The Taurus you picked up was supposed to arrive at a rental agency in Lexington, Kentucky, this morning. The driver never showed. However, a woman fitting your description returned a car—the one you should have had—to the Richmond rental agency this morning around 6:00."

John interrupted. "What do you mean when you say 'fitting your description'?"

Thompson continued. "The man at the rental agency said she was a young woman in her twenties with short auburn hair and dark eyes."

Well, that certainly clarified the situation. I hated to pee in his Cheerios, but personally I couldn't help but wonder how many thousands of women in their twenties with auburn hair and dark eyes were passing through Virginia at any given moment.

Besides, the only time I ever had auburn hair was one summer when I had the unfortunate incident with a bottle of "Sun-In" at the beach. My hair is decidedly brown. A guy I once dated even called it "chestnut." It's also very curly and falls just below my shoulders, not exactly what I'd call short.

I tactfully gave it a whirl. "Sheriff, I think we all know exactly where I was this morning at 6:00. I wasn't in any condition to leave the hospital, pick up a car I didn't know I had, and return it to a rental agency in Richmond." As an afterthought I added, "And besides, my hair is brown."

Thompson nodded. "I stand corrected, Miss Kelly, I'm not quite up-to-date on my fashion color descriptions. I'm not suggesting that you pulled an elaborate stunt to return the car. I merely find all these coincidences very hard to swallow."

"If Karen Kelly returned the car this morning," I asked, "where did she go from there?"

His frown locked in tight. "The clerk said she waited around for a while, then someone picked her up in a car across the street. He couldn't remember the model."

"So we're back to square one," John sighed.

"Not necessarily," I said. "When I reserved the car a few days ago, they asked for my address and phone number. Why can't we track Karen Kelly down that way?"

"I'm a step ahead of you, Miss Kelly," Thompson replied. "I know where Karen Kelly lives." He reached for a Styrofoam cup holding coffee that looked as black and syrupy as tar being laid on the highway on a hot July day. He took a sip and made a face that said it wasn't exactly a premium brew. "Karen Kelly is a student. She lives in a dormitory on the William & Mary campus." He paused and looked directly at me. "What do you think of that, Miss Kelly?"

Williamsburg. Just my luck. This was getting more bizarre as time clicked by. I wasn't sure what Thompson wanted me to say next. I almost expected Rod Serling to walk by and announce that we had just entered the Twilight Zone.

I shook my head. "I agree, Sheriff, this is rather odd, but how could this be connected with my accident?"

He sighed. "Remember, we found a great deal of money at the scene. Now, since you say it doesn't belong to you, that makes me wonder if it wasn't intended for Karen Kelly."

John laughed. "What would a college student be doing with money like that? I never had that kind of cash when I was in college."

It hit me where the sheriff was heading. "Do you think she was involved in something illegal? Drugs? That might explain why someone would want to run her—or me, as it turns out—off the road. I think we need to pay Karen Kelly a visit."

"Exactly," Thompson said. "Except *we* won't pay her a visit; *I* will do it. You have no need to be involved, Miss Kelly."

That's what he thought. "I'm on my way home to Williamsburg right now. I could accompany you and hear Karen's version myself."

I thought the idea was splendid. Thompson didn't.

He shut the file, sighed again, and shook his head defiantly. "The answer is no. This is police business, not yours."

"I agree," John interjected. "What you need to do is rest. You're in no shape to play Nancy Drew. I'm sure Sheriff Thompson will call you with the information he receives from Karen Kelly. Won't you, Sheriff?"

Thompson stood. "You can be assured that I will keep in touch."

"Okay," I said as I opened my purse. I usually refer to it as the "great abyss," given the mishmash of objects hiding inside, and unfortunately it was living up to its name as I rummaged for a business card. "I can't find a business card right now, but I know I have some in my camera bag. That brings up an important point. Where is my luggage?"

The sheriff walked over to a closet sandwiched between two file cabinets. He opened the door and pulled out my bags, which were tagged "evidence." Thompson noticed my raised eyebrow and snapped off the tags. "Standard procedure only, Miss Kelly."

I took the bags from him and quickly sorted through the contents. Other than being rather disheveled, everything seemed to be there. I heaved a sigh of relief when I inspected my camera and film canisters. The hydroplane story had survived. I dug out a card and scribbled dad's phone number on the back.

Thompson took the card and shoved it into his chest pocket. "Everything okay? Is there anything missing?"

"No, I think my luggage made it in one piece." I decided to try one last time. "You know, you could get to the bottom of this in one meeting. There'd be no reason to backtrack and get in touch with me again."

Thompson smiled. "Take her home, Dr. Donovan. See that she rests quietly this afternoon. Thank you for coming by today."

John and I were soon on the road. I directed him through the old neighborhoods on the outskirts of the tourist area of Williamsburg, and we finally came to the tree-lined street I remember so well from my childhood.

"What a beauty," he said, letting out a low whistle as we rolled to a stop in front of my parents' house. "How old is this place?"

"Oh, it's a young pup by Williamsburg standards," I said as I stepped onto the sidewalk. "Only 110 years old." I stopped and looked appreciatively at the house. John was right, it was beautiful: a white, three-story Victorian showplace dotted with stained-glass windows and wrapped on two sides with a covered porch that holds my mom's prized white wicker furniture.

When we reached the porch, I turned to John. "If you'd like to come inside, I could fix some sandwiches and give you a grand tour."

He leaned against the porch railing. "That's tempting, but I'm afraid I'll have to take a rain check. I have some things to take care of this afternoon, then I need to drop by the hospital for a while." He glanced at his watch. "I promised someone I'd cover part of his shift late this afternoon. Maybe I could drop by later tonight to, you know, see how you're feeling."

It was my turn to smile. "That would be very nice. Since you're working late, I could fix a little dinner for you. Consider it a thank-you for your help this afternoon." As I said that, I bit my lip. Cooking isn't exactly one of my great talents. I don't think I've poisoned anyone yet, but let's just say Julia Child has nothing to fear.

"Oh, I wouldn't want you to go to any trouble," he replied. "Besides, you promised me you would rest this afternoon."

"Honestly, it's no trouble. You'd be surprised at what I can do with a freezer and a microwave."

John laughed, but he didn't realize how serious I was. He ran his hand from my shoulder to my elbow. "Fine. You get some sleep, then I'll call you around seven."

He trotted down the porch steps to his car. He opened the car door, then paused. "Should I call your dad first and ask permission to see you tonight?"

Dad. I hadn't thought about that. Ah, the perils of living at home again. "Oh, I'd only worry if you have evil intentions," I shot back.

John grinned. "I'll work on that. See you later."

He drove off, and I went inside. I dropped my bags at the foot of the staircase, then rummaged through the stacks of mail scattered across the antique table near the door.

I crossed over to the library, which doubles as Dad's home office and has always been my favorite room in the house. Bookshelves bubbling over with dog-eared copies of novels, reference books, and textbooks line one wall and reach to the twelve-foot ceiling. The far wall is hugged by a huge stone fireplace, bordered on either side by impressive looking, but infinitely comfortable red leather wing-back chairs. On the opposite wall, Dad's imposing antique mahogany desk sits grandly before a beautiful stained-glass bay window looking out into the garden.

I dropped into the chair behind the desk and reached for the phone. I dialed the number to Dad's office and was rewarded with his voice mail: "Hello, you have reached the office of Dr. James Kelly, Department of History. Please leave a message and I will return your call shortly."

I left a quick message, assuring him I was home in one piece, then hung up the phone and headed for the kitchen. I rummaged through the white-pine cabinets in search of something easy and quick I could fix for John. I should have known better. The shelves were nearly empty.

Whenever Mom is out of town on assignment, Dad tends to eat most of his meals in restaurants. I think my abhorrence for cooking was inherited from him. When all else fails, there's always pasta.

I located a box of angel-hair pasta and an unopened jar of spaghetti sauce. It was even a "chunky garden" version, full of bits and pieces of vegetables. Great. It would look like I really put some thought and effort into dinner.

Satisfied that I had the makings of a romantic meal, I left the kitchen and passed through the dining room, heading for the sitting room across the hall from Dad's office. As much as I hated to admit it, I was pretty tired. I scooped up a copy of *Southern Living* magazine and flopped on the emerald-and-pink chintz couch that faced Mom's gleaming black baby grand piano. I paged through a few sections of the magazine but decided instead to give up the fight and take a nap.

"If you're going to sleep all night, dear Katherine, the least you could do is sleep upstairs in that brass bed your mother and I bought you when you were 16."

I opened my eyes to see Dad towering above me, hands on his hips. He was wearing a navy polo shirt and khaki pants, which for Dad was akin to wearing cut-off shorts and a beer T-shirt. That told me in one glance that he'd been home for a while.

"What time is it?" I asked, sitting up. "How long have you been home?"

"It's a good thing I'm not an intruder. I've been banging about the house for over an hour. It's nearly 7:30. I thought you might like some dinner."

"Dinner!" I exclaimed. "Seven-thirty, oh, this is not good."

John had said he'd call at seven. I was sure that I looked like a mess, and dinner was still slumbering quietly in the kitchen cabinets. Not good. Not good at all.

"You see, Dad, Dr. Donovan was going to drop by—"

My demented ranting was interrupted by the ringing of the phone. I looked helplessly at Dad, who smiled and said, "The good Dr. Donovan, I presume."

I stuck my tongue out, raced across the hall, and answered. The voice on the other end confirmed my fears.

"Kate, it's John. How are you feeling?"

"Much better. You'd be proud of me. I slept all afternoon. I'm as good as new."

"That's good to hear," he said. There was silence on the other end. "Kate, look, about dinner, there's something you should know." His voice was strangely flat and emotionless.

I wasn't prepared for what came next. He cleared his throat. "Kate, I just met Karen Kelly."

"Oh," I replied. "What did she have to say for herself?"

"Not much," John said quietly. "She's dead."

Chapter 4

DAD SPENDS MOST OF HIS DAY giving lectures. You'd think by the evening he'd want to rest his voice. Hardly. I received quite a lecture as we raced toward Woodbury Memorial. Dad insisted on accompanying me to the hospital because he was sure I was in some kind of unforeseen danger. I stared out the car window as I listened to a litany of reasons why I should quit my "globetrotting" and come home and get a "calm, respectable job" with the local newspaper.

He was still going strong half an hour later as we crossed the hospital parking lot. "You just don't know what this girl was involved in," he continued.

In the emergency room the chorus of high-pitched tones from life-saving medical equipment mingled with the rush of nurses, doctors, and technicians scurrying past. Gurneys and wheelchairs braced the hallway as if they were supporting the walls.

We turned a corner and came upon two familiar faces. John sat on the edge of a waiting room couch, his elbows resting on his knees, his fingertips wearily massaging his temples. Sheriff Bowman Thompson sat opposite John, coffee cup in one hand and clipboard balanced on one knee.

Thompson looked up from his scribbles. "Well, Miss Kelly. I had a feeling I'd be seeing you again today."

Dad was in no mood for idle chitchat. He strode over to the sheriff and extended his hand. "I'm Dr. Jim Kelly, Katherine's father. I'm very concerned about this situation. I'd like to know how you plan to resolve it."

Thompson raised an eyebrow. "Well, Dr. Kelly, you have my word I'm trying to get to the bottom of this. I don't take very kindly to people dying under odd circumstances in my town."

I was anxious to hear what the "odd circumstances" were, but my query was interrupted by a tall, elegant woman who was standing in the corner. She rushed up to Dad. "Did you say your name was Dr. Kelly? Are you Karen's family? Oh, I'm so dreadfully sorry." She dabbed her large hazel eyes with a crumpled tissue. "She was such a lovely young girl."

Dad took a step backwards. "No, ma'am, I'm sorry, I'm not related to the young woman. We merely share the same last name."

"Oh," she said quietly. She started to say something else but stopped and turned her gaze to the door. A man entered the room, carrying two cups of steaming coffee.

He was a burly yet refined man I guessed to be in his early fifties, with wavy silver hair laced with traces of black. His small, deep-set blue eyes were almost lost to sloping cheekbones bolstered by a firm chin. His chiseled features were covered with deeply tanned skin that hinted of a living made outdoors. Another clue came with his muddy boots, riding pants, and wrinkled knit shirt. A small rip crept from his collar and spread across the shoulder seam.

The woman, on the other hand, was dressed impeccably in a cool, emerald linen suit. A flowered silk scarf swept across her shoulders and was clipped firmly with a large pearl and emerald brooch. Something told me the gems sparkling were the real thing, not a Liz Claiborne knockoff. Straight blonde hair was secured by a large green bow at the nape of her neck.

She tucked a stray wisp of hair behind her ear. "Darling, this gentleman's last name is Kelly. I thought he was Karen's father, but he said they're not related."

"I'm Chase Merriman, and this is my wife Constance," the man replied. "Karen Kelly worked for me. Sheriff, is there a connection here I should know about?"

Thompson nodded. "Why don't we all have a seat?"

Constance Merriman sank gracefully into a nearby chair. Her husband remained standing. Dad and I joined John on the couch.

"You look beat," I whispered to John.

"Tell me about it." His tie was AWOL and his loafers had been replaced with old, scuffed, high-top tennis shoes. His wrinkled lab coat fell open to reveal a muddy stain on the right side of his shirt.

I scraped my fingernail across the caked stain. "What happened here? Indulge in a little mud-wrestling on the side?"

He sat upright, closed his coat, and answered quickly. "Oh, just a little accident. I was messing around in my yard when I was called in. I didn't have time to change."

Thompson cleared his throat. Class was in session, in the stilted, police-style cadence I recognized from my days at the *Virginia Tribune*, covering too many accidents and crimes to mention.

He briefly explained to the Merrimans the circumstances surrounding my accident, then turned to the rest of us. "I visited the dormitory of the deceased, Karen Kelly, this afternoon, but her roommate explained that she was working as a companion for Mr. Merriman's invalid mother. I proceeded to drive out to Merriman Farms."

Dad's ears perked. "Merriman—I knew I recognized the name. Merriman Farms is one of the largest forestry and landscaping companies in the state. Are you Robinson Merriman's son?"

Chase smiled. "One and the same. I apologize for my appearance. I spend far too much time locked away in our corporate office staring at shipping orders and bottom lines. I much prefer to be on the farm, managing the actual production process that keeps my wife in such comfortable surroundings."

Constance didn't appreciate her husband's comments. Ice dripped from every well-heeled syllable. "Dear, someone had to take over the corporate division when your father passed away."

Chase shrugged his muscular shoulders and took a sip of his coffee. "I try to make it out to the farm at least once a week. In fact, I was there when Sheriff Thompson arrived."

Thompson picked up the story. "I wanted to discuss the rental car switch with Karen Kelly. Mrs. Merriman informed me that Miss Kelly had left the premises to take a walk."

"Mother Merriman was napping," Constance interjected. "And I'm not used to having the police show up on my doorstep, so I called Chase on his cellular phone. He returned to the main house, and he and the sheriff took off to look for Karen."

Chase cleared his throat. "Karen is—was—a very outdoorsy kind of kid, always wandering the grounds in the afternoon while Mother rested. We have over a thousand acres, most of it heavily wooded, so I had no idea how to even begin to search for her. We questioned a few of my staff, and one said he saw her heading down the azalea trail."

"Is that significant?" I asked.

He wrinkled his nose. "Not particularly. In addition to our forestry division, we also specialize in flowering shrubs. The azalea trail is merely a section where we grow most of the flowers. It's a nice place, and I know Karen had a particular fancy for that trail."

He quickly glanced at his wife. "The sheriff and I walked the entire trail for several minutes. We couldn't find Karen—until we came to the lake."

"We found Karen Kelly's body in shallow water," Thompson said. "Mr. Merriman and I administered CPR and mouth-to-mouth resuscitation until the paramedics arrived, but unfortunately, it was too late."

John spoke up. "She had been in the water for quite a while. There was nothing more I could do."

The blunt reporter in me surfaced. "Do you think her death was an accident, or a suicide?" I also wondered if the person who ran me off the road had realized his or her mistake and had come back to finish the job at the lake.

Thompson answered very evenly. "That's still under investigation, Miss Kelly. We found the young lady's tennis shoes and T-shirt on the shore. There was the appearance that she left on her shorts and, ah, lingerie for an impromptu swim."

"I just don't understand," Constance said, clenching her tissue. "Karen knew she was always welcome to use our pool. We have an entire selection of swimsuits in the pool house, so that wouldn't be a problem."

Chase shook his head. "It's a hot, sticky day. Maybe she was over-heated by her walk and thought she would jump in the lake to cool off. It's very secluded; no one would see her. However, the depth of the lake is very deceptive. It's shallow around the edges, but it has a steep drop-off about ten feet from shore. If she wasn't a strong swimmer, she could have panicked when she realized how deep the water was."

A thoughtful Sheriff Thompson chewed on his bottom lip as he scribbled notes on a legal pad. "Dr. Donovan, you and I both noticed the presence of contusions on Karen Kelly's upper torso. Her T-shirt was also stained with mud, indicating a possible struggle. Did you detect any evidence of sexual assault?"

Chase fingered the tear at his collar. "Sheriff, what are you imply-ing? Merriman Farms is quite secure. We've never had any trouble. You're out of line if you're suggesting someone attacked Karen."

"There was nothing to indicate sexual assault," John said. "As for the contusions, it's difficult to say. The discoloration of some indi-cate that the bruises may be a few days old, others seem to be newer. Anyway, they're not that widespread. They could have come from any bump here or there."

Constance closed her eyes and rested her head on the back of her chair. "This is just so awful. What on earth are we going to tell Mother Merriman?"

Her query went unanswered. Dr. Mason Shelby burst into the wait-ing room. "Constance, Chase, I heard there was an accident at the farm. Is something wrong with Mrs. Merriman? Chase, I'm your moth-er's damned personal physician. I demand to know why I wasn't called."

Storm clouds surfaced on Chase's face. "Mason, my mother is fine. However, the young lady who keeps Mother company drowned at the lake this afternoon. There was no time to call you; we brought Karen in by ambulance."

"Who was the attending physician?" Mason barked.

John stood. "I was, why?"

"You? You're a kid."

So much for the friendly little episode earlier.

Mason's gaze fell on me, and his ice-blue eyes narrowed to slits. "Karen, you say? You, Miss Kelly, we met earlier today. You must be her sister."

"No, I'm not," I said. "We have the same last name, that's all. I've never met Karen Kelly."

Constance spoke up. "Mason, of course you knew dear Karen. She was always with Mother Merriman when you'd arrive for your visits. She thought very highly of you."

"I wouldn't know," he said. "I focus on the care I give Mrs. Merriman, not schoolgirl crushes. I would just hope that in the future, someone remembers to inform me of incidents at the farm." As an afterthought, he added, "My condolences to her family, whoever they are."

Chase's tanned neck was singed with red. Had we been born in another era, he probably would have challenged Mason to a duel. Instead, he clenched his straight, white teeth. "Mason, I think I can handle events at my home quite well, thank you. Right now, my concern is breaking the news of Karen's death to my mother. They were quite close. Perhaps you should come out to the house in case Mother needs something to calm her nerves."

"It's late," Mason replied. "Tell her in the morning. I'll be out at my regular time to check on her." He swept his eyes across the room. "I'll see you tomorrow."

His abrupt exit left us all with frowns usually reserved for those times when you have a bad taste in your mouth—like when you're craving a sculptured mound of expensive chocolate-covered nuts and bite into the piece of candy, only to discover a maple-cream filling inside.

Thompson shook his head slowly and said in a stage whisper, "Yep, it was a sad day in Woodbury when old Doc Shelby died and left us with his son."

An angry Chase concurred. "If it wasn't for Mother, that man wouldn't set foot in my house."

John tentatively joined in the conversation. "Well, I can't say much for his bedside manner, but I do agree that perhaps you should wait to tell Mrs. Merriman the news in the morning." He looked at his watch. "It's late. We could all use a good night's rest. I'm assuming Sheriff Thompson will want to speak with us again tomorrow."

"You assume correctly." The sheriff nodded. "Chase, if you don't mind, I'd like to come out to the house first thing to take another look around."

The muscles around Constance's mouth raced to pull themselves back to her ears, and her brow was furrowed like a freshly dug field. "It's just so distasteful to have the police poking around your private property. What will people say?"

Thompson sighed. "Death is distasteful, Mrs. Merriman."

There were still too many unanswered questions for me. How did Karen Kelly really die? And who had tried to make mincemeat of my car? Something told me the answers could very well be at Merriman Farms.

But how to get myself on that property? My mind was racing through several possible methods when Dad, who had been sitting quietly, solved my problem. He stood and said, "We really should be going. My daughter is still recovering from her accident, and I have several papers for my history class waiting for me."

History! That was the answer. I fished around my purse until a business card floated to the top. I pressed it in Chase's hand. "Mr. Merriman, I think I can divert your mother's attention from this terrible tragedy. I write for *Travel Adventures* magazine. My specialty is small-town history."

That was a stretch. My specialty was writing whatever my editor assigned me.

I took a deep breath. "I'd like to do an article on Merriman Farms. Perhaps if I busy your mother with interviews on the history of your family, she'll be able to keep her mind off Karen's death."

A smile finally broke across Constance's face. "Oh, Chase, that's a wonderful idea. You know how Mother Merriman enjoys reminiscing. Why, she could speak for hours on the history of the house." The color was quickly returning to her pale skin. "It's so kind of you to take an interest, Miss Kelly."

I smiled back at her, but something told me I'd have to do a bit more to convince her husband.

Chase eyed me carefully. "Yes, Miss Kelly, it is very thoughtful of you to be so concerned."

He paused for an agonizingly long moment and stared at my card. Either he was having trouble reading the printing or he still didn't know whether to trust me. I hoped it was the first one.

He finally focused his eyes on mine. "All right, we'll try it. Come out to the house tomorrow morning around ten. You must understand, though, if Mother doesn't wish to proceed with this, you'll have to leave."

Success at last.

I ignored the dumbfounded looks on Dad and Sheriff Thompson. "Thank you, Mr. Merriman."

He wasn't convinced. "We'll see."

"Well, I think it's a lovely idea," Constance said. She stood and collected a Gucci bag bigger than most briefcases I've seen. "Chase, dear," she continued as she walked out the door, "it's been such a dreadful day. I can't bear to spend another minute in this place."

Chase looked hard at me. "I trust, Miss Kelly, that you can procure directions to the farm on your own. If not, I'm sure the sheriff can give you an idea. You must understand, Miss Kelly, it's nothing personal, but I have a general mistrust of reporters. They usually do nothing more than stir up trouble."

Dad aligned himself with Chase. "That's true. It's best to leave some things alone, Katherine."

Thanks so much, Dad. Don't forget, your wife and only child are both reporters.

"Your father is right," John agreed quickly.

What was this, a conspiracy? It was obvious that the gentlemen surrounding me didn't want me to pursue this any further.

Their minds were made up.

So was mine. "So, Sheriff, about those directions. . . ."

Chapter 5

THE LANDED GENTRY. I believe that's what my high school history books called that rarefied group of obscenely wealthy families who dot the landscape of Virginia. There's Wellington Warfield Wilson VI, whose family lineage is directly traceable to the 25th Earl of Shaftsbury, who undoubtedly was someone of enormous importance. Or so his heirs would like to imagine. His family fought in the Revolutionary War and then met up with Poopsie Petersen Pottinger's family, and together they created an American dynasty.

Most of these families exist today on the remnants of trust funds and legacies so old, family members are hard-pressed to answer exactly where their money originated. This is the gilded set that revolves around polo fields, the best schools, and exclusive country clubs. These families truly do prefer Grey Poupon, and to them, the Ivy League is much more than a garden club.

The Merrimans were members of this privileged class.

Before leaving home, I grabbed breakfast and delved into Dad's books on local history. Unfortunately, his research material dealt primarily with the Williamsburg settlement; Woodbury barely rated a passing glance.

However, Woodbury's fifteen minutes of fame in the reference books was thanks to the Merriman family. King George III granted a Merriman ancestor several thousand acres of land which eventually evolved into the town of Woodbury. In the ensuing decades, the Merrimans managed a profitable working farm, and they parceled off plots of land to interested settlers.

Woodbury, which sits nestled in an enclave between the hills just off I-64, was a sleepy farming town until the turn of the twentieth century, when Chase Merriman's grandfather, Barringer Merriman, grew tired of being a gentleman farmer and created the Merriman Forestry Company. He shrank the size of the farm and concentrated on harvesting the hundreds of acres of woods surrounding his property. His son, Robinson, matched his savvy business and marketing talents with Barringer's physical sweat and toil, and together they created a forestry and landscaping company that today ranks as one of the most profitable in the Southeast.

As the only child of Robinson and Winifred Merriman, Chase is the sole heir of the vast family fortune. After his mother passes away, he will hold controlling interest in Merriman Farms, Inc., not to mention ownership of all the remaining land and the antebellum mansion. Not exactly small change.

Armed with this information, I set out for the estate in my mother's car. Merriman Farms wasn't that difficult to find. The corporation's clever marketing gurus opened an outdoor flower and shrubbery market across from the entrance to the farm. There you can purchase the same flowers and plants sold in any Virginia garden center, with the added attraction of the massive gates to the private estate in the background of the cash register.

Chase would be proud—business was booming as I drove past the market bustling with armchair gardeners. I pulled up to the guardhouse sitting before the grand black wrought-iron gates emblazoned with a large gold "M." Chase would not be so proud—inside the tiny guardhouse sat a uniformed guard, fast asleep.

I tapped lightly on my horn and startled the old fellow so much, he dropped his newspaper to the ground. "This is private property. The parking lot for the flower place is to the left."

"My name is Kate Kelly," I said. "I have an appointment with Mrs. Merriman this morning."

"Is that so?" He whistled. He pulled a notebook out of a small drawer, licked his forefinger, and flipped through several pages. "Nope. I don't see no Kate Kelly here for Mrs. Merriman." He gave me a superior smirk which faded as quickly as it appeared. A thought wrestled itself through his creaky cranium, and he reached under the telephone for a small piece of paper. "Oh, you're with all the mess with the police yesterday."

He pushed a button, which swung the gates open with a loud screech. Before me lay a long, solitary drive which snaked up the side of the hill. The private estate sat high above Woodbury like a medieval castle looking down on its little fiefdom. The Merriman house was traditionally Southern, reminiscent of Tara from *Gone With the Wind*. Six grand white columns hugged the front of the two-story mansion, while nine sets of red shuttered windows stretched across both floors of the massive façade. I parked the car and climbed the steps to the wraparound porch, half expecting Scarlett O'Hara herself to answer the stained-glass double doors.

Instead, a short, plump Hispanic woman dressed in an aproned gray-and-white maid's uniform greeted me. "May I help you?" she asked.

"Hello, my name is Kate Kelly. I'm here to see Mrs. Merriman."

The maid didn't have time to reply. Constance emerged from the left. "Hello, Kate, please come in, we've been expecting you. Maria, please bring Ms. Kelly an iced tea."

As the maid quickly disappeared, Constance reached for my hand. "You had such a nice idea last night," she said as she led me through the door and into a sitting room directly to the left.

Constance was walking so quickly, I barely had time to take in my surroundings. The entry hall's marble floor reminded me of fudge ripple ice cream. At the center of the hall was a grand staircase, sweeping up to a balcony that circled the second floor. At the top of the stairs, a pair of floor-to-ceiling French doors, which led onto a verandah, allowed sunlight to stream into the entrance foyer and dance off the crystals suspended from the chandelier.

The sitting room I entered was no less grand. The eminently taste-ful room, painted a pale cornflower blue, was bordered in sculptured white crown molding. A fireplace lined with blue and white tiles took a center spot on one wall and was topped with a white mantel. A large oil portrait of a stately woman in a light blue evening gown hung over the fireplace.

"I see you're admiring the portrait." Constance settled into a white cushioned wing-back chair. "That's Mother Merriman, several years ago. Quite a stunning woman, isn't she? She's always had such good taste. She's responsible for most of the decorating in the house. Some of it is a bit out of fashion I would imagine, but we dare not change a thing without her approval."

If these surroundings were "out of fashion," I shuddered to think of what Constance would say about my apartment. I like to think of my decorating style as falling somewhere around the class of dead-great-aunt-leftover-furniture-accented-with-Kmart-curtains. My mother once delicately described my apartment as having a "very lived-in look." It may never make the pages of a magazine, but it works for me.

"We told Mother Merriman about Karen this morning," Constance continued. She brushed her hands absentmindedly across her lap, smoothing out nonexistent wrinkles on her pale yellow silk palazzo pantsuit. "She's very upset, but actually, I think she's taking it bet-ter than we all expected. Mason is upstairs with her now, although I don't think she really needs to see him."

Maria carried two tall glasses of tea on a silver tray into the room for us, then left without saying a word.

"Is Mrs. Merriman ill?" I asked. "I noticed last night that Dr. Shelby said he'd come by at his usual time."

Constance sipped her tea. "Well, not exactly. Mother Merriman is in her late eighties. She suffered a small stroke about a year ago, which slowed her down some, but for a woman her age, I'd say she's doing quite well." She tossed her shoulder-length blonde hair and leaned in toward me. "My husband is an only child. He's very close to his mother and is understandably protective of her—to a fault sometimes. He'd do anything in the world to protect her. That's why he insists on having Mason visit once a week to check on her."

Constance wrinkled her nose. "It's very kind, of course, but I think the only real benefit involved is to Mason Shelby's wallet. I mean, unless I'm at the club or in town, I'm here most days. We had Karen here in the afternoons, not to mention our regular staff. I think we could keep a sufficient eye on her and call in Mason when it's needed. But she's not *my* mother, so I'll keep my mouth shut."

She sank farther into the chair cushion and glanced out the window to her right. "We didn't tell her about the sheriff nosing around here today. He and Chase have been down at the lake most of this morning. I don't know what else he could possibly want. After all, it was an accident. There's just no telling what people will think if they hear Sheriff Thompson was here two days in a row."

We were interrupted by the deep drawl of an elderly voice at the door. "Constance, why is there a police car in the drive? And who is your guest?"

So much for keeping the sheriff's visit a secret.

I turned to see an older version of the portrait over the fireplace. Mrs. Winifred Merriman was a diminutive woman, about five feet two, but she carried a regal presence which towered over us. She was still attractive, with clear blue eyes and high cheekbones. Long silver hair was woven into a thick, solitary braid that wrapped around her head like a tiara. Despite the heat outside, she wore a long-sleeved, black linen suit with large white buttons down the front of the jacket. A wooden cane, topped with the carved head of an eagle, rested in her hand.

Constance rose quickly from her seat. "Mother Merriman, I thought you were going to rest this morning. Where is Mason? How did you get downstairs?"

Mrs. Merriman leaned on her cane and briskly clopped over to where we sat. "Constance, where are your manners?" She turned to me and extended her hand. "Hello, dear, I'm Winifred Merriman. You must be the reporter Chase told me about this morning. What was your name again?"

"It's Kate Kelly, ma'am."

She sank onto the couch across from my chair. "Oh, yes. Chase did say you had the same last name as poor Karen. But you didn't know her, did you? Such a tragedy, such a tragedy." She paused, then looked at her daughter-in-law. "For heavens sake, Constance, sit down. You needn't worry about me; Maria helped me down the back lift. I am capable of moving about my own house."

Without a word, Constance obediently sank into her chair.

Mrs. Merriman reached for my hand. "Now tell me again about yourself. My son was very vague."

He was vague for a reason, thanks to me.

Glancing at Constance, I bubbled up an explanation. "I'm a writer for a travel magazine. Merriman Farms is so well known in this area, I thought it would be nice for our readers to hear the story of how it began."

"I see," Mrs. Merriman replied. Her piercing blue eyes ran the length of me. "I will buy that. Now, tell me, dear, what happened to your forehead?"

Constance nearly choked on her tea.

Given Constance's spasm, I decided to skip most of the more colorful details. "I had a bit of an accident the other evening. I'm not completely familiar with the roads in this area, and I'm afraid I took a bad turn."

Mrs. Merriman nodded. "I see. If you need the services of a physician, I can recommend my doctor, Mason Shelby Jr."

Mr. Personality himself. Ugh.

"Thank you, Mrs. Merriman, but I'm under a doctor's care."

She patted my hand again. "Very well. Now, why don't we get on with this business of your story. I think the easiest way is to show you this house my husband treasured."

Constance leapt to her feet. "I'll go along. You might need my help."

Without any assistance, Mrs. Merriman deftly pulled herself off the couch. "That won't be necessary. I have my wooden friend and Miss Kelly's arm if needed. I don't know why everyone thinks I'm so frail. I have an old body but a young mind, which will triumph every time." She looked at me and smiled. "I know they mean well, but I will decide when I am tired. I have enough sense left to know my limits."

Constance waved her hand in the air. "Go on, then. I'll be in here if you need anything." The smile had faded and she looked like a woman used to bowing to the wishes of her mother-in-law.

I reached for my purse and pulled out a notepad, pen, and my microcassette recorder. I showed the recorder to Mrs. Merriman. "Mrs. Merriman, if you don't mind, I'd like to record our conversation. It's much more natural for us just to talk, instead of having me constantly scribbling notes. The recording also helps me keep things accurate."

She peered at the recorder. "Isn't that amazing how tiny they make things these days? Look, Constance, isn't that interesting?"

A tight-lipped smile crawled across Constance's face. "Why yes, Mother Merriman, it is interesting." She looked at me. "I hope you have enough tape. Mother Merriman is quite the historian. She'll talk your ear off."

Mrs. Merriman laughed and motioned for me to follow her into the hallway.

We stood at the foot of the grand staircase, which was wide enough for at least three or four people to walk up it side by side. The cherry banister gleamed with hours of polishing.

"My husband, Robinson, treasured this house," Mrs. Merriman began. "Of course, it was the only home he ever knew. The Merriman family has lived in it ever since the house was built around 1830."

She rubbed her wrinkled hand along the end of the banister. "This house has seen it all: wealth, droughts, illness, slavery, wars, grand parties, and babies born. Just think of everyone who has stood in exactly the spot you're standing right now. It makes you think, doesn't it?"

I had to agree. You could feel the ghosts. "It sounds like you love this house as much as your husband did."

Mrs. Merriman grinned. "Oh, I do. It's been my life." She walked over to a bookcase that sat underneath the rising staircase and picked a small crystal vase off the shelf. She held it up, catching a beam of sunlight that sent a rainbow dancing across the floor. "This vase is over one hundred years old. My husband had a passion for antiques. His business travels took him all over the world. He would always return from those trips with an antique to add to our collection. Most people might think it's a bunch of old junk, but my husband had an excellent eye. There's a great deal of money surrounding you here, my dear."

She placed the vase back on the table. "My husband was a shrewd man. We lived through the Depression. It scared everyone. Robinson figured that even if the farm went down, we could still live off the money generated by selling off these antiques."

As we slowly walked down the hallway toward the back of the house, Mrs. Merriman continued her story. She explained most of the history I had already unearthed, adding, "As far as the details of the business, you'll have to check with Chase. I'm sure he can provide you with most of that information. I never bothered much with it; I left that to my husband. I much preferred to walk the grounds and admire the flowers and trees.

"It was a different time, you see," she went on. "My job was to look pretty, arrange the flowers, and host the ladies auxiliary twice a month. I didn't have the opportunity to strike out on a career of my own, like you have done."

"And what would that career have been, Mrs. Merriman?"

She chuckled. "Oh, my, I really don't know. Perhaps I would have opened a florist shop. My love for flowers is what prompted Robinson to create a flower division for Merriman Farms. But we shall never know, will we?"

A wistful look crossed her face. She was lost in thought, then suddenly brightened. "Why, I haven't told you about the legend, have I?"

"Legend? No, but it sounds like something that would add a nice touch to my article."

A new energy seized Mrs. Merriman. She slipped her arm through mine and we continued down the hallway. Her eyes glinted as she began her story. "The Merrimans have owned this land since the late 1700s, but this house was built by Carter Merriman in 1830. He was quite the character, a bit of a rogue. Rumor had it that he was a smuggler, always disappearing to the coast and returning with jewels and cash he acquired from less-than-legal means. In his later years, he was also quite a gambler. He was too old to travel much, so he would hold grand parties here at the house. There would be much gambling, with Carter usually winning the stakes. He was very ruthless. If you didn't have cash to pay up on your debt, he would simply take furniture or other objects from your house—whatever caught his fancy."

She laughed and waved her hand around the room. "In fact, I believe many of the paintings and furnishings in this house today are the result of Carter Merriman's hobby. Apparently, though, his luck ran out. Around the time of the Civil War, he became embroiled in a scandal involving a great deal of money. He had angered one too many people, and they were all out for revenge. Fearing for his life, he supposedly hid a treasure trove of some sort somewhere in this house or on the grounds. He left a very confusing riddle, then disappeared one night, never to be heard from again."

"That's a wonderful story," I said, "but do you actually believe it? It sounds too good to be true."

Mrs. Merriman shook her head. "I'm sure it's gained embellishments over the years, but I do believe the core of it. We had the note he left, you know."

My ears perked. A photo of the riddle would make a great centerpiece for my article. For that matter, I could see the legend as the story's theme. I could pop out an article with my eyes closed and then concentrate on the real reason I was visiting Merriman Farms.

I tried to contain my excitement. "Could I see the riddle?"

Mrs. Merriman frowned. "Oh, no. My husband destroyed it after all the bother it caused."

"What happened?"

"A local reporter got wind of the legend. One of our staff gave him a copy of the riddle, which he promptly printed in the paper. The farm was overrun with fortune hunters. It was 1952, Chase was just a little boy. The crowds frightened him. Strangers tried to bribe him with candy and toys, thinking he knew where the treasure was. My husband was furious. He installed those electric gates at the bottom of the hill and burned the riddle in the fireplace one evening."

Dear Robinson Merriman.

"Haven't you ever wondered where the treasure is?" I asked.

"Oh, no, dear," she replied. "I'm quite well provided for in my old age. I have no use for buried treasure. Let someone else have the thrill of finding whatever it may be."

I was going to question her further, but an agitated voice I recognized as belonging to Dr. Mason Shelby Jr. rose from behind a closed door nearby. "Don't worry, I'll have it for you. All I need is a little extension. I'm on to something. I can't tell you about it, but it's going to be very profitable for us."

He paused, as if he were on the phone. "Don't tell me that. I don't have the time or the inclination to bother with your problems. I have enough of my own. Just do what I said: two-fifty on the first and five hundred on the other."

He paused again. "Of course I know. It will all work out. Just let me handle it."

Mrs. Merriman looked perplexed. "Why, that sounds like Dr. Shelby. I thought he had left. You should meet him." She snapped open the door to reveal a stunned Mason on a cell phone. "Mason, I thought you left a long time ago."

He stared at us, then said to the person on the line, "I'll talk with you later." He clicked off the phone. "I needed to make a phone call, Mrs. Merriman, and check on a patient's condition."

Yeah, right. You were checking on a patient, and my next interview is with Cary Grant. His conversation sounded like many things, but my top-ten list didn't include a benevolent doctor checking on an ill patient.

Mason wasn't overly excited to see me. "It's you again," he said less than politely. "You're turning up everywhere these days."

Mrs. Merriman glossed over his rudeness. "Oh, Mason, have you already met Miss Kelly? She was injured recently, and I told her if she needed a physician, I could recommend you."

"We met at the hospital," he snapped. "Another doctor is on her case. She seems to be doing quite well to be up and about so quickly."

"I am feeling much better, thank you," I replied.

What had I ever done to Mason Shelby? He was staring at me the way you stare at a roach crawling across your plate in a fancy restaurant.

"Miss Kelly is a writer," Mrs. Merriman continued. "She's doing a story on the farm, Mason. We've just been having the most delightful conversation. I've told her all about the legend."

His eyes twitched. "The legend? You're not going to dredge that up again in your article, are you?" he asked me.

I gave him a very even look. "I don't know. I never discuss my articles with anyone until they are completed." Especially not with arrogant, rude doctors.

"Well, I don't think you should bring up that story again. It will only cause problems." He looked at his watch. "I have to go. I have an appointment in town."

We followed Mason into the hallway, where we found Chase and Constance deep in a hushed conversation. Chase barely nodded at me. "Mason, what are you still doing here?" he asked.

Mason didn't mince words. "I was just leaving."

Chase's gaze fell to the recorder in my hand. "What's that for? What are you recording?"

My poor recorder. "I use this to keep accurate records of my interviews, Mr. Merriman, that's all," I replied.

Mrs. Merriman interrupted. "Isn't that a wonderful little invention, Chase? I so enjoy talking with Kate."

He nervously ran his hand through his hair. "I don't think that recorder is absolutely necessary. This isn't the White House, you know."

"Oh, Chase, let Kate do her job," Mrs. Merriman admonished. "I'm enjoying her company. She's helped me keep my mind off of poor Karen. Let her record what she wants."

Sheriff Bowman Thompson stepped into the hallway from the sitting room. He stopped short when he saw Mason and me standing with the Merrimans. From the look on his face, I'm sure his thoughts would melt a minister's collar.

I wiggled my fingers at him. "Afternoon, Sheriff."

He opened his mouth but no sound emerged. His face wore a sour expression, then he turned to Chase. "I'm afraid I had a disturbing conversation with the coroner. The autopsy results on Karen Kelly are back. Drowning wasn't her only problem. Her windpipe was severely damaged. It appears she was strangled and then tossed into the lake."

Thompson looked at each of us before summing it up succinctly. "Folks, Karen Kelly was murdered."

Chapter 6

"NO! YOU'RE MISTAKEN, it was an accident," Constance nearly screamed. Her skin was as pale as her pantsuit, and a vein in her neck imitated the pulsating beat of a Caribbean rhythm.

Mrs. Merriman wavered a bit. "Murder? That's never happened on Merriman Farms."

Chase eyed his mother and reached for her arm. "Come on, Mother, let's go into the other room."

That obviously wasn't in Mrs. Merriman's game plan. Her back stiffened. "Chase, this is my farm and my house. This matter concerns the welfare of the family. I will be present for all discussions."

It was Chase's turn to sport the throbbing vein in his neck. "Mother, please."

The wrinkles in her face tightened, and she defiantly shook her head.

Chase swept his hand through his hair. "Mason? Don't you think Mother should rest?"

Mason glanced at Chase. "She'll be fine. You worry too much. Look, I'm not a part of this family. I have nothing to hide. I do, however, have things to do in town. I'll be in touch."

He turned and Constance followed quickly behind him. "Mason, don't say anything like that in town." Her voice raised an octave. "We have nothing to hide."

Mason completely ignored her and let the front door snap shut in her face. She turned and bore her large hazel eyes into Thompson. "Sheriff, we have nothing to hide."

"I've never suggested that you do," he said.

Chase interrupted. "Constance, dear, why don't you take Mother into the sitting room? We'll join you shortly."

Call me a cynic, but there was about as much affection in the way Chase said *dear* as in the feeling I get when I squash a spider.

"Miss Kelly," Chase continued, "I think we've had enough interviewing for one day. I'm sure you can find your way down to the main gates."

Things were just getting interesting. Why leave now?

It was pretty obvious when Thompson talked about the damage to

Karen Kelly's windpipe that she had been strangled, but I decided to push a little further. "I thought you said she'd removed her T-shirt and shorts to go swimming? What makes you think she was strangled?"

Thompson looked at me like I'd just asked him how to tie my shoes. He hadn't anticipated teaching "Murder 101" today. "What makes me think she was strangled? It's a little something called the coroner's report. It appears the killer choked her until she lost consciousness, then pushed her into the lake to create the appearance that she drowned while swimming."

"But why would anyone want to hurt poor Karen?" Mrs. Merriman asked.

The sheriff glanced at her and chose his words carefully. "Or, perhaps she was involved in a romantic situation gone wrong. She could have died during a, um, domestic situation."

A secluded spot. A pretty college student. Kinky sex. Murder. A cover-up. It sounded plausible to me.

Chase's hand shot up to his shoulder. I remembered that gesture from the night before when he was overly preoccupied with the tear on his shirt collar. "I told you last night, Bowman," he hissed. "Affairs of that sort don't happen at Merriman Farms."

Constance licked her lips and sighed loudly. Her gaze intently studied the chandelier above our heads. "My husband is right. Affairs of that type don't normally happen here."

It would have taken a blind and deaf man to miss the pointed stare she shot in Chase's direction, not to mention the emphasis placed on the word *normally*.

Thompson noticed as well. He gazed at her with squinted eyes. "I don't mean to be rude, but do you know all your employees' activities at all hours of the day?"

It was Mrs. Merriman's turn to speak up. "Our people would never tarnish the Merriman name with insidious activities."

Poor Thompson. The rich and powerful Merrimans were closing ranks. People in the South, though, are trained to wade through mounds of glop without ever losing their composure. Southerners have the uncanny ability to sugarcoat their answer until it's enough to send a diabetic into shock.

The sheriff was a consummate pro. "Ma'am, I wouldn't think of tarnishing the proud Merriman name. But you see, there are a few nasty fellows out there who can fool us with their charm. They are good at sneaking into advantageous situations, then causing all sorts of harm."

Thompson picked up his tan cap off a chair and held it over his chest. I thought for minute he might break into the national anthem.

"Now, don't you worry," he said soothingly. "I'll take care of this matter in no time. Perhaps Constance can see you to your room."

That looked like the last thing Constance wanted to do, but after a hasty nod from Chase, she frowned and took her mother-in-law's arm. "Come on, Mother Merriman, we'll visit with everyone later."

Mrs. Merriman seemed as happy to be leaving as Constance. "I expect a full update on this matter this evening, Sheriff."

He nodded his head reverently. "As you wish, ma'am."

We watched the two women disappear into a back hallway. The minute they were out of sight, Thompson returned to business. The sugarcoating was gone, and his voice was downright salty. "Chase, I want to talk to everyone who was on this property yesterday. Hell, I'll even talk to the mailman. I'm also calling the county ETU boys out to go over the house and the lake."

ETU—I'd worked at the newspaper long enough to know that meant the Evidence Technician Unit. Those are the grim-faced cops who sweep onto a crime scene wearing their rubber gloves and carrying brushes and plastic bags. They may look like well-dressed housekeepers, but they aren't sweeping dust balls into their bags. They're looking for clues like fingerprints, or murder weapons, or bits of body.

Chase rubbed his neck nervously. "The house? Why would you need to poke around the house?"

"I want to cover every spot Karen Kelly was yesterday," Thompson said.

Chase rubbed his neck harder. "Uh, fine, Sheriff. Whatever you say." He was more blunt with me. "You can leave now, Miss Kelly."

So much for Southern hospitality. I mumbled my good-byes, gathered my purse, and slipped out.

As I drove down the winding drive, I tried to concentrate on how Karen Kelly died, but questions pelted me instead. Who had Mason Shelby been arguing with on the phone? Why were Constance and Chase so nervous? What was the deal with this legend?

As I paused at the bottom of the hill, something just beyond the guardhouse caught my eye—the Woodbury Municipal Library. I knew what my next move would be.

It was time to hunt for buried treasure.

I parked the car on the street and took the steep steps of the library's stone entrance two at a time. The library was housed in a large, airy building anchored with a cornerstone reading "1887." Inside, I saw a massive wooden counter in the center of the room, balancing two additional rooms which flanked the main lobby. Rows of old card-catalog cabinets lined the right side, and brightly colored mobiles in the children's section hung to the left. The desk ahead looked deserted until I walked closer. A tall, rail-thin woman was kneeling beside a bookcase, busily stacking books on the floor.

She stood, anxiously smoothing her pastel, flowered, cotton dress. She had short, curly, sandy hair and a pleasant but forgettable face with paper-thin pale skin dotted lightly with freckles. Light gray eyes demurely rested behind wire-rimmed glasses.

Her voice was soft and fragrant with the Southern freshness of the flowers in her dress. "Good afternoon. I'm Mrs. Chatworth, how may I assist you?"

How could she assist me? Good question. "I'm doing some genealogical research, and I was wondering if you had records of the local newspapers from the early 1950s? I'd like to scan them and see what data I can gather."

Where did that come from? Sometimes I'm amazed at my ability to come up with little white lies. Maybe I should run for public office.

Mrs. Chatworth smiled sweetly. "Why, of course we have those records. They're in our microfiche department. Won't you be kind enough to follow me?"

She led me past the card catalogs and into the next room, which was lined on all sides with rows and rows of wooden bookshelves. We passed the biography and fiction sections and stopped at a small antique oak desk resting in front of a picture window. The "microfiche department" consisted entirely of this one desk and a small projection screen which read the film.

"You wait here," she said. "I'll fetch the film you need. We have both the *Virginia Tribune* and the *Woodbury Chronicle*. What years would you like?"

"Just 1952," I replied. "I'm looking for something specific."

She returned a moment later and readied the machine for my search. She gave me basic instructions. "Now, turn this knob to scan the pages. If you want to print out anything, just call me."

I thanked her and set to my task. Mrs. Merriman had said a local reporter got wind of the legend, so I chose the *Woodbury Chronicle* first and quickly scanned the pages. The events of 1952 flashed before my eyes: King George VI dies, the Korean war raged on, Eisenhower elected president. Locally, nothing very interesting took place. There were the usual deaths and marriages, an occasional fender bender in town, and plenty of ads for Merriman Farms plants and flowers. Small-town life at its most boring.

I was ready to give up when I struck gold. November 22, 1952: "Mysterious Riddle Promises Treasure at Merriman Farms." I hungrily read the gossipy report of the secret riddle which the Merrimans had allegedly hidden for decades. According to the paper, the riddle promised great wealth and treasure for the person who cracked the case.

"Robinson Merriman," the article said, "could not be reached for comment." I smiled as I recognized the old reporter's phrase. "Could not be reached for comment" is reserved for those people you'd like to ignore. To cover yourself, you at least let the subject's phone ring once or twice, before you hang up and insist that they couldn't be reached. That sneaky tactic is unfortunately becoming harder to swing in this age of voice mail and beepers.

The article included a picture of Robinson and Winifred Merriman and their son, Chase, but I couldn't tell which parent Chase resembled. He had Winifred's high cheekbones, but other than that, he could have been any little kid. He certainly didn't resemble his father. Robinson Merriman was a Nordic blond with a full beard that probably covered numerous chins. The man's girth no doubt matched the circumference of some of the older oak trees on Merriman Farms. When people said he was a giant, they weren't just talking about his business sense.

Like in the painting over the fireplace at the Merriman estate, Winifred Merriman presented an elegant image. She had the same regal hairstyle, yet her hair was dark and her skin smooth and sculptured. She wore gloves with a dark fitted dress and a three-strand pearl choker. She looked every inch the wealthy society wife of the 1950s.

The end of the article held the riddle. I read through it once, then pulled out my notebook and scribbled the jumbled phrases onto paper:

> The treasure you seek
> Is both plentiful and rich,
> But deserving to only a few
> Who can divine the magic of an old witch.
> The location you'll find,
> Not from a wise old maid or a young dumb waiter;
> Nor in the fire of the sun, where flowers wilt from the
> heat;
> But instead to a place where you may bid a welcome
> retreat.
> With this wealth, you'll find the power you're due
> For behind it, the history of the world awaits you.

I always enjoyed riddles as a child, but the more I read, the less sense it made. No wonder the treasure was lost. This one was going to take some work to decipher.

I glanced at the rest of the page and discovered a small article about a new hat shop owned by a Sue Ellen Shaw. I decided that would serve my purposes, so I called over Mrs. Chatworth.

"I'd like this page printed, please," I said. "I believe I've found what I'm looking for." I looked directly at the librarian and didn't blink an eye. "I'm doing research on the Shaw family in this area."

"I see," Mrs. Chatworth said. "I love to dig into genealogical research myself. My husband and I have managed to trace his family back to seventeenth century England. I think it's a very—" Stopping mid-sentence, she peered closely at the page. "Well, isn't that odd?"

She pulled her glasses down her nose a bit and stared at me. "Very few people find a need to look through these old papers, but just a few weeks ago, a young lady came in and asked to scan old newspapers. She selected this very page. She was very interested in the Merriman riddle."

Mrs. Chatworth's brow furrowed. "She looked a lot like you as well, except her hair had a bit more red in it—you know, more of an auburn color."

Something in my stomach jumped. I heard my voice squeak, "Really?" followed by an equally unconvincing, "What is the Merriman riddle?"

I think I should keep my day job. I certainly wasn't that great a liar after all.

Mrs. Chatworth stared at me and said, "The story just above the one you want. The riddle is supposed to lead to great wealth, but to my knowledge no one has ever found it. This story caused quite a ruckus when it was printed. I thought it was strange that this girl would know about it." She frowned. "You mean you didn't notice this story at all?"

I could feel my face turning red. "Oh, I glanced at the headline, but I was concentrating on looking for the name Shaw."

That was swift. I should be nominated for a best-actress Oscar any day now.

Mrs. Chatworth nodded slightly, then set the machine to print the page. She handed me the copy. "That girl certainly resembled you. Do you know who she might be?"

"No, I'm afraid not," I bluffed. "I guess I just have a common face. Thanks very much for your help." I took the page and scooted my chair back so quickly, it made a horrific belching noise. I whispered, "Sorry," and flew past Mrs. Chatworth.

Once in my car, I thought about the librarian's reaction. She had to be talking about Karen Kelly. Mrs. Merriman had probably told Karen about the legend. Her job as Mrs. Merriman's companion gave her the perfect excuse to snoop around the house and grounds. What college student wouldn't love to find a lot of money to use to pay off student loans? But did she get close enough to the treasure that someone killed her?

What made it so special that someone would kill for it?

Chapter 7

MY MIND WHIRLED as I drove out of Woodbury. Did someone murder Karen Kelly because of the legend? Was I heading in the wrong direction? Or did the riddle hold the key to everything?

When I want to clear my mind, a carefree drive usually does the trick, so I rolled down the windows, turned up the radio, and turned onto Higgins Pass. The sun was bright and the temperature was climbing into the low eighties. Trees were blushing with the first hints of rustic autumn hues, and the wildflowers were spurting their final blooms.

I saw a sad irony in that. Karen Kelly was young and vibrant, full of life; but someone prematurely brought that life to a crashing end. She'd never again smell the scent of burning piles of autumn leaves or see the delicate dance of snowflakes. That angered me. Who took her life, and why? I felt like I'd known Karen for a long time, yet I had never seen her face. Slowly, I'd begun to piece together a portrait of Karen Kelly.

I knew there had to be more to her story. No one had mentioned her family or friends. I remembered Thompson said he had spoken with her roommate, so I decided to head toward William & Mary. Surely the roommate couldn't be that hard to track down. I glanced at my watch. It was barely noon.

I stopped at a railroad crossing and spied the tiny hamlet of Taylor Point and the entrance ramp to I-64. You could probably fit the entire town of Taylor Point inside a city park. Once past the railroad crossing, the world reverted several decades. Across the street sat an old Chevron station, complete with thick, old-fashioned pumps. Next, on the corner, was a large brick building, cluttered with piles of lamps, vases, and chairs pressing against the windows. A dining room table and matching chairs sat outside the door and shared the sidewalk with a white wicker porch swing and the hulking frame of a king-sized, carved cherry bed.

I peered closely at the sign painted on the window: WALENZA'S ANTIQUES—FINEST SELECTION IN VIRGINIA—REASONABLE PRICES, FINE QUALITY. Despite my better judgment, I turned the steering wheel in the direction of the store. I have a terrible weakness for antique stores—particularly cluttered, dusty, hole-in-the-wall establishments. I often can find the most wonderful treasures in these worn-down shops.

I sat in the car for a few minutes, arguing with myself over whether or not I should go inside. I was hungry, and I wanted to get to William & Mary to track down Karen's roommate. I didn't have time for a shopping expedition. More importantly, what if I saw something I wanted? My MasterCard was in my apartment on my nightstand, and I barely had enough cash for a drive-through flight at McDonald's. But the inside looked really dusty and disheveled, which was an instant clue that great things could be found beyond the glass door.

Desire won. I was greeted with the musty smell of dust-covered books, boxes of china and glassware, and rusty kitchen utensils that were as foreign to me as the *Hong Kong Daily News*. The store consisted of two large rooms, the first displaying hundreds of knick-knacks, costume jewelry, dishware, and books. The second room toward the back of the store held large pieces of furniture. A glass-topped counter with an old cash register sat to the door's left.

I worked my way over to a table displaying trays of costume jewelry. I'm a sucker for pretty pins and pearls. My grandmother had an enormous selection of jeweled pins that she kept in a shoe box in her dresser drawer. She would pull them out for me to play dress-up when I was little. I spent hours imagining that the glass baubles were real jewels, and given my current salary, I'd have to keep that youthful imagination sharp.

I was busy fingering an ice-blue star pin when I heard a voice. I glanced up to see a couple of older women quietly shopping in the back room, but no one else was in sight.

The raspy voice floated through the room. "Hello, my fine friend. I wanted to get back with you on the questions you had on the fine, fine items from this honorable store."

I looked toward the entrance and saw a man standing behind the counter. He must have been bent over when I entered.

He spoke rapidly into an old black rotary phone. "Now, you are a fine, fine person and a leader in your community. You obviously recognize the importance of these items. They are quite a collector's find. I would never cheat you. I'm sure you'll be pleased to hear the value of those pieces, and because I am such a fine, fine businessman, you know I won't double or triple the prices just to make a profit. I care about my customers. You are an important person to me. Without you, I am nothing. Profit is secondary to me."

Right, I thought with a grin. *Profit is always secondary when you're trying to snag a gullible customer.* He was quite the salesman.

"Oh, I simply couldn't let those go for that amount. You should consider the valuable historical importance of these fine, fine items. History is very important.

"It's not every day you'll find these," he continued quickly. "After all, these Elvis salt and pepper shakers are worth at least, oh, $20. He was the King, you know."

Elvis salt and pepper shakers?

"Yes, well, I think you have made a wise, wise choice," he bubbled on. "I think you will be proud to own this piece of Americana. Now, I must go; a very important customer just entered my store, and I must attend to her needs immediately. Rest assured, I will put these fine, fine items in a safe place until you can purchase them."

He hung up the phone and carefully lifted a small box off the shelf behind him. He scribbled a name on the box and replaced it with the care a scientist would use handling a vial of the Ebola virus. I almost didn't see him heading in my direction. I was still trying to get over the way he pronounced *Americana*. It was something like "A-meer-ee-cane-a." My eyes focused also on a framed sign hanging behind the counter. It read simply in large black letters, WALENZA'S ANTIQUES—YOU DIE, WE BUY.

"How do you do, madam? My sincerest apologies for being on the telephone apparatus when you entered the establishment." He smiled "You know how it is when Rupert Q. Walenza speaks with a client. I had a great reluxance to depart from my conversation. You can understand, I'm sure, the importance of balancing the self-esteem of *all* of one's clients."

Reluxance? That was one word I'd missed in my vocabulary classes.

Rupert Q. Walenza was in his late sixties, about five feet eight, with a bulbous nose and a shock of gray hair that stuck out at wild angles around his ears. He wore thick, white socks in huarache sandals, tan chinos, and a bright green Aztec-print cotton shirt that was unbuttoned far enough to spy a white undershirt and two heavy gold chains. He had large black-framed glasses that were probably in need of a prescription change, since he tilted his head at an unnatural angle to get a good look at me.

He grasped my hand and said through a dense New England accent, "I'm so glad you chose to visit today. We've received several new pieces in the past week which I'm sure you'll be interested in. Business has been a tad slow—not too bad, mind you, but a slight decrease from past weeks. I suppose it has to do with this weather. Terribly hot, isn't it? Cooler weather is much more conducive to shopping, don't you think?"

He paused to take a breath, and I interrupted. "I'm just glancing around today. If I need any help, I'll be sure to call you."

I wasn't going to get off that easily. He let go of my hand but continued to follow me at a close distance. "See anything that strikes your fancy? You know, it's been a productive month. Three major passings—the Winthrop, Edleson, and Colbert estates—all in one month. That's quite unusual to have a windfall like that. Of course, that means my black suit has been to the cleaners three times in a month. Imagine that." He leaned over the table I was behind and whispered, "Three funerals, two in one week alone. I hate to be out of the shop so much, but one does what one must."

"Yes, one does," I replied. I could not believe I was having this conversation. I moved around the table and tried to appear immersed in a stack of old *Life* magazines.

He picked up a vase and reached into his back pants pocket. With a flourish, he whipped out a large white handkerchief and began to buff the vase. "You know," he continued, "I must apologize again for remaining on the phone as you arrived. It's so annoying when someone won't stop talking."

He had that right.

"But, every customer deserves my utmost attention and respect. Don't you agree?"

"Of course," I said. "I appreciate your interest, but, like I said, I'm just looking today."

"Oh, by all means," Walenza enthused. He looked ready to spurt yet another eloquent comment, but he sucked it back in his throat. He pressed the vase to his chest. "Oh, my goodness, dear. What, may I ask, happened to your forehead? Have you been injured? Do you need to sit down? Let me get a chair." He hastily put down the vase and pulled up an orange vinyl-covered kitchen chair.

"Really, I'm fine. You don't need to do that."

"No, no, please, sit. I insist," he said as his hands pushed me down onto the chair.

It truly wasn't any of his business, but I explained. "I had a small accident the other evening. I bumped my head, but I'm fine now. It looks much worse than it is." I gingerly rose from the chair. "I appreciate your concern, but I really should be going."

"My apologies," he said. "Unfortunately, my eyesight is not what it used to be." Walenza laughed to himself. "I didn't realize it was you at first. Sometimes I wonder if these glasses are doing me any good. I'm glad you're feeling better and in the mood to shop again. Will your gentleman friend join you today? He said he'd be by in the next few days."

He smiled triumphantly and pointed his finger at me. "Your hair, that's it. You've altered your hairstyle, haven't you?"

"No one is joining me today." I decided to take a leap. "What do you like different about my hair? I'm flattered you noticed."

His greasy smile returned and he folded his arms across his chest. "It's curlier, and the color, you've darkened it, haven't you? Myself, I always thought darker hair was more seductive, you know, like Jane

Russell. I'm sure your gentleman friend likes that. He seems sophisticated."

Here was another person who thought I was someone else. Had I lost my identity completely in the state of Virginia? Surely he didn't think I was Karen Kelly. Or did he? Taylor Point was smack in between Woodbury and Williamsburg. It's possible that Karen could have stopped here. Who was her "gentleman friend"?

Walenza interrupted my thoughts. "I shouldn't have said that. That innuendo is out of place in a business setting. Regardless, I think the change looks nice. It makes you look older."

That was a backhanded compliment, especially if he thought I was the college-aged Karen.

He continued, undeterred. "I merely mean that a sophisticated look is nice, especially when you're with your gentleman friend. Incidentally, have you come across any new finds that I might be interested in purchasing? Your friend has such good taste, and you know that I pay top dollar for quality items."

"I don't know," I said hesitantly, groping for a way out of this. Walenza appeared to be a very thorough businessman who probably kept meticulous records. "You know, I can't remember the last few things we brought in. We have so much. Could I see your records?"

His bushy eyebrows shot up in an arch. "Why, of course." He walked quickly toward the front of the store, his huarache sandals flopping out a rhythmic cadence. He stepped behind the counter and reached for a large, leather-bound ledger book. He elaborately licked his finger and flipped through a few pages, then chose a section and ran his finger up and down the columns.

A puzzled look clouded his face. "Well, surely you remember the last item, the figurine? You brought that in just a few days ago. An exceptional beauty, I can tell you. Remember? You said you wouldn't accept less than $200." He shook his head. "I generally don't pay my suppliers that much, but I know when you and your friend bring in something, it's very valuable indeed."

I peered over the counter at the spot where his finger rested. There, in a thick, messy scrawl was written, "Sept. 12—K. Kelly—Girl w/ dog—1897 dated figurine—$200 cash." It was followed by an elaborately scribbled "RQW"—Walenza's initials.

Where was Karen Kelly getting her hands on expensive antiques? My eyes ran the length of the list. I saw at least four "K. Kelly" receipts on that page alone.

He snapped the book shut. A mini-tornado of dust swirled upwards, creating a thunderous sneeze from Walenza. He whipped out his handkerchief and rubbed it under his nose. "You've had a profitable couple of months, haven't you? Of course, your friend is very shrewd. It's all a buy, sell, buy market. Why, some of these things don't spend any time at all on these shelves. Your friend picks them up, you sell them to me, then I sell them to someone else. Supply and demand economics, that's what it is. One man's junk is another man's treasure."

He laughed. "Of course, some things have more treasure value than others. I like the ones with the high value. It allows me to live quite comfortably and buy nice clothes and jewelry for myself and Mrs. Walenza." His sense of style could be classified somewhere around "South Florida tourist," as opposed to Armani.

"Did my friend say when he was coming by?" I asked.

Walenza tapped his finger on his nose. "Let's see, he said in the next couple of days, so that would be possibly today or tomorrow. Of course, that's if he meant it literally. He could have meant it figuratively, so in that case it would be, well, it could be anytime."

He looked at me and smiled. "If you've been ill, he probably didn't want to bother you with bringing something in. Don't worry, you'll be back in business soon."

"Yes, I'm sure we will."

I wondered if Sheriff Thompson knew anything about a boyfriend. This made things very interesting.

As chatty as Rupert Walenza was, I wondered what would happen when he told the boyfriend that I had been in the store. That would be quite a feat, since technically Karen Kelly wasn't in a shopping mood anymore.

I also wondered about the money Karen was making selling antiques. Two hundred dollars for a figurine isn't exactly small change. That would be a nice little addition to whatever salary she was making as Mrs. Merriman's caretaker.

One of the other shoppers from the back room wandered into the front of the store. Walenza shoved the ledger book back onto the shelf and reached for my hand again. "I do so sincerely hope you're feeling better soon. What a terrible thing to happen to such a pretty young lady. Please come by again when you're feeling, shall we say, up to par." He leaned in closely. "That's a term used in golf. I don't have much opportunity to play it, but I'm sure it's a respectable game."

Glancing over my shoulder at the other customer, he said to me, "Please give my best to your gentleman friend. Now, if you'll excuse me, a very important customer needs my assistance. Do take care of yourself, dear, and visit Walenza's Antiques again soon."

I made a mental note of the location of the ledger book and slipped out the door. It would help matters if I could get my hands on that ledger. I was anxious to see just how profitable Karen's "business" had been. It crossed my mind that I could return with John and have him occupy Walenza's attention while I borrowed the book. It was devious, but I wanted to know how many things Karen had sold him. I only hoped John would be willing to help.

The morning had been busy but full of interesting information. I still had to find Karen's roommate at William & Mary. I didn't have time to worry about some stupid nuisance like the remnants of a concussion and aching muscles. Maybe if I got something to eat, my headache would disappear. I put the car in reverse and pulled out onto the road. The ramp to I-64 was only about half a block down the street.

As I waited at a stoplight, I watched life in Taylor Point go past—which wasn't saying much. A young woman pushed a baby in a stroller down a sidewalk to my right, passing two elderly men sitting in front of the Cut and Shave Barber Shop. The only other sign of life was three cars which passed me heading in the opposite direction. The first was a rusty, old Ford pickup truck. The second, a Jeep loaded with teenaged boys, reverberated with the pulsating sound of a rap song.

The third car sped around the corner just as my light changed to green. The sun hurled a beam which reflected off the chrome of the silver convertible Mercedes and bounced off my window. It was blinding for only a second, but not long enough that I missed the driver. I watched in my rearview mirror as the Mercedes ground to halt in front of Walenza's Antiques. The car door opened, and Chase Merriman stepped out into the sunshine. He locked the car and marched into Walenza's shop.

I was desperate to return to the store, but I was startled by an angry horn blast from the car behind me, and, like a robot, I turned onto the expressway entrance ramp. As I drove down I-64 my mind raced. What was Chase doing at Walenza's Antiques?

I shook my head. I was too obsessed with this small-town intrigue. Chase was a wealthy man with a house full of antiques. He probably visited antique stores on a frequent basis. Walenza's was the closest antique store to Woodbury. But, my subconscious argued, Chase was a wealthy man who probably shopped at large, expensive antique dealers. He wouldn't bother with a junky little store like Walenza's.

All this thinking was really making my head throb. Within a few minutes I reached the Williamsburg exit and headed into familiar territory. As if on autopilot, I drove to Jefferson Avenue and pulled into the lot at The Colonial Grill. I had spent many hours as a college student at this little restaurant.

The Colonial Grill is a small diner tucked between several souvenir shops. The food is basic, cheap, and rated somewhere in the "danger" category of the American Dietetic Association listings. It's populated mostly by William & Mary students and weary travelers looking for a quick bite to eat before heading for the tourist attractions.

I slid into a booth and grabbed a laminated menu as a waitress appeared. Her pink, ruffled apron clashed horribly with her brown, cropped T-shirt and long gauze skirt. Her blonde hair was separated into two thick braids, and a large silver peace-symbol pendant rested in the folds of the apron. She looked like Heidi lost at Woodstock.

"What can I get for you?" she asked.

"I'll have a turkey sandwich on white, a Coke, and some aspirin if you have it."

She glanced up from her order pad. "You know, white bread is really horrible. You'd be much healthier if you ate whole-grain wheat bread. Pills are bogus too. You should try some herbal tea instead, but if you insist on filling your body with chemicals, there are little bottles of aspirin at the cash register."

She turned on her heel and strolled lazily toward the kitchen. Maybe I was grumpy because my head hurt, but I certainly didn't need advice from a flower child. I slid out of the booth and walked over to the cash register. A small case filled with candy, gum, lip balm, and sample-size bottles of medicine lined the counter.

As I paid for the aspirin, I noticed a newsstand to my left. It held the *Virginia Tribune,* the *New York Times, USA Today,* and the *Williamsburg Student Sentinel.* My eyes zoomed in on the student newspaper, whose headline screamed out in large block letters, SORORITY MEMBER FOUND DEAD IN WOODBURY. Below the headline, a picture of a smiling, attractive student stared out at me. Karen Kelly finally had a face.

I grabbed the paper and rushed back to my table. Heidi was opinionated but quick. My sandwich—on wheat bread—was already waiting for me. I swallowed an aspirin, took a bite of my sandwich, and pushed the plate aside. I pored over the article but was distracted by the picture. Karen Kelly did look like me. We could have been sisters. I stared hard at the photo, haunted by her image.

Her hair was cut in a short, straight bob with a fringe of bangs that brushed across her forehead. She had large, dark eyes like mine, and a fresh, happy smile. In the black-and-white photo, her hair looked dark, but the article referred to the "bubbly, redheaded Sigma Gamma" who was an honor student majoring in business. She was vice-president of her sorority and a "well-liked and respected athlete."

The article explained how Karen worked for the Merrimans and was found by Chase at the lake. There was no mention of Sheriff Thompson's presence, or my accident. More interestingly, there was no mention that Karen had been murdered. The article merely said she had "died of injuries" sustained while she was at the lake. To the uninitiated, Karen had drowned.

Students at William & Mary were said to be "in a state of shock" over the popular coed's death. The Sigma Gamma house, where Karen lived, was closed to reporters. Karen's roommate, identified as Annalee Chisolm, was quoted: "I'm devastated. Karen was a wonderful friend and an asset to her school and sorority."

Well, there I had it. Not only did Karen Kelly have a face, she now had a roommate with a name and an address. I wolfed down my sandwich, left Heidi a tip, and flew out the door.

Soon I was driving along sorority and fraternity row on the William & Mary campus. I passed several well-kept gingerbread houses adorned with various Greek letters. I had attended enough parties during my college days that the signs weren't at all Greek to me. I must admit the sorority life was never my style, although I knew several girls who loved their sororities; and it goes without saying that the fraternities managed to plan several memorable evenings.

I parked the car at the Sigma Gamma house and climbed the steps of the large front porch. The double wood-and-glass doors were ajar, so I walked into a lobby smothered in shades of peach and teal, from a bright teal carpet with a peach border, to the peach ruffled curtains, peach pinstriped wallpaper, and teal-and-peach plaid wing-back chairs.

A perky blonde, wearing teal shorts with a peach polo, poked her head out from a side hallway. "Can I help you, ma'am?"

Ma'am? I turned around and looked for my mother.

I reminded myself that I was less than ten years older than this fresh-faced ingenue. "Hi, I'm looking for Annalee Chisolm. I need to talk to her about Karen Kelly."

That response brought the curious Sigma Gamma fully into the hallway. She studied me with a pained face. "Oh, wow, you must be— Oh, I'm so sorry. I didn't realize you were family."

Tears were already brimming in her bright blue eyes. "Annalee is upstairs, the second door to your right. She's very upset. We all are. Karen was one of us. When one dies, we all die a little. Not that any of us have died before, but, well, you know what I mean." The tears flowed freely and she held a trembling hand under her nose. "I'm sorry. I just can't believe this has happened." She turned and disappeared down the hall.

I stared after her for a minute, not sure how to proceed. It was much easier in the car, but now there were friends and emotions and tears involved. I had begun to feel a kind of kinship with Karen, and I wasn't sure how to handle the grief of her friends. I was doing a good job of ad-libbing today, so I bit my lip and stoically climbed the teal carpeted staircase. I'd figure out something. Soon.

The peach and teal theme continued upstairs. The long, narrow hallway was papered in peach roses and lined with composite photos of years of smiling sorority sisters. The door to Karen's room was shut, but I could hear movement inside. Music that I didn't recognize pounded loudly and was peppered with thuds, as if someone might be doing some heavy moving or cleaning.

I knocked lightly on the door and was rewarded with a shouted "Go away. I told you guys I want to be alone."

That didn't deter me; I simply knocked harder.

No answer.

I rapped once more just as the door was wrenched open. I almost gave Annalee Chisolm a bloody nose. I pulled my hand away as she angrily spewed, "Look, I told you, I want to be left—" The rest of her sentence was lost in a sharp shriek.

Just call me the Welcome Wagon.

Chapter 8

ANNALEE BACKED AWAY as if I had a ring of rotten eggs draped around me. She blinked several times, then squealed, "Oh, wow."

"Hi, I'm Kate Kelly," I said, figuring I may as well plunge in before she had a chance to scream again.

"Well, like I didn't know that already," she said in a more normal tone of voice. She reached for a pair of thick, wire-rimmed glasses sitting on a peach painted dresser, and tripped over a pile of clothes as she switched off the stereo.

She cursed under her breath, swept the errant clothes into her arms, then unceremoniously dumped them into a far corner of the room. The dorm room was small and cluttered with books, clothes, Sigma Gamma paraphernalia, and an abundance of houseplants, which covered every available surface not occupied by remnants of college life. Twin beds with matching ruffled peach spreads sat in the midst of the houseplant jungle. Annalee picked up a cardboard box off one bed and placed it on the floor.

"You can have a seat here," she said. "My name is Annalee Chisolm. I was Karen's roommate. I'm sorry I was so rude. I wasn't expecting any of Karen's family to show up. I guess you're her cousin? She talked about you guys a lot, even though you barely saw each other anymore."

I was in this far anyway, so I continued the ruse. "I was just coming through town and thought I'd surprise Karen. I didn't know about the accident until this morning when I saw it in the paper."

Annalee's eyes grew large and misty. "Oh, wow. That's totally awful timing. I thought you knew already." She fiddled with the bottom of her T-shirt and gazed uncomfortably at the floor. "Uh, have you talked to the sheriff from Woodbury yet? He's been here a few times to talk to us about Karen's, um, accident."

"I briefly talked to him after I read the article. I'll see him later today. I wanted to come here first. I have to let things soak in, I guess, before I meet with the police."

"Oh, I completely understand," she said quickly. "It must be such a shock. I don't think it's actually hit me yet. I keep expecting Karen to walk through that door, and when I saw you there, I guess my subconscious just freaked out."

I studied Annalee. She had long black hair and wore jeans and a teal T-shirt emblazoned with the sorority's Greek letters. Her violet eyes were red from crying, and a liberal dose of freckles danced across her nose and cheeks.

"Were you and Karen close friends?" I asked.

"Well, of course we were. We were SG sisters, after all." Annalee's shocked look changed to one bordering on pity. "You were never in a sorority, were you, hon? You just don't understand. That's okay, though. The Greek system is just a wonderful bonding experience. I'm sorry you weren't a part of it. I'm sure you would have been a good sister."

"Yes, well, I think I've managed all right," I feebly replied. I couldn't believe I was defending myself like this. It was definitely time to change the subject. "You know, sometimes it helps to talk about a person's good points when you're grieving. It's been a while since I've seen Karen. Too long, actually. What was she like as a friend?"

A smile spread across the girl's face. "Oh, she was the best. She could make you laugh at anything, and she'd go out of her way to help you. Everyone adored her. She was so smart and had so much ahead of her." Annalee's voice trailed off as she briskly wiped a tear from her eye.

"I guess, as a business major, she studied a great deal?" I prompted.

"Oh, tons. She always had her head buried in a book. We didn't have any classes together, but I know she had good grades."

"What are you majoring in, Annalee?"

She tossed her hair over her shoulder again. "Liberal studies. I intend to have a well-rounded degree. I plan on entering law school when I graduate. Of course, if I fail the entrance exam, I'll go to med school. I think. I may become a teacher, but I hate kids, and the only thing it's really got going for it is that I'd have the summers off."

She smiled proudly. "I have very definite goals in my life. That was Karen's problem. She just always said she'd go into business. That's not definite. Business could mean anything. Don't you agree?"

"Well, I guess it depends on how you look at it," I said slowly. "Did Karen have a job?"

Annalee shrugged her shoulders and sank onto the edge of the bed. She reached for a ruffled throw pillow and cuddled it in her lap. "It wasn't a real job, you know, in a business. She baby-sat for some rich old woman up in Woodbury. That's where she, um, had her accident. I always told her she should just get a real job in the mall or something, but she insisted that she wanted to work for this family."

She looked at me very seriously. "These people, the Merrimans, are loaded. Jaguars, Mercedes-Benzes, a mansion, and a beach house in the Caribbean. The old lady has control of it all. She lives in this incredible house with her son and daughter-in-law, but they're never there. They're always off to some party or trip to the beach. If I were them, I'd never leave. Karen snuck me inside a few times. Wow, the place is just too cool. It usually just seemed to be her, the old lady, and all these uniformed servants. I thought it made Karen look like one of the hired help, but she insisted she was a personal assistant and not a well-paid maid."

Annalee waved her hand around the room. "You've heard of Merriman Farms, I'm sure. You know, the plant and tree people? Well, that's the family she worked for, can't you tell? I told her if she brought another plant home, I'd kill her."

Realizing what she'd said, she cupped her hand to her mouth. Tears streamed down her cheeks. "I can't believe I just said that. Oh, I feel awful. She should have never worked for those people."

"It's okay. I'm sure you didn't mean anything by that." A box of Kleenex sat between us, so I plucked a tissue out and handed it to Annalee.

She took off her glasses and flung them onto the dresser. As she wiped her eyes and loudly blew her nose, my eyes wandered to a small bookcase covered in framed photos of Karen, Annalee, and their friends. Smiles abounded at dances, parties, on boats, and by the water.

Behind the row of pictures were four golden swim trophies. I peered closely at them. "Do those trophies belong to Karen?"

Annalee blew her nose again. "Of course. You know what a great swimmer she was. She was practically a fish. We're really going to miss her talents on the swim team this year." She crumpled her tissue in her fist. "That's one of the things that's so weird about her death. Of all people, Karen—one of the best swimmers I know—drowns at a dinky little lake. It just doesn't make sense."

It would make more sense, I thought, if she knew Karen had been strangled first.

"I know this sounds strange," she continued, "but I'd understand it if she'd died in a car crash. That's how she always said she'd die, you know, karma and all that stuff. I guess after her mom died in that crash that paralyzed her dad, that's all she thought about. Is he still in a nursing home?"

"Who?" I said stupidly.

Annalee looked at me strangely. "Karen's dad, your uncle. She never wanted me to go with her when she visited him in Ohio. She said it was too sad, that she wanted to remember him as he was before the accident. It didn't matter to me, because I'd never met him before, but Karen felt very strongly about it."

Boy, I was quickly digging myself into a pickle barrel. "Uh, yeah, he's still there. It's a very sad situation."

Annalee frowned. "My parents are very alive and healthy. I can't imagine what it must be like to basically lose both of them at once. I know it's a horrible tragedy, and I don't think Karen ever really got over it. She was really obsessive about safety, especially when it came to her car. She was a repairman's dream. She took it to the shop all the time, just to make sure nothing was wrong. She was convinced that she'd die in an accident, just like her mom. She said something about meeting up with her in the afterlife that way because they never had the chance to say good-bye. It really gave me the creeps when she'd talk like that."

Annalee stood and strode to the window. She leaned her head on the glass and drew an invisible picture on the windowpane with her finger. "That's another weird thing. Why hadn't I thought of that?"

"What's that, Annalee?"

She looked at me blankly. "The car. I couldn't believe she did that."

Not only was I moonlighting as one of Karen's relatives, but now I had to assume the guise of mind reader. I returned the blank stare. "I don't know what you're talking about, Annalee. Why don't you start from the beginning?"

She turned and leaned against the window. "Karen hasn't been herself the last few months. I ignored it at first, but in the last couple of weeks she's really had a rough time. As usual, it was all over a dumb guy."

My ears perked. Enter the elusive boyfriend. "Was she seriously involved with someone?"

Annalee shrugged. "When wasn't she? I hope you don't mind me saying this, since you're family and all, but Karen had terrible taste in men. I mean, there are plenty of great guys in the fraternities here at school. The Kappa Epsilon Gammas are great prospects, and the Phi Deltas are always a lot of fun, but Karen had a thing for old men. All they did was use her and break her heart."

Remembering my encounter with Annalee's sorority sister downstairs, I gently pried, "Just how old is old?" I steeled myself for the probable answer of something ridiculous, like 25.

She came close. "Well, some of them were probably, gosh, nearly 30. But there were several who were a lot older than that. Abby Swain, one of our SG sisters, is a psych major. She says that Karen was dating all these old guys because they reminded her of her dad. I don't know if that's the case, but I can't imagine having sex with someone that old, can you?" She made a face like she'd taken a sip of sour lemonade.

I felt my skin wrinkling on the spot. Quick, call out the Oil of Olay police. "What's all this have to do with a car?"

"Oh, yeah," Annalee said. "See, she'd been dating this old guy for a while and wanted to break up with him. They made plans to go out of town for a few days, but instead of picking her up, he told her to meet him at some hotel. I didn't think that was right, but Karen said it was fine because she was going to tell him it was over and then leave." She scratched her chin. "Like I said, Karen was obsessive about her car. It was her baby. She wouldn't let anyone else drive it, and she certainly never drove another car. However, she got a rental car to go meet this guy. She got really defensive when I asked her why she did that."

"Did she tell you why she rented the car?"

"It was his idea. He set up the entire thing," Annalee said. "He was real specific about which car she should get, and said he'd have a package for her in the car."

I wondered if the package was the money in my trunk. I filed that thought and listened to the rest of her story.

"She made me drive her all the way to the Richmond International Airport to pick up the car," Annalee continued. "That's so ridiculous; there are plenty of car rental agencies here. It was almost like she was in some kind of spy movie or something. She was supposed to pick up the car at the airport Sunday night, then meet him at some hotel in Richmond. I didn't understand it at all."

"Why Richmond?" I asked. "Why rent a car in Richmond if that's where you're staying?"

"Oh, that's not where they were going to stay. Richmond is only where they were going to meet. I think they were going to drive to Kentucky for a few days."

Why not fly to Kentucky? I wondered. "But why meet at a hotel? Why not meet at the airport, then drive to Kentucky? What about his car? Why not just take the car he drove?"

Annalee rolled her eyes. "Honestly, I didn't pay that much attention to all the details. Karen was always running off here or there with one of her old guys. Who knows what their motivation was? Maybe he wanted a quickie before they hit the road for Kentucky."

Karen was a bit more colorful and rebellious than the newspaper article described. I looked at the picture on the bedside table. Karen stared at me with wide eyes and a bright smile. It was easy to see why men would be charmed by her.

"If she was going to break up with him," I said, "why agree to go out of state with him?"

Annalee sat on the edge of the bed. "Well, she wasn't really planning on going away for the whole time. She had been real stressed out lately and had been making lots of late-night phone calls to this guy. She'd drop everything for him, then ultimately return here and cry herself to sleep. Something major was going on with them."

She reached for another tissue. She pulled it out of the box, but instead of using it, she merely twisted it around her fingers. "It was like—I don't know—like she was scared of him. Personally, even though he was supposedly pretty rich, I think he was a real jerk."

Looking at me with haunted eyes, she nervously whispered, "I think he knocked her around a bit. She would never admit it, but there were times she'd come home really upset, and then the next day, she'd wear long-sleeved shirts and stuff, even if it was hot outside. Once, she had a really nasty bruise on her chin, just like you'd get if someone slugged you. When I asked her about it, she said she bumped into a door. I think his fist bumped into her face."

I thought back to the hospital and Sheriff Thompson's comment about bruises on Karen's chest. "Couldn't someone in charge of the sorority say something to her? Someone should have tried to help Karen."

"I know, I know, but what could I do? Karen denied that he hit her. Was I supposed to embarrass her by accusing her boyfriend of abuse? Besides, what if it got out to the other sororities that something so awful was going on? That kind of stuff doesn't happen in good sororities."

I was furious and dumb struck at the same time. "Annalee, the sorority should have helped her. There's no reason to be embarrassed by it."

I hit a nerve that Annalee knew well. She shut her eyes tightly and took two deep breaths. Her eyes still screwed shut, she whispered, enunciating each word, "I know that now. Believe me, I think about it all the time."

She slowly opened her eyes, blinking salty tears out of a tangle of wet eyelashes. "They had a huge argument last Wednesday, then he sent her flowers on Thursday and they arranged for this trip. I guess he was trying to make up for whatever they fought about. Karen really freaked out when he told her about the rental car, but then she decided that she would rent the car, go to the hotel, tell him good-bye, and leave. That way, he'd still have to pay for the car rental. I guess it was a small piece of revenge in her eyes."

"Is that how it happened?" I asked. I couldn't say I blamed Karen for sticking him with the car rental. It was the least he deserved if he was beating her. Personally, I could think of many things to do to him. If he was wealthy, $60 for a car rental probably didn't scratch a notch in his money clip.

Annalee shook her head. "Well, yes and no. I took her to the airport Sunday, and she went to the hotel like they planned. Apparently, he went ballistic when she told him she was breaking up with him. She said she ran out of the hotel and started to head back to Williamsburg. Once she hit the highway, she thought he'd probably try to follow her back here. She said she was really upset and didn't know what to do, so she just kept driving."

So, Karen and her boyfriend had a fight, and in his rage he followed her onto the highway. However, she must have lost him and, instead, he mistook my identical rental car for Karen's and decided to play vengeful bumper cars. What a sweetheart.

"She didn't come home at all that night," Annalee said. "Of course, I didn't know what to think. I was worried, but then I thought maybe she went ahead and made up with him. You could never tell what Karen would do when it came to guys."

"When did you see her next?"

"The next morning. She said she drove all night, trying to clear her mind and decide what to do. She took the car back to the agency, then called me to pick her up. Talk about an early wake-up call. It was only six in the morning. I could have killed her."

There was that phrase again.

Annalee burst into tears. "Why do I keep saying that? I'm so sorry. You never think about how words can mean so much." She sobbed, her face buried in her hands. She raised her head. Tear-stained strands of her hair were plastered haphazardly on her cheeks, like lines on a road map intersecting at strange angles. She didn't bother to push the strands away. "I brought her home, and she crashed. She hadn't slept all night and was exhausted. I had to go to the library on campus, so I woke her up about an hour before she had to go to work at Merriman Farms. That's the last time I saw her. . . ." The rest of her sentence was choked with more tears.

I felt so uncomfortable. I reached over and squeezed her hand. Annalee's story had gaps in it, but overall, it seemed vital. It gave me a motive for my accident and placed a mound of suspicion on the boyfriend. If we ever figured out who he was.

"Annalee, have you told Sheriff Thompson this story?"

She reached for another tissue and blew her nose twice. She honked so loudly I found myself glancing out the window lest a flock of geese should descend on the room in search of companionship.

She finally pushed the wayward strands of hair off her cheeks. "Yeah, he came by here yesterday. I told him everything I've told you."

I asked the obvious question. "What was Karen's boyfriend's name?"

Annalee sighed again and turned her eyes toward the ceiling. "Oh, geez, the sheriff asked that also. I don't know, Bob, Bill, John, Joe, something. Like I said, Karen had a lot of boyfriends. I can't possibly be responsible for all their life histories."

I looked at her with incredulous eyes. Annalee was probably the only person who could finger Karen's murderer, and she couldn't think of his name? "You seem to know a lot about this guy. Surely Karen said his name."

"Like I told the sheriff, Karen got around. Some were single, but a lot of them weren't. Maybe it's not the most politically correct thing to do the deed with a married guy, but she at least had the dignity to use assumed names for them."

"What do you mean by assumed names?"

Annalee blinked several times. I waited for her to say "Duh?" She rose above the occasion. "Just what I said. Fake names, made up stuff. Some of these guys were big movers and shakers in town. She couldn't risk being caught in some kind of scandal."

I tried again. "So, this guy was married? Do you know what kind of work he does?"

Annalee's cheeks flushed. "No, I don't have any idea. It's apparently a pretty nice job, because he bought Karen lots of nice stuff. Some of the flower arrangements he sent probably cost well over a hundred dollars. As for being married, you got me there. She never really said. If I had to guess, I'd say he was married. Most of her relationships with the old guys were pretty hush-hush, but this one practically met CIA standards for secrecy."

This was getting me nowhere fast. "So I guess you've never actually met him face-to-face," I concluded.

"Are you kidding?" she replied. "Even when he'd call, he'd never talk, just say, 'Karen, please.' If she wasn't here, he wouldn't even have the decency to say thank you; he'd just hang up."

I grasped at straws. "What was his voice like?"

Annalee looked at me like I'd asked her to add up the national debt without a calculator. "He had a guy's voice. What do you expect?"

She had a point.

I looked around the room again, and my gaze landed on a chipped porcelain vase. Something clicked in my mind. "Did Karen talk about antiques much?"

"No, why?"

"She didn't like to visit antique stores and pick up old objects?"

She shook her head. "The only old objects she liked were her old men."

I winced. I recalled the comment about some of Karen's boyfriends being "nearly 30" and pictured my hair going completely white as we spoke. I was afraid to look in the mirror.

"Look," Annalee said, "I hate to be rude, but I have a class. I'm really sorry about Karen's death. She was one of my best friends. I know your family must be really devastated. I just don't know what else to say. Feel free to look through Karen's stuff. Her books are on the shelves over there, and she kept boxes of letters and notes in the bottom of her closet."

She walked over to a narrow door in the corner of the room. She turned the knob and revealed a closet overflowing with clothes, shoes, and cardboard storage boxes. "It's kind of a mess. Take all the time you need. Just close my door behind you when you leave."

She painted on a weak smile. "It was nice to meet you, even though the circumstances are terrible. Please call us if you need anything. The Sigma Gammas are always ready to help."

I mumbled my thanks and stared at the closet as Annalee headed toward the door. "Annalee, did the police search Karen's closet yesterday?"

She spun around. "No, why would they want to do something like that?"

"I don't know," I fibbed. "I was just curious."

My question clearly unnerved the girl. She reached for her glasses and her purse and clumsily knocked over a perfume bottle. She swung the purse over her shoulder, sending a bottle of nail polish and a notebook tumbling off the dresser. "I've got to go," she said quickly. "I hope I see you later."

She shut the door with a thud. My conscience rapped loudly at my thoughts. I had no legal right to be alone in Karen's room. Contrary to popular opinion, I was not related to the deceased. I had no reason to plow through her private possessions, other than to feed my morbid curiosity. If Thompson had known I was standing in Karen's room, he would have had a stroke.

But, I was a reporter with a story to cover.

Or uncover.

It was my journalistic obligation, right?

I headed for the closet.

Chapter 9

I STARED into Karen's disheveled closet. A mountainous pile of sweat-shirts and sweaters on a narrow shelf towered above a thin rod which sagged under dresses, jeans, and blouses shoved together like tourists on the monorail ride at Disneyland. Perhaps it was some kind of physics experiment, to see how much could be smashed into a tiny space. If so, Karen deserved an A on her report card. A succession of tattered cardboard boxes lined the floor and were topped with plastic shoe racks. Shoes, however, seemed optional, since most of them lay in mismatched piles between the racks. I should be such a critic. Karen's closet-organizing skills (or lack thereof) weren't that far removed from my own.

She had me beat on sheer quantity, though. While I'm not exactly hurting for clothes, my closet tends to hold looks which are more comfortable than Karen's collegiate, preppy collection. I could be eternally happy living in a pair of jeans and a sweater. Better yet, I hope to spend eternity in thick, fleecy sweat pants, an oversized sweatshirt, and fuzzy slippers.

I thought about poking through the pockets of her clothes, but that could have taken ages. Instead, I ran my hand across the garments as if they were keys on a piano. They swayed back and forth gently but didn't reveal anything.

The boxes on the floor, however, begged me to inspect them, so I rummaged around the pockets of Karen's coats until I came up with a pair of gloves. With all these weird coincidences swirling around me, the last thing I needed was for my fingerprints to appear over all of Karen's belongings. That would make Thompson's day. He'd probably polish the electric chair just for me. I pulled on the black Isotoners and set to work.

I yanked the shoe racks onto the floor next to me and shoved the loose shoes into a corner. The first box held old notebooks from accounting and business management classes. I flipped through each one, in case she had inserted anything interesting, but it was to no avail. Two department-store sweater boxes held more notebooks. Karen saved everything possible. I found receipts for books, dinners, clothing, and Sigma Gamma membership dues.

I carefully replaced the notebooks and moved on to a flowered, cardboard file box. This one was more interesting. Several envelopes of pictures were scattered through the box. There was an assortment of weddings, college parties, sorority picnics, the usual stuff. The only two people I recognized were Karen and Annalee. I looked for a pattern of pictures of Karen with a man, but the only ones I could find were group shots from picnics or fraternity parties. There were no photos of Karen's "old men."

The last file box held stuffed animals. I pawed through a veritable zoo of turtles, teddy bears, horses, and mice, but came up empty. The bottom of the box was lined with a dog-eared collection of trashy romance novels. Brawny, bare-chested men with biceps the size of Montana clutched lusty, well-endowed heroines on each cover. I flipped through the books quickly and smiled at the folded pages and inked arrows directing the reader to the juiciest parts.

This breaking-and-entering business was harder than it looked on television. I hadn't found a thing that hinted at why Karen was dead. I carefully replaced everything, even to the point of scattering her shoes haphazardly across the tops of the boxes.

The bookcase next to Karen's bed held more knickknacks than books, and the only thing living under her bed was a colony of dust balls next to two empty Coke cans. My last hope was the dresser. I quickly searched through the four drawers but found nothing more interesting than an enormous collection of lingerie in every conceivable color, fabric, and design.

I returned to the closet as I removed the gloves. As I shoved them back into the pocket of a burgundy Lands' End windbreaker, I looked up at the shelf full of sweatshirts. It was the only thing I hadn't examined. Oh, why not? I slipped on the gloves again and pulled over a small, badly nicked desk chair. It didn't look very sturdy, but I stepped onto it and held the side of the closet in case my foot went through the seat. The seat survived, and I gingerly balanced on the chair, which wobbled a bit on uneven legs.

The sweatshirts and sweaters were neatly folded and shoved tightly together on the plywood shelf. I lifted and gently shook each sweater and sweatshirt, hoping that something would appear out of the blue. It was useless. I wasn't sure I'd even know a clue if it fell on my head. If something did fall on my head, it would only add to the headache that had returned with the force and annoyance of a door-to-door salesman. I rubbed my forehead for a moment and tried to think of where I would hide something important if I were Karen.

"Oh, give up, will ya?" I said aloud. I shoved a row of sweaters toward the wall and stepped off the chair. I heard a clunk in the back of the closet and saw something slip from a corner and slide down the wall. I dropped to my knees and pawed through my artful arrangement of shoes. A stenographer's notebook dangled between the heel of a red leather pump and the laces of a pair of mud-stained Nikes.

I pulled it out and lifted the cover. The first part of the notebook hadn't been written in, but when I fanned the mint-colored sheets, I discovered that the middle section revealed several pages of writing titled "Special Project." In a large, rounded script, Karen listed three pages of items and corresponding prices. I scanned the list, which read like an inventory for someone's house: "Blue glass ashtray—$25, three silver teaspoons (engraved)—$75, tea cup and saucer (labeled "Nippon, Japan")—$50, crystal vase (early 1800s?)—$165, two knives (match teaspoons)—$50."

The list went on to include picture frames, glass eggs, a few more figurines, and an assortment of vases and silverware. The final page was titled "Good Stuff" and included several pieces of jewelry which brought three- and four-figure prices.

I wanted to believe that Karen simply purchased these things at various antique stores or flea markets and sold them for a profit. It is a hobby many people have. Why shouldn't she enjoy shopping for treasures at the plethora of flea markets which spread across the Virginia countryside like kudzu each year? There's no harm in doing that. However, the cynical side of me nagged that there was probably much more to the story.

All the items had two things in common. They were all small enough to slip into a pocket or purse, one at a time, so that they wouldn't be missed right away, and each piece was of the variety that if the owner discovered it missing, he or she might simply think it had been misplaced. It might never occur to the owner that the item had been stolen and sold.

The Merriman house was full of antiques, and Karen was there every afternoon. I assumed she had gained the complete trust of everyone there. They considered her a sweet, honest college student who took care of Mrs. Merriman, the matriarch of the town's most important family. Constance herself had said that Chase was protective to a fault when it came to his mother.

Why risk being caught stealing from the most prominent family in a small town? The resulting scandal would probably be social suicide to a sorority member. It goes without saying that an arrest and conviction for stealing probably wouldn't sit well with the college administration either. Why jeopardize your entire future on a small cache of pilfered antiques?

I pulled out my reporter's notebook. Some people fill their purses with lipstick, gum, and money. I have the gum and, on rare occasion, the money; but I also carry a narrow white notebook and a microcassette recorder. Carrying those items not only makes me feel like Lois Lane, but at least I know where they are at all times on the off chance I get to interview Superman. I flipped open my notepad and copied the list of items from Karen's notebook.

Now, more than ever, I wanted to get my hands on the ledger book at Walenza's Antiques. I had a very strong hunch that the lists would match. I flipped to the next page of Karen's notebook and found it covered in calculations. Two columns, labeled "Me" and "Him," figured the take. After a few calculations of my own, I discovered that Karen took only a 10% cut of the money made selling antiques. The remaining 90% went to "Him." In the same rounded scrawl and underlined several times, she had written, "This is bullshit!" near the totals.

The next part of the notebook was empty, but I soon came upon more writing. Once again, things got interesting. The Merriman riddle, in all its glory, adorned a sheet. Karen had scribbled several notes to herself in the margins and crossed them out so fiercely that I couldn't read them even when I held the page up to the light.

The riddle puzzled Karen as it had generations of treasure hunters. I stared at her version. Next to the phrase "But deserving to only a few who can divine the magic of an old witch," Karen had drawn a crude cartoon of a witch and labeled it "Constance." I wondered if Constance's tears over Karen's death were genuine.

Where the riddle read, "The location you'll find, not from a wise old maid or a young dumb waiter," Karen had circled *dumb waiter* several times and put an exclamation mark next to the words. She had figured something out, but I couldn't follow her train of thought.

What caught my eye was the next line: "Nor in the fire of the sun, where flowers wilt from the heat." Karen had underlined each word with blue, black, and green ink. She'd emphasized it so much that it was difficult to read the line below. For good measure, she also circled *where flowers wilt from the heat.* I remembered Chase had mentioned that Karen fancied the "azalea trail" at the farm. I wondered if that or the lake had anything to do with her predilection for this part of the riddle.

I leaned against the closet door and closed my eyes. My afternoon was coming together quickly. Not only had Karen visited the library to copy the Merriman riddle, she also appeared to be Rupert Walenza's favorite antique customer. I hoped I was wrong, but I had a strong suspicion that she was stealing from the Merrimans.

The largest question still loomed. Who was "him"? There were so many references to his existence, yet no solid proof, like a picture or phone number, address, or, most importantly, a name. As I turned the next few pages of the notebook, my breath caught in the back of my throat and eked out a surprised squeak. I stared at a letter which began, "My darling."

It read, "First I want you to know how important you are to me. I admire you so much for everything you've taught me—about business, about the world, and about love. I have never met anyone as exciting as you. You are so mature and smart; nothing like these stupid fraternity boys in my classes. You're a man—I have no use for boys anymore."

There's nothing like feeding a guy's ego, is there?

It continued, "I am so proud to be a part of your life. I want to share you with the world, even though I know that's not possible. I wish it were! I want to tell my friends about you and all the exciting things we've done. You're so devious! Just think, someday it will all be ours!"

I wondered if "it" was the Merriman treasure. I filed that thought and read on, discovering a more ominous tone: "Darling, you know I'd do anything for you, but I'm scared that someone might find out about our project. Don't you think it would be better to be more secretive about it? I know it makes you angry when I bring this up, but I'm afraid of being caught. I know you'd defend me and make everything all right, but I have to cover my back as well. Please don't be angry with me; I hate to see you cross, but I think it would be best if I stopped working on our project."

The pleading tone of Karen's letter made me very uncomfortable. I could imagine what seeing him "cross" or "angry" would entail. Karen was just a scared, abused kid. She was bargaining for her freedom and safety in this letter that apparently never made it to the intended party.

The handwriting in the next paragraph became messier, as if it had been written through tears. "You know I love you, but I think it would be wise if we stopped seeing each other for a while. Your temper frightens me, and I think things are getting you too stressed out. Maybe it would be better if we both could have some time off to think about how we can eventually be together without all this mess. You know you can trust me always. Don't worry—your amazing secret is safe with me. I'll be at the farm each day this week. Please, let's talk about it in a quiet, rational way. I'm only suggesting this because I love you and want the best for you. I hope you know that in your heart."

That was all. Either Karen never finished the letter or she abandoned the entire idea of sending it. It held a lot of information, but it still didn't help me figure out who the mystery man was. It also made me extraordinarily curious as to what his "amazing secret" was. Had Karen and her boyfriend solved the Merriman riddle? Or was it something else that could harm him if Karen spilled the beans?

I was aware of an advancing crawl of heat down the back of my neck. It extended to my palms, which were now swimming in sweat inside the black gloves. My breaths were coming in deep, pounding sighs, and my stomach tightened as if a block of cement were pushing down on it. The notebook shimmied with a slight tremor. I looked at my hands and realized they were trembling.

This letter and all the other notes scared me. I had entered a very private, personal world where a seemingly innocent affair and adventure had wound up in murder.

And now I was tangled in the thick of it.

I looked around the room again and jumped when someone ran down the hall outside and slammed a nearby door. I shut my eyes and took a few deep breaths. My head was pounding, but I wasn't sure if it was from fear or my lingering reminder of the car accident that was intended for Karen.

The sound of a U2 song from someone's stereo thumped on the wall facing me. I looked around the room for a clock. I had no idea how long I'd been alone in Karen's room. Annalee could return any minute, and I didn't think it would look too innocent to find me sitting on the floor, wearing black gloves and reading Karen's private notes. How would I explain that one?

I shut the notebook and rapped it nervously on my knee a few times. I tried to justify "borrowing" it for a while, but then I visualized an angry Sheriff Thompson locking me up in the county jail and providing me with plenty of extraneous reading material. Such as how to defend yourself on various charges like breaking and entering, tampering with evidence, concealing evidence, and disturbing a crime scene.

I climbed on the chair and sandwiched the notebook between a teal SG sweatshirt and a speckled gray sweater. I put the gloves back into the windbreaker pocket, then shut the closet door with my elbow, being careful not to touch the door handle. I decided that the next time I saw Thompson I would casually inquire if he had searched Karen's dorm room. Hopefully, that would give him the hint and allow him to "stumble" upon the notebook.

I plucked a couple of tissues out of the box on the bed and used them to cover my hands as I put the chair back in place. I shoved my notebook and pen deep into my purse and glanced around the room one last time. Everything looked exactly as Annalee had left it.

I cracked open the door enough to peer down the hallway. I could hear voices in some part of the sorority house, but no one populated the entry hall. I flew down the carpeted steps, past the framed, toothy smiles of decades of SG composite photos. I was out the front door in a blur without being seen by anyone.

Anyone inside the house, that is.

I bounded down the porch steps and rounded a large evergreen. My car was only steps away, but I managed to crash into someone walking in the shade of the evergreen. Our bodies slammed together clumsily.

My ankle bowed inward and my keister hit the sidewalk. My conspirator in this latest collision of mine fared better.

He wobbled for a second, then squatted to the ground. "Kate, are you all right? What the hell are you doing here?"

I stared at the face just inches from mine. Dr. John Donovan.

"The question is, John, what the hell are *you* doing here?"

Chapter 10

JOHN STARED AT ME. "Are you sure you're okay? You look like you've seen a ghost."

The boy was cute, but he obviously had a hearing problem.

I rose to my knees, sank back on my heels, and brushed dirt from my jeans. "John, I'm fine, even though I feel a little silly sitting here in the middle of the sidewalk."

He stood and offered his arm. I reached for it and he pulled me up to a standing position.

Trying to ignore how dizzy I felt, I put on what I call my mean-schoolteacher face: I squinted my eyes and pursed my lips as if I'd just swallowed a state-fair-sized prize lemon. It always worked for Mrs. Wampler in the fourth grade. "I asked you a question. What are you doing here?"

It was obvious John wished that I had asked him something else, like if there really was a Santa Claus. He looked around the street, pointedly avoiding my gaze. After a ten-second or so stall, his eyes lit up. "Library. I was at the library on campus. Doing research. Medical stuff. Yeah, the library."

He was trying his hardest to be sincere, but something told me he probably never did very well when he had to play truth or dare as a kid. He should have given up, but he babbled on, his dark eyelashes flapping like a fan in the sweaty hands of a country churchgoer singing gospel hymns.

"I was doing some reference work on blood diseases. At the library, over there." He pointed over my shoulder, then quickly jerked his hand over his own shoulder. His smile continued a downward spiral. "I mean, over there. The library is, uh, over there."

"I know," I replied. "I went to school here." Why was he lying? I decided to test him. "This is quite a walk from the library. Where's your car?"

I knew exactly where his car was. I could see it parked along the street about thirty feet from where we stood.

"It's right back there, but you know that, don't you?" He looked toward the sorority house and quickly changed the subject. "Were you an SG when you were here?"

"No, I was an SAS."

His eyes flopped back to me. "SAS? I don't remember hearing of that sorority."

I grinned and shrugged. "Sororities Are Silly. I managed to survive college without a taste of the Greek life."

John's smile returned. This time it was warm and genuine. "Yeah, I was the same way. I was too wrapped up in med school to worry about getting drunk and naked each weekend."

That conjured up a pleasant image. I felt my cheeks turning red, so I tried to erase that vision from my brain. It wasn't an easy task. What was that phrase? "If only I had a jug of wine and thou?" And how. I decided the only way to get back on track was to stick to the hard, unpleasant truth. The jug of wine would have to come later.

"Karen Kelly was an SG. I just met her roommate, Annalee. She thinks I'm Karen's long-lost cousin. You know, family resemblance and all."

John nodded. "Clever move. I, uh, didn't know Karen was an SG. I heard she was in a sorority, so I thought I'd try and find out which one. I don't know why, I just feel like something about this situation isn't right."

His eyes softened to the shade of warm cocoa as he reached for my hand. His grip was firm and he ran his thumb absentmindedly across my knuckles. "Kate, I don't know how to tell you, so I'll just say it. We ran an autopsy on Karen. She was murdered, Kate. Strangled. I had suspicions before, but I didn't want to say anything until we knew for sure."

"I know," I said. "I heard about it this morning when I was at Merriman Farms. Sheriff Thompson took the call from the coroner there. He's not exactly in a great mood right now. I think he'd rather leave murder investigations to jurisdictions other than his."

"I can't say I blame him," John said. "I hate to sound provincial, but things like that really don't happen around these parts." He frowned. "Kate, I know you're curious about what happened, but I think you should let it go. Let the police take care of things. You didn't even know Karen Kelly. You should just walk away from it all; consider it a bad memory. After all, we're talking about a murder. You could be in danger, and I don't know what I'd do if, if. . . ."

I watched John's gaze shift quickly to something behind me. Before I could turn to see what was so interesting, he dropped my hand and impulsively cupped my chin in both of his hands, then pulled me forward into a warm and deep kiss. It was sudden, but certainly not altogether unwelcome. His fingers slid up my neck and made a detour into my hair. I was only partially aware that someone was walking past us. For all I cared, it could be a marching band—with elephants bringing up the rear.

That changed, however, when the person stopped and tapped John on the shoulder. "Hey! It's you! I haven't seen you in ages! Looks like things are going great for you." The squeaking voice intruding on my little reward of passion giggled at a pitch that would send dogs six blocks away scurrying for cover.

It also sent the flame out the door. We came back to reality and turned to the Human Dog Whistle. She had short, layered, black hair that was in need of a cut—or at least a healthy combing out—and thick glasses that magnified her eyes to the size of fried eggs. It didn't surprise me that she was wearing a teal shirt with the Greek letters ΣΓ spread across it.

"I'm just really, really glad to see you here again," Dog Whistle gushed. "I didn't think I'd have the chance anymore." She pierced the air again with the excruciating giggle. "I mean, you know, there's really no reason for you to be here. Like, I didn't mean it like that, but, well, I'm just glad you're here."

I think we had established that fact.

The feeling wasn't mutual. John's eyes narrowed, and the muscle in the corner of his jaw clicked like the second hand of a watch. He took a breath, then said very slowly, "And it's nice to see you again. . . ." He tilted his head toward Whistle as if to solicit a response.

She quickly took note. "Shannon. Shannon Mulavill, remember? That's okay, it's been a while. You know, anytime you'd like to come by, feel free. You're always welcome." She looked at me less enthusiastically and added, "And you can come too, if you really want."

"Well, thank you, Shannon," John said very politely. "I'll keep that in mind, but right now, we've got to be going. Have a good day." He grasped my elbow and propelled me toward his car. In a flash, he whipped out his keys, opened the passenger door, and deposited me in the seat.

The Whistle known as Shannon remained in her spot and managed a tentative wave to John. "Don't forget my invitation, now, okay?"

He glanced over his shoulder. "Yeah, right. I'll remember." He slid into the driver's seat and gunned the engine. As we swerved onto the roadway, he shook his head fiercely. "Man, that was annoying."

"Old girlfriend?"

He looked at me in horror. "No, no, no! She was, uh, a patient. I vaguely remember her. How could I forget a laugh like that? I think they brought her into the ER one night after some party. To put it bluntly, she puked her brains out all night after consuming most of the alcohol available in Virginia."

"That's pleasant," I said. "Why did she come all the way to Woodbury? Williamsburg Community Hospital is only a couple of miles away from here."

Wrong question.

John's foot met the floor, and we lurched onto North Henry Street. "How should I know? If they're sick enough to come to the ER, I guess they go wherever they think of first. It was just weird that we ran into her like that. Coincidence, that's all."

Coincidence—my favorite word these days.

"You got that right," I said. "The last few days have been very weird. Now, you know very well how much contact I've had recently with our buddies in blue, so forgive me if I ask you something."

John glanced uneasily at me. "All right, shoot."

"Correct me if I'm wrong, but isn't this considered kidnapping?"

His eyes clouded, then brightened quickly, and he laughed. "You're right. I did just drive off without exactly asking you if you wanted to come along. Hell, I don't even know where I'm heading now." His smile widened. "I won't hold you for ransom. You've had a rough enough week without having to worry about that. I guess you'd like me to take you back to your car?"

I wanted to say, *No, you can drive me anywhere. And, oh, by the way, just what did that kiss mean?* We'd never had the chance to comment on that significant event.

It was still uppermost in my mind, but it seemed to have floated out of John's gray matter. It has always annoyed me to no end how men can switch their feelings on and off with the speed they click a remote control. Was the kiss genuine, or was it merely a way to busy himself so he could avoid contact with our friend The Dog Whistle Named Shannon, who, strangely enough, was an SG?

Like Karen. And didn't she say something like, *It was great to see you here again?* Was she implying that he'd been to the SG house before?

I made an executive decision. "Since I'm here anyway, and it is getting late, how about dinner? You can drop me off at my car later."

"It's a deal," John replied. "Where would you like to go?"

I thought for a moment. "Is the Armadillo Roadhouse still around? I practically lived there when I was in college." Remembering how old everyone thought I was lately, I quickly added, "Which wasn't all that long ago. College, that is."

"I feel like I've been in school my entire life, but that's what happens when you decide to pursue medicine." He was quiet for a few seconds. "And of course the Armadillo is still around. That place will never shut down. It sounds great to me." He looked over his shoulder, switched lanes, and headed toward the freeway.

The sky was already mottled with splotches of burnt sienna, which is a color I've loved to use since my Crayola days. Saying it makes me feel smarter. It's so much nicer than just picturing a sunset as ordinary orange. The summer was quickly fading.

I glanced at my watch—it wasn't even 6:30 yet. Pretty soon we'd all be begging for long, lazy summer nights when the sun stays bright until nearly 10:00. I made a mental note to check into story ideas in the Deep South in the coming months, somewhere like Key West, or maybe even down around the Caribbean. It didn't matter where it was, as long as it had sunshine and warm temperatures.

The Armadillo Roadhouse is the type of restaurant I always look for on my travels. It's simply a fun, warm place with friendly people and decent, spicy, melt-your-margarita-glass Tex-Mex food. It's far from trendy and is reasonably priced, so if you wanted to impress a date or drag along your family, you could easily succeed on both accounts. It's always busy and very noisy, crowded with the discordant rhyme of dishes gone haywire, loud laughter, and ESPN blaring the latest sports scores from above the bar.

The Armadillo was the place to hang out when I was in college. My friends and I frequented the restaurant so much the waitresses actually knew our voices on the phone when we'd place the rare take-out order. More often than not, though, we'd shore up in one of the oversized wooden booths, order a few rounds of margaritas, and gossip until the kitchen closed.

The prospect of spending the evening at the Armadillo not only put a smile on my face, it also reminded me how hungry I was. My subconscious also zinged forward to remind me that the Armadillo was a bit off the beaten path from Williamsburg.

That's why it's so popular with the locals. The hordes of tourists who swarm around our fair city every day have yet to discover this local treasure. The restaurant is off I-64 on the outskirts of Williamsburg. There are no signs advertising it, so you have to know where you're heading once you turn off the highway and hit Higgins Pass.

My subconscious whapped my head once more. Higgins Pass. Why, that leads right past Walenza's Antiques and heads directly into Woodbury. I could enjoy a nice dinner with John, then we could cruise past Walenza's, just in case the urge to go antiquing hit for any reason.

John flipped a switch, and a soft buzz whirred above my head as the sunroof lazily eased open. "So what's this about your appearance as Karen Kelly's long-lost cousin?"

"I've had quite a day," I began. "After I left Merriman Farms, I stopped for lunch at a diner nearby. I saw a copy of the student newspaper, which told all about Karen's death. It quoted her roommate, so I decided to pay her a visit."

"That's the reporter coming out in you," he said.

"You must have a bit of reporter in yourself as well," I replied, "since you decided to hunt down her sorority."

John flashed a look at me. "Yeah, well, I just thought that would be the most logical place to start."

What didn't seem so logical was John's selection of the SG house as his first visit, since it was literally in the middle of the row of sorority houses. "How did you know to begin with the SG house?" I asked. "Had you been there before?"

"At the SG house?" He frowned. "No, why should I go there? I, uh, saw the same newspaper as you did this morning. I just thought I could maybe talk to the roommate, like you did. That's all, really."

Okay, that sounded plausible. I believed him, but something still bothered me about why he had lied earlier. "I have to admit that I was a little shocked when I saw Karen's picture in the paper. Why didn't you tell me how much she and I looked alike?"

"Honestly, it didn't really register that much with me," John replied. "I hate to sound crass, but I work in the ER, Kate. I see dozens of people every day, and usually they don't look that great. I concentrate on whatever the medical problem is first, then I get to know them." He winked. "You should know that. You're one of my patients. I think a lot of the resemblance comes in your eyes, and, well, Karen never regained consciousness. I never saw her animated and inquisitive like you."

I hoped that was a compliment. I glanced out the window as we flew down the exit ramp onto Higgins Pass. The Armadillo was just a few stoplights away.

"Actually," I said, "her roommate was very helpful, whether she knew it or not. I've learned a great deal today. I think there's a lot more to this murder than most people are letting on."

"Sounds intriguing," John replied. "I can't wait to hear all about it."

We luckily hit green lights along Higgins Pass, and the familiar neon-lit cactus at the entrance to the Armadillo Roadhouse blinked merrily ahead. Like the bells ringing for Pavlov's dogs, the neon blink triggered something in my mind and signaled an appreciative gurgle from my stomach. Damn the diet; burritos and *queso* would soon come to the rescue.

"Geez, would you look at this parking lot," John said as his wheels crunched the gravel lot. The Armadillo was living up to its reputation. Even though it was a weeknight, there wasn't an empty spot in view.

People of all ages lined the wooden porch, talking loudly and drinking margaritas and beer. A group of women in low-cut T-shirts and painted-on jeans bopped in the far corner of the porch to the sounds of the Rolling Stones blaring out from the loudspeakers. Mick Jagger's refrain of "Jumpin' Jack Flash, it's a—" was interrupted by a crackle of "Buchanon, party of four" over the intercom. The interruption didn't disturb the dancers. They merely laughed, twisted their hips some more, and sloshed another wave of beer out of their mugs.

John rolled to a stop near the porch. "I'm anxious to hear about your day, but why don't you go put our name on the list while I try to find a place to park? It looks like I might have to head across the street or something, so it might be a few minutes."

I popped the door open. "Sure, be glad to. Can I get you a beer while I'm waiting?"

"Sounds delightful. Make it a Heineken. The next round will be on me."

"I hope you make it back before the first round is over."

John laughed. "Yeah, well, if I'm not back in fifteen minutes, call the sheriff and add a missing person to his to-do list."

I shut the car door, and he headed off to parking spaces unknown.

I bounded up the steps to the porch and pushed in the heavy wood doors. Merriment and mayhem abounded as waitresses in jeans and white T-shirts performed delicate balancing acts with trays full of drinks and food, leaving the enticing scent of green chilies and onions in their wake as they wove in and out of the crowd near the bar.

A hazy film of smoke floated through the air, and a preppy, manicured sports anchor's commentary was lost forever amid the boisterous conversations taking prominence under the TV set perched above the bar. Beer and boasting probably had a lot to do with the volume, but it could also be related to the stereo system, which was thumping out strains of classic rock. It was so noisy and crowded that it took great effort to hear yourself think.

Life was good at the Armadillo Roadhouse.

A hostess was nonexistent. Hoping to find a waiting list for tables, I maneuvered my way up to the bar. I also placed an order for two Heinekens. In a practiced move, the bartender tweaked off the bottle caps and handed me the two ice-cold beers. To my shouted inquiry about a waiting list, he shouted back, "You need to talk to Susan. She'll get your name. Just look for her over there."

I turned to see nearly thirty or forty people "over there," none of whom looked like they were working or even remotely interested in taking my name for a table. I worked my way closer to where he had pointed and was scanning the crowd for the elusive Susan when I caught the eye of a waitress quickly heading my way.

Short and stout, she had obviously packed away her share of burritos over the years. Her straight, dishwater blonde hair was tied tightly in a ponytail secured by a rubber band, and a light fringe of bangs, beaded at the roots with perspiration, stuck out at wild angles across her broad forehead.

She waved brightly from across the smoky room. "Hey! Woman! How're you doin'?" The waitress squeezed past the little tables and groups of people standing in every conceivable spot, and made it to within a few feet of me. She stopped and covered her mouth with a pudgy hand.

The grin appeared again, and she wiped her hand on the white apron covering faded jeans with holes in the knees. "Whoops, I'm sorry, ma'am," she said with a twang that sounded more Georgian than Virginian. "I thought you were someone I haven't seen in a while. I guess it's just too smoky and crowded in here tonight. Must be messin' with my eyesight. Welcome to the Roadhouse. You got yourself a table yet?"

I took a gamble. "Are you Susan?"

She smiled brightly, her chubby cheeks popping out on either side, as if she had two huge peaches shoved beneath her gums. "That would be what my momma named me. Man, you really do look like one of my old customers. I thought for sure it was her. She ain't been in here recently, and I was gonna give her a ways to go for not visitin' sooner."

Not again.

"What was your customer's name?"

Susan made a face and scratched her chin. "Now, you would go and ask that wouldn't ya? I used to talk to her all the time, you know, recognizing her face and all. Let me see, I think it was Kathy, or Carmen, something with a *C* or a *K*. Isn't that terrible of me? It's just that I know so many faces, but not always their names."

"Was it Karen?"

"That's it!" She snapped her fingers. "College girl, real book smart, and right nice. Do you know her? Where in the hell's she been lately?"

I didn't feel like ruining the hostess's night, so I ignored the last question and saddled up my stock fib. "I'm her cousin. I'm here for a visit and thought I'd grab a bite to eat."

Susan's multi-watt smile returned. "I knew you had to be kin to her. How's she been? We used to talk all the time; she's such a nice person." She paused and rumpled her pug nose. "Now, I know I didn't have her name right earlier, but we did talk lots about stuff, so I hope you don't mind me askin', but is she still dating that hoity-toity jerk?"

I blinked and camouflaged a smile. "Which hoity-toity jerk?"

She laughed loudly and slapped her hand on her leg. "Well, now, I see you do know about all her men. What a woman, she has more followers than Jerry Falwell! Every time she comes in here, she has a different guy on her arm. I always tell her, that's the smart way to eat right—let someone else pay for your food."

Susan wrinkled her nose again, and her grin spread as wide as the Mason-Dixon line. "And you know what? They are all handsome, too. And some of them—what's the phrase? Sugar Daddies? You know, older, real sophisticated-type men. She sure knows how to go for the big bucks! Although, if I was her, I'd have the rich ones take me somewhere's fancier than this place." She glanced around the crowd, then put her hand on my arm and nodded toward my beers.

"Now, honey, are you goin' double-fisted tonight, or is someone joining you?"

John. I'd almost forgotten about him. "He's parking the car. He should be here soon."

"You ain't been here recently, have you? If he can't find a place in the lot, I sure hope he has his cross-trainers on, 'cause he'll park a month of Sundays away from here." She turned and stared toward the steps leading into the dining room just as a waitress appeared in the doorway. "Hey, Jolene," Susan called. "Is the calf missin' from the barn in the South 40?"

I was glad Jolene could decipher that cryptic phrase. She bent her head into the dining room, then squealed, "That's affirmative, Susan."

Susan nodded wisely and turned back to me. "That's good. Come on with me, I'll go ahead and seat you now. There's a table waiting just for you and your friend."

Glancing at the crowd of people surrounding me who were growing cobwebs, I began to fear for my safety. "But there are a lot of people ahead of us waiting for tables."

"I know," she said matter-of-factly. "That's why I'm the hostess. You're kin to my friend Karen. You just follow me and I'll see that your friend finds the table." She turned on her heel and marched toward the dining area.

I pointedly tried to avoid the gazes of the other would-be diners and followed closely at Susan's heels. Sure enough, there was a lone, empty booth along the side wall. "Tell me more about the hoity-toity jerk," I said as I slid into the seat.

She whipped a dish towel from her back pocket and busily wiped errant remnants of someone else's dinner from the table. "Well, it was the last guy she brought in here. Like I said, there's a new one practically each time, so I notice these things." She shook her head and rubbed a spot of salsa away. "There's just something about him I don't like. I can't explain it, it's just a feeling I get. He looks like he's someone important, a big wingdinger. Karen looked just over the moon that night, but he didn't seem quite as affected. Just kind of blasé. You know, cute little girlfriend, plaything, whatever. I just thought that after what she'd told me before, he'd treat her a little nicer."

That sounded interesting. "What had she told you before?"

Susan chewed her lip, then grinned. "Your cousin gets around a lot. Shoot, I been married since I was 18, and we don't even want to go where I am right now. I married the only guy who'd take me to my senior prom. Here we have Karen, who's what, 21 or 22? She's got all these cute guys just twisted around her finger. I kind of respect that, in a way. She told me how she got all those guys." The grin returned. "Let's just say that she scrambles their eggs real, real nicely. You follow me?"

I followed, but I had never heard it phrased quite that way before. "Do you know this latest guy's name?" I asked.

"Nah, I just know them as Karen's guys. He's older than she is. You know, sometimes she'll bring in a college guy with her, but usually it's someone older. Like I've told her: 'You go, girl. The older ones die quicker and leave you more money.'"

In another situation, I might have laughed along with Susan, but she didn't realize the irony in what she said.

"Could you describe what the latest guy looked like?" I pried.

"Oh, I don't know, they all look like they belong on the cover of *GQ* magazine."

As she laughed, I looked over her shoulder and saw Jolene pointing John in our direction. He spotted me at the same time, smiled, waved, and began to head toward the booth.

Susan turned and bundled up the dish towel. Her eyes grew large and she whistled. "Well, lookee here. Why don't you ask one of her boys himself? He just walked in. I wouldn't forget a face like that."

Her smile faded when she realized John was approaching the table. She raised an eyebrow. "Well, now, this is your friend? Keepin' it all in the family, I see. Hey, this is Virginia—I don't ask no questions. Y'all have a good dinner. Tell Karen I said 'hey.'" Susan walked away quickly and turned to stare at John with wide eyes as she passed.

Her eyes weren't the only ones that were wide with surprise.

John slid into the seat across from me. "What's up? You've got that ghost look again. Did something happen?"

You could say that.

Chapter 11

WHAT WAS I GOING TO DO? Whenever the cat I had as a teenager was spooked, he'd run and hide behind something large but woefully apparent to anyone looking for him. Following that animal instinct, I reached for the menu shoved between the salt and pepper shakers, held it in front of my face, and flipped through the laminated plastic pages. I tried to corral the thoughts sloshing through my confused brain but, instead, found John's hand pulling the menu away from my face.

"Kate, what's wrong? Did something upset you?"

I took a deep breath. "Why, no. I just thought you got lost and weren't coming back. It would be awfully embarrassing to be dumped in a crowded place like this."

He smiled. "Is that all? I'd never do that to you. You wouldn't believe where I had to park. It's ridiculous; I can't get over all the people here tonight. I sure would love to own stock in this place." He looked around the crowded dining room. "How on earth did you get a table already? What did you do, slip the hostess a twenty?"

"Something like that," I replied. I wasn't ready to tell him about my encounter with Susan. I still couldn't decide what it all meant.

It sounded like an old pick-up line, but I asked, "So, do you come here often?"

"Yeah, pretty frequently. It's the only Mexican restaurant near Woodbury, and a lot of doctors and nurses from the hospital meet here after work." He reached for his beer and took a drink. "Thanks for the beer, it tastes great. You know, it's funny, especially in a small town like this, but I have to watch where I eat and drink. People think that because you're a doctor, you eat nothing but vegetables and drink juice. I can't tell you how many patients I've run into who are shocked to see me eating junk food or drinking beer. But, hey, I'm human. I live for my junk food."

"Now, don't you go callin' our stuff junk food," said Jolene, who appeared beside the table. "You know better than that. Susan told me to take real good care of this table tonight, just for her. Now, how 'bout some hot *queso* and chips to go with your beers?"

"That sounds wonderful," John said, then he looked at me. "Do you like fajitas? This place has a great deal on a huge dinner for two people."

Even though food was now the farthest thing from my mind, we were sitting in a restaurant, and it was the usual habit of people in this type of establishment to eat. "That's fine with me. It sounds good."

Jolene nodded and scribbled on her notepad. "Artery glue and siz-zlin' veggies coming right up." She looked at me with a devious leer. "Y'all have a real, real good dinner, ya hear? I'm sure you have lots to talk about. I'll be back in a bit."

She sashayed away, pausing to check on a nearby table. Satisfied that the diners were enjoying their dinner, she made a beeline, not to the kitchen with our order, but to Susan, who was hovering expec-tantly in the doorway. Their heads were bent in a conspiratorial whis-perfest which was topped off with two loud laughs and quick gazes in our direction.

It was time for me to take a drink of my beer. A long drink.

"Who's Susan?" John asked. "Is she a friend of yours?"

I took another drink. "She's the hostess. I just talked to her a lit-tle before you came in; she's very friendly. That was Susan walking away from the table when you arrived. Haven't you seen her here before?"

"I really didn't pay that much attention to her. I guess I might be able to pick her out of a police lineup, but I can't say she's a close per-sonal friend."

No kidding. He especially wouldn't think that if he knew what Susan had just told me.

I decided it was time to learn a little more about my doctor. The nurse at the hospital made it sound like John was a near social recluse, but now Susan was telling me he was robbing the cradle with college girls. One particular, dead college girl, in fact, who resembled me and had thrown me into the midst of a murder investigation.

Jolene returned with the chips and the bubbling *queso*, which she placed on a small metal pedestal over a tea candle. She lit the can-dle, all the while staring hungrily at John. I admit that wasn't a hard task; he was easy on tired, old eyes.

He couldn't be involved in this, I thought. It just wouldn't be fair. Unfortunately, it would fall right in line with my traditional streak of rotten luck with the male species.

John fingered a tortilla chip and dipped it into the thick, peppery cheese. He held up the chip and grinned. "A chip for your thoughts? You've got a very serious look on your face."

I reached for the chip. "I'm sorry, I don't mean to look solemn. I must be hungry." I put the chip to my mouth. "So, this is where you spend your free time?"

He shrugged his shoulders. "Free time? What's that? I'm afraid I don't have much of a social life, Kate. I'm chained and married to my work. I love my job, and I think it's important to establish relationships with my patients. Doctors today are too impersonal and concerned only with pushing as many patients through their doors as possible. I like to spend a lot of time at the hospital, checking up on patients and their families. I enjoy visiting with them and getting to know what their lives are like."

"Then you take them out to dinner," I interjected.

"No, that happens rarely, if ever. I hope you don't think I'm like that, Kate. I just, I don't know, thought I'd like to get to know you better. I'm sorry it had to be under these circumstances, but I can't help that."

I hoped not. I actually didn't know what to think. He seemed honest and sincere, but why had he lied about knowing Karen?

"How long have you been in Woodbury?" I asked.

John popped another chip into his mouth, chewed quickly, and calculated. "Let's see, nearly two years, I guess. I completed my residency in Chapel Hill, then came here. It's not too far from North Carolina, which is where I grew up, and despite the small-town setting, Woodbury Memorial actually has a great reputation in medical circles. I guess that has a lot to do with Mason Shelby's reputation."

"Mason Shelby Sr., I assume," I said, thinking of my friend, Dr. Congeniality.

"Oh, of course," John said. "I mean, Mason Jr. is a fine doctor, who went to the best schools and all, but with his personality, no way. He's respected for his medical knowledge, but his reputation rests in his acidic personality. No, like I said before, Mason's father was a legend of sorts. His son will never live up to that."

The sound of sizzling chicken and vegetables interrupted us as Jolene reappeared with a tray sagging under the weight of the fajitas. Steam swirled around us and dampened her hair as she set the plates on the table. "Now, y'all watch out, this here is one hot baby. I wouldn't want you to burn your lips or nothing and not be able to, uh, talk." She laughed and turned to John. "How 'bout I bring a couple more brewskis around?"

"That would be great," he said.

As Jolene walked away, John reached for a tortilla and began loading it with food. "Enough about me and the hospital stuff. I want to hear about your day. What was it like up at the Merriman mansion? Is it as incredible as everyone says?"

That was a welcome strike one to my troubling theory. If John hadn't been to the mansion before, how could he have killed Karen?

I reached for a tortilla. "It is quite the showplace. There are servants running around everywhere, and the rooms look like pages out of *Architectural Digest*." I spooned still-steaming chicken onto the tortilla. "Haven't you been there before?"

His eyes searched my face quickly. "Well, yeah, but I haven't been inside the house. I've been out there a few times when Merriman employees have fallen out of trees or played with one too many power tools."

So much for strike one.

I asked, "Have you been to the lake where they found Karen?" *Well, Kate, you can't be much more blunt than that.* I took a bite and mumbled, "I just wondered what it was like out there."

John's eyelids fluttered several times. He took a bite and chewed for an exceedingly long period. "Maybe I have; I'm not sure I remember. It's a huge farm, and I never really know where they're taking me when I've been out there." His gaze darkened. "Why did you ask me that?"

I didn't have a respectable answer, so I quickly changed the subject. "While I was talking to Mrs. Merriman, she told me about a famous legend involving Merriman Farms. Have you heard about it?"

Batter up. The pitch was thrown, and I hoped for a strike.

"Is that the one about all the hidden treasure?" John asked as I continued to lose my appetite.

"That's the one. It seems Karen was diligently trying to solve the puzzle."

"Really?" he said. "I've heard people talk about the legend, but I don't know a lot about how you're supposed to find it." He stabbed an errant piece of pepper which had slipped from his tortilla. "Isn't it some kind of riddle? How does it go?"

I told him about my visit to the library and related as much of the legend as I could without pulling out my notebook. Just as I was reciting the riddle, Jolene brought two more beers.

She interrupted with a salacious smile. "Oh, cute. Poetry." Her tip factor was on a rapid landslide in my view. She grinned and flashed a toothy smile in John's direction.

"Wow, that's pretty bizarre," he said, once Jolene had rushed off toward Susan's post, no doubt to relate the latest. "Do you think that Karen found something at the lake? Maybe it's sunken treasure in a trunk or something?" His large eyes grew. "Do you think someone didn't want her to crack the riddle?"

"Could be," I said quietly.

John put down his fork. "You know, she was a champion swimmer. Maybe she was diving in the lake looking for the treasure, and when she came up the killer was there waiting for her."

Oh, why did he have to say that?

I stared at his eager face and took a deep drink of beer. I set the bottle down, counted slowly to ten, ran my finger around the bottle's rim, and said, "John, how did you know she was a champion swimmer?"

He looked everywhere except my eyes and mumbled unconvincingly, "I don't know why I said that."

Sure he did. He may not have meant to say it, but he obviously had gleaned that morsel of information somewhere. I was just afraid of where he had learned it.

I stared at my plate and knew what I had to ask. The uncertainty of wondering just how John was involved in all of this was maddening. To be having dinner with a murderer was one date I had never experienced. I nudged a piece of chicken on my plate and pushed it aimlessly around a roadblock caused by a strip of green pepper.

John was staring just as hard at his food. I certainly knew how to create an uncomfortable lull in conversation. My next comment took care of that as I spewed, "Could it be that you really do know Karen?"

He looked at me with wild eyes, then turned toward the center of the room and shut his eyes for a moment. Then he turned back to me, his eyes opening slowly. His gaze was cold and hard. "Yes. I did know Karen. All right?" He reached for my hand and enveloped it tightly in his. "But I didn't have anything to do with her death, Kate. You have to believe me."

His grip was so firm, my wrist ached. He stared at me, then let go of my hand. He leaned against the back of the booth, ran his hands through his hair, and let loose an exasperated sigh. "The girl at the sorority earlier—that was true. She did come in the ER a while back, with that good old college ailment of acute alcohol poisoning. Karen and a couple of other sorority girls brought her in. They were frantic, afraid she was going to die. The girl's father is a doctor at Williamsburg Community, and for obvious reasons they didn't want him to find out how stupid his pride and joy had been. So they drove into Woodbury."

John drank from his beer. "Karen was the one who was in charge. The others were pretty drunk, crying and making themselves sick. I can imagine the hangovers they must have had the next morning. Karen was sober and the one who talked to me."

He grinned sheepishly. "I should have known better, I guess. She was very pretty and seemed bright. I should have thought about how young she was, but I was stupid. I had recently broken off a very serious relationship with a girl I knew in North Carolina. We had dated for over four years, and I truly believed she was 'the one.'"

"What happened?" I asked, still trying to sort out the truth.

"I mistakenly believed that she loved me as much as I loved her. Unfortunately, she neglected to tell me a minor detail. It was nothing much, just another guy who appeared on the scene." John stared blankly at his beer and unconsciously picked at the label. "They got married two weeks after she told me about him."

He snorted and shook his head sadly. A sticky, wet section of the beer label clung to his fingers. "It threw me, Kate. Did you ever believe in something so much that when you discovered it wasn't true, you couldn't bring yourself to accept the fact?"

It wasn't a question that needed an answer.

He continued. "I was angry, hurt, and confused. I shut myself off from everyone and concentrated on my work. Karen and her friends just happened to hit me at a very vulnerable point. I felt like nothing, just a lump of flesh, but here was Karen, with her bright eyes and interest in me. She asked me all kinds of questions, as if I was the smartest man on earth. She made me feel special, like someone really important."

From what I'd learned, Karen had an almost magical knack of casting a spell on men. I envied her for a second, until I realized that her magic had turned deadly.

John took a halfhearted bite of his dinner. "She seemed a lot older and mature for her age. She was intelligent and she made me laugh. We only went out a couple of times. It was nothing serious by any means. Just a few dinners, that's all. I came to my senses pretty quickly."

"Oh?" I asked. "What prompted that?"

"It's pretty embarrassing, really. After we went out one time, she invited me back to campus for a party. It sounded like fun, so I agreed to go. I'm not a stick-in-the-mud, Kate. I've done my share of partying in my time." He laughed self-consciously. "You know, I think that was the appropriate phrase."

He lost me on that one. "What phrase?"

"'In my time.' The party was at a fraternity house. The place was packed to the rafters, and there was a stereo on each floor turned up as loud as it would go. The music was awful, I didn't recognize any of it. The older, wiser physician in me was upset with the amazing combinations of alcohol being consumed, and everyone there looked at me like I was an alien."

"Hooch?" I asked, remembering from my college days tubs filled with a nauseating combination of grape juice and eight or nine (or however many could be found) different liquors.

"Excuse me?"

"Never mind," I replied. "Bad college flashback. John, you're not that much older than Karen."

"I know that, and you know that. But believe me, I felt ancient at this party. I realized then that the relationship was a big mistake. I broke it off a few days later. I was afraid she was going to be hurt, but she took it very well."

I hated to tell him, but I had a feeling he was just one stallion in Karen's stable. I'm sure she made a notch in her lipstick case and moved on without any problem.

"I didn't see her again until the other day. It was awful." He looked at me with deep, almost black eyes and enunciated each word slowly and clearly. "I want to find the person who did this to Karen as much as you do, Kate. You have to believe that."

It probably wasn't the wisest thing to do, but in my heart I did believe him. I guess I'm just a sucker for a good story. And large, brown eyes. And the heady scent of a musky cologne.

However, the suspicious little investigative journalist demon that lives deep inside me somewhere knocked annoyingly at my conscience. "Why didn't you say anything before now?" I asked. "It just doesn't make sense."

There you go again, Kate. Kill the moment. I manage to do that so well.

His frown returned. "Look, I'm a 35-year-old guy, who was dating a 21-year-old girl who winds up murdered not long after I dump her. What conclusion do you draw? I'm sure the sheriff would jump on that, since he doesn't seem to have any other suspects. I know that I'm innocent and that our relationship had nothing to do with her death, but how does it look to people who don't know the whole story?"

He finally managed to peel the label off his beer. "I can't risk ruining my career for something like that. It may not be the most mature way to handle this, but it's what I'm doing. I hope you can respect that."

"But what if she said something to you that could lead to the killer? Maybe she dropped a clue somewhere along the way?" I couldn't give up that easily.

"Believe me, I've gone over it and over it in my mind since I saw her in the ER. I've tried to think of every conversation we had, everything we did, but I come up dry each time. Our relationship wasn't that intense. Like I said, we only went out a few times, had a few laughs, that's all. I wish more than anything that I could think of something crucial to the investigation, but I can't."

"Did Karen talk about the Merriman legend at all?" I prodded. I pushed my plate aside. It was time to get to work.

John shook his head. "She may have mentioned it once, but I never knew she was seriously trying to solve the riddle. She certainly never said anything about coming close to the solution. Karen didn't really talk much about her work at Merriman Farms. She was proud to be a member of their inner circle, but she downplayed the fact that she was an employee. I guess she liked to think that she was a family friend, not a staff member."

"I guess she didn't talk about relationships with other men, huh?"

John looked hurt. "Why, no. I guess I must have been naive, but I kind of thought I was the only one at the time. What makes you ask?"

I stumbled for the answer. "Well, from what I've learned today, she was involved in a pretty nasty, abusive relationship with an older guy."

John's voice hardened. "I can't believe you'd think it was me. I'm a doctor, Kate. I would never purposely hurt someone."

"I didn't mean to imply that it was you," I said quickly, trying to soothe his anger. "I thought maybe she cried on your shoulder about an old boyfriend."

I tried to redeem myself. "I would never accuse you of being abusive, John." I might not accuse him, but I could put out a mean hint. I smiled weakly and, I hoped, endearingly.

"No, she never mentioned anyone else," he snapped.

Jolene appeared again to remove our plates, and John said, "We'll take our check now, please."

"Now, that was said like a man in a hurry," Jolene drawled as she pulled out her order pad. She made a couple of quick calculations, then ripped the check from her pad and slid it near John's hand. She tapped a pointy, red, manicured nail on the table. "Just pay me when you're ready, darlin'. Y'all have a good night. Don't do nothin' I wouldn't do." She sauntered away with a dirty little grin.

I wasn't getting anywhere, so I made my last attempt. "What about antiques?"

"What about them?" John said vacantly. He pulled out his wallet and fished for cash.

"Did Karen talk about collecting or selling antiques?"

He paused. "Well, she never said anything about selling them, but she did talk a lot about all the antiques at the Merriman mansion and how much she admired them."

I stared at John and considered my options. I wanted to believe him, but in case he was the elusive boyfriend, I didn't want to let him know how much information I had gathered.

"Are antiques significant somewhere?" he asked as he placed a couple of bills on top of the check.

Damn, those eyes. John Donovan wasn't capable of murder. At least I hoped not.

"I think Karen was stealing antiques from the Merrimans," I explained, "and then selling them for a profit. I stopped at an antique store today, just down the road in fact, and the owner mistook me for Karen. He was very chatty and spilled all kinds of information about her and her antique sales. I'm assuming from his descriptions that she got the antiques from the Merriman mansion."

John's eyes grew large. "She didn't strike me as the type who would steal anything. Are you sure? How can you be positive it was Karen?"

"Oh, I'm very sure. I played dumb and asked what the last thing was that she had sold. He showed me a ledger book filled with Karen's signature. Her side business has been quite profitable the last few months."

"Wow, that's pretty serious," John said quietly. "Do you think someone caught her stealing something?"

I had been concentrating so much on the boyfriend and the legend that I hadn't equated Karen's death with the antiques. I knew the antique scam was an important element in the secret relationship, but I hadn't considered that she might have been caught with the stolen property. I felt a shudder go through me when I thought of Chase Merriman's arrival at Walenza's store.

"John, I have to get my hands on that ledger book. It may hold very valuable information. Let's visit the antique store. It's just a little bit down the road from here." I was talking as quickly as my mind was racing. "You can distract Walenza, the owner, while I borrow the ledger book. It won't be hard. He's as blind as a bat and will talk forever if you just say hello. He'll never see me with the book."

John held up his hand. "Tonight? I don't think that's a good idea. Maybe we can go another day." His frown returned. "And maybe I should stay in the car. Someone might recognize me, and if I'm caught helping you steal the book, it could hurt my career."

Where was his sense of adventure?

"I'm not stealing the book, John, I'm only borrowing it for a bit. I'll return it, hopefully after I have good information to pass on to Sheriff Thompson."

"Why not just tell the sheriff? That way, he can look for it. It's his job, after all. You shouldn't get involved, and neither should I."

"Oh, come on, it will be exciting, and we won't hurt anything. You said you wanted to help find Karen's killer, so here's your chance. It will only take a few minutes."

I was ready to go. I stood and tugged on his arm. "Just maneuver your way into one corner of the store and start talking to Walenza. I'll come in a few minutes later, slip behind the counter, and be gone. No one will know we're together. Don't worry, your career is safe. I'm good at being sneaky."

John stood. "I don't know, Kate. What if we're caught?"

I looked deep into his eyes and tried my most seductive pout. "We have to strike when we can. It wasn't right that Karen was killed, was it? What if the killer beats us to the book? Then my theory is kaput. Come on, John, you know we can do it. Do it for Karen. Do it for me."

He wasn't happy about it, but a few minutes later we were heading north on Higgins Pass. I had won, but my accomplice was still stubbornly reluctant. "We really shouldn't go tonight, Kate. Let me take you back to your car."

I was preparing to spurt my argument once again, when our attention became riveted to the scene in front of us. The black night sky was pierced from all sides with the flash of blue and red emergency lights. Two police cars, one ambulance, and a few assorted cars crowded a small parking lot just ahead.

The parking lot for Walenza's Antiques.

"Oh, man, what did I tell you?" John whistled as he pulled slowly to a stop in front of the building. "We better keep going. We shouldn't be here."

I swallowed as I watched two uniformed officers stringing yellow tape reading POLICE LINE—DO NOT CROSS across Walenza's storefront. "No, we've got to find out what happened."

"Read it in the paper tomorrow," John hissed. "Let's get out of here."

We were both startled by a tap on the driver-side window. Sheriff Bowman Thompson peered inside, and he was scowling like he had heartburn from hell. He tapped on the glass again and motioned for John to roll down his window.

"Oh, shit," John mumbled.

Chapter 12

AS JOHN ROLLED DOWN the window, he turned to me and said, "I told you this was a bad idea."

Super. I'd managed to have our first date and first fight in the same night. Remind me again why I'm still single?

Thompson bent down to the window and stuck a flashlight in our faces. I thought that was a bit of overkill, given the streetlights and the flashing emergency lights bathing the car. "Dr. Donovan, sir," he said, "please move your car over there."

John's skin melted to the shade of a cadaver. "Sheriff, is there a problem?"

"Dr. Donovan, I asked you once nicely. Park your car on the right and remove yourself from the vehicle."

Thompson was right. The first time was definitely done in a much nicer tone of voice. The first time was merely a grumble. This one was tantamount to a growl.

John gripped the steering wheel. "Kate, I hope you have a great explanation ready."

I stared ahead. "I'm working on it, okay? It would help if we knew what was going on."

"You better think fast." He turned off the ignition. "I told you we shouldn't have come here tonight."

We got out of the car and I slammed the door. "You've made that abundantly clear, Doctor."

John turned to Thompson. "Sheriff, I notice an ambulance over there. Do you need me to offer some assistance?"

"That won't be necessary," he replied. "Will you both join me over by my car?" Thompson's tone was more of an instruction than a request.

The sheriff leaned against the side of his car. The scanner inside squawked loudly, and the flashing lights painted streaks of blue and red across his face like a bad disco light.

"Miss Kelly," he said, "Woodbury is a quiet place. I like to keep it that way, but when an out-of-town pest comes buzzing through my county, I tend to pull out my bug spray. With you, I'm beginning to think I need some extra-strength repellent."

John's eyes grew so large, I thought for a minute they might swallow his face.

I shifted my weight. "Thank you, Sheriff, but you need not change your shopping habits. I have no intention of causing a problem for you, or anyone in your county. On the contrary, I am the one who has been inconvenienced."

John's mouth dropped open, and he put a hand on my arm. "Kate, don't—"

I ignored him. "I had no intention of visiting your fine community. I did not choose to wind up in a ditch with my car wrapped around a tree like a big 'Welcome to Woodbury' bow."

Thompson cocked his head to one side as I boiled over. "I would appreciate a little less homespun sarcasm and a little more information as to why we are being detained," I went on. "Dr. Donovan and I were out to dinner and merely passing by. Now, pardon me if my Southern law is rusty, but since when is that a felony?"

The sheriff looked at John and said, "Funny how all reporters are so smart-mouthed. She's awfully feisty tonight, doctor. Shouldn't she be home resting and recovering from her accident?"

John avoided both our eyes. He knew he was in a no-win situation.

I took a deep breath. "Look, Sheriff, I don't appreciate—"

Thompson stuck his finger in my face. "Appreciate this, Miss Kelly. The last homicide in my county was in 1989. In the space of two days, I have a suspicious hit-and-run and two homicides. That upsets me. And, I see one constant variable." He paused. "You."

I felt a queasy feeling brewing in my stomach. "Two homicides?"

"That's right, Miss Kelly. The old man who owns this shop didn't come home for dinner tonight, you see? He's quite a creature of habit, always walks through the door at 5:17 P.M. sharp. When 6:00 comes and goes, his wife thinks that's strange, so she drives over here to see what's amiss."

He looked toward the storefront. "She wanders into the store, looks around to the right, then the left, calls out her husband's name. No answer. You know why? She takes a few steps over toward his cash counter and finds his body on the floor. Her husband has his head bashed in. Little bits of flesh flung here and there. It's not a pretty sight, folks."

I leaned against John, who quickly slipped his arm around my waist.

"Miss Kelly," Thompson continued, "you don't look very well. Is there something you'd like to say?"

"No, I just didn't expect—"

"That's what makes murder so bad, young lady. No one ever expects it to come knocking."

John's grip tightened around my waist. "Do you think it was an armed robbery?"

The sheriff shrugged. "I doubt it. Nothing appears to be missing. The cash register is full. All the jewelry cases are intact too. I can't say much for the rest of the place, though. There's junk piled everywhere on tables."

I peered toward Walenza's door. Two men in white uniforms hovered near the entrance. They were leaning against a metal gurney, white sheet ready to cover its latest victim. One of the men finished a cigarette and flipped it into parking lot, while the other ambulance attendant studied the organisms growing under his fingernails. Just another night on the job for them. They'd probably grab a burger and fries on the way to the morgue.

Through the front window, I could see officers moving around inside, congregating near the register. A flashbulb popped, illuminating their faces for a split second. Photos of the crime scene to be used during a trial, I thought. But whose trial?

Thompson caught me staring. "Miss Kelly, have you ever been inside this antique store? I think I know the answer, but I want to hear you say it."

Before I could answer, a beefy deputy rushed over to our cozy little group. "Sheriff, they need you over on the other side right away," he said urgently. "There are some people gathering where they shouldn't be."

Thompson barked, "Isn't that something you're capable of dealing with? Tell them to move on, and if they don't, arrest them for trespassing." He shooed the deputy away with his hands like he was swatting at flies at a picnic. "Can't you see I'm busy?"

"Uh, sir, some of the folk is family and neighbors, and one of the TV stations just pulled up."

"How the hell did the TV people find out about this?" Thompson screeched.

It would have behooved me to keep my mouth shut, but the reporter in me automatically answered. "Easy. Police scanners—every newsroom has at least two or three of them. A 10-80 means a dead body; it's the first code you learn."

Thompson spun on me, his eyes on fire. "For your information, in this county, 10-80 is a stolen car. You don't know everything." He shook his head like he couldn't believe he'd stooped to quoting police codes. "You two stay put. Don't move. I am not finished talking with you, do you understand?"

He stomped away.

John was looking decidedly green. "Now what, Sherlock?"

I stared at the store. "I want to go inside."

"You what?"

I didn't look back as I sprinted to the door. I was met across the yellow tape by an equally curious officer. "Excuse me, ma'am, but can't you read? This tape says, 'Do not cross.'"

I dug into my purse and quickly flashed my press ID.

Quickly is the operative word, since closer inspection would reveal that it expired three years ago. If I cup it in my hand just the right way and execute a finely tuned flip of the wrist, no one can tell what it is.

"It's okay," I said authoritatively as I shoved the ID back into my purse. "I've talked to the sheriff."

"Honey," the officer said, "don't you think I've heard that one before? You press people never cease to amaze me."

I glanced over my shoulder and saw John still in place, hands on hips and looking decidedly unhappy with his dinner date. I peered around the officer and tried to look inside. The police photographer just inside the door snapped another shot and stepped away. I blinked when I recognized a pair of white athletic socks and worn huarache sandals sticking out from behind the counter.

It was Walenza.

Had Karen's boyfriend visited the store like Walenza thought he would? Did Walenza innocently tell his killer that I, "Karen," had been in the shop asking questions? Was he dead because I pretended to be Karen?

I shut my eyes to hold back the nervous tears struggling to escape. "What's wrong, kid, you a virgin?"

My eyes flew open. "What did you say?"

"Are you a rookie reporter? A dead-body virgin? I thought all reporters your age had seen at least one stiff by now, some charred flesh, mangled wreckage. You guys love that kind of stuff."

I shut my eyes briefly again and tried to control my temper. I did not feel like delivering a treatise on journalistic ethics, nor did I care to respond to the slam about "reporters your age" or whether I was a virgin of any type.

I squared my shoulders and stared directly at the officer. "How did he die?"

The officer's eyes actually glinted. "In a very unique way. This wasn't your usual zip-lock body-bagger."

My nerves were raw. "Sheriff Thompson said he died from a blunt trauma to his head."

"Yeah, he did, apparently," the officer confirmed. "Poor guy was whacked in the back of his head with a table lamp shaped like Elvis Presley. He probably never saw it coming. I guess you could say he had his lights knocked out." He actually laughed.

I didn't.

One of the other investigators called for the officer. He nodded, then turned back to me. "I've got to go, so I hope I can trust you to stay put on your side."

So I was alone, more or less. I leaned over the yellow tape as far as I could to get a good look. I could see two uniformed officers, a police photographer, a homicide detective, and the backs of the ambulance attendants, who were bent behind the counter. I tried to spy the all-important ledger book, but that was nearly impossible since the officers were blocking my view of the shelf.

Walenza had died in an inconvenient spot. How was I going to sneak over there and grab the ledger book?

I shifted my attention to the tables of antique pins I had looked at earlier. The chair Walenza had plopped me into was still in the same spot. The sheriff was right, it was hard to tell if anything was disturbed. The entire store looked disturbed. Antiques and junk were simply stacked wherever there was an empty spot.

"What are you doing here?"

I was so startled by the rough voice at my side that I jumped and, in the process, ripped the precious yellow tape in half. One half of it now was housed in my tightly clenched and very sweaty palm, and the other half floated to the ground, where it landed across the shoes of Dr. Mason Shelby.

At first glance it looked like he was off duty. His $900 suit was gone, replaced with jeans and a plaid shirt. On second glance, however, it was hard to miss the bloodstained rubber glove he was slowly peeling off his left hand.

I swallowed. "So, are you the coroner, too?"

Mason's eyes twitched. "No. Dr. Elliot isn't available tonight, so I am the most qualified person to fill in." He snapped the glove off his hand and began working on the other one. "If I were you, Miss Kelly, I'd be a little more careful where I show up in this town. You seem to bring trouble wherever you are."

"I don't see it that way," I replied.

He bundled the soiled gloves into a ball and tossed them into a trash can inside the door. "Things are very complicated right now in Woodbury, and you seem to have a lot to do with it. This is a small town, Miss Kelly. People talk. The sheriff listens. I would watch what I say and do, very carefully. If you know what's best for you, you'll go back to wherever you're from and leave Woodbury alone."

I gave him a level stare. "Is that a threat, Dr. Shelby?"

He didn't flinch a muscle. "Consider it a consultation with advice, free of charge. There's not much free in this world. Take what you can get."

The arctic air of his stare froze me solid. He probably loved giving patients shots in the most unspeakable regions of their bodies.

"Miss Kelly! What in the hell do you think you're doing?!" The words behind me were spit out in rapid fire.

Uh-oh.

Sheriff Thompson stomped up to Mason and me and grabbed my hand, which held the torn yellow tape. "I can arrest you right now for tampering with evidence. Do you understand me?"

The slightest hint of a smile danced on Mason's face.

Thompson asked him, "Dr. Shelby, was she bothering you?"

Mason's grin grew to expose teeth. "No, Sheriff. My work is finished here. I was just offering the young lady some advice." He turned his gaze to me and narrowed his eyes. "Isn't that right, Miss Kelly?"

I didn't respond.

Curiosity killed the cat and also got the best of John. He tentatively joined us on the doorstep. He made a face as if to say *I told you so*, then turned to Thompson. "Sheriff, I can take Kate home now, if you'd like."

Thompson let go of my hand. "I'd like nothing better, but I need to talk to you both some more. Dr. Shelby, sir, I don't want to keep you. I appreciate your coming out here on such short notice."

Oh, please, I thought. *Kiss up to him some more, why don't you?*

The sheriff continued, "Is there anything else I need to know before tomorrow?"

Mason shook his head. "Nothing that isn't already in my report. Blunt trauma to the cranial region, crushed skull." He looked right at me. "Excessive blood loss. He didn't have a chance. The killer did a nice job, as far as these things go."

"I see," Thompson said quietly.

Mason tilted his head to one side. "Any idea who did this?"

Thompson looked at each of us first before replying. "What is your opinion, Dr. Shelby?"

Mason shrugged. "It's hard to tell. It had to be someone with a pretty good aim and swing, but not necessarily someone of equal height or weight. The body can provide amazing surges of strength when it's angry or overexcited." He looked at me. "Even someone of Miss Kelly's stature, if provoked, could successfully commit murder in this fashion."

Wait just a minute! "What is that supposed to imply, Dr. Shelby?"

"It's just a forensic quirk." Mason was enjoying this entirely too much. "A man will shoot you or stab you—something quick and clean. A woman, however, often uses unusual objects or means. A lamp, for instance. Or poison. Something more drawn out."

"Oh!" I shot back. "So this is a clinical fact which can stand alone in court?"

John interrupted. "You can quote any number of odd behaviors or methods. It's pure conjecture, that's all."

Thompson nodded. "There's another one as well. Have you ever heard the one where the killer actually returns to the scene of the crime to get a sick charge from watching the aftermath?"

Again, all eyes turned to me. This was going way over the line as far as I was concerned.

"What? Why are you staring at me? Am I supposed to have all the answers here?"

Thompson knew how upset I was. He folded his arms across his chest. "Why don't you take a stab at a few answers, Miss Kelly, and we'll see if they're correct or not."

I gritted my teeth. "Ask me whatever you want. I'll be happy to help you in any way I can."

John looked nervously at his watch. "We should go. It's getting late. We need to leave."

Thompson raised an eyebrow. "I'm not finished, Dr. Donovan. I'll tell you when you may leave." He turned to Mason. "Dr. Shelby, have you determined a time of death yet?"

Mason glanced at me. "I won't know for sure until tomorrow, but it's safe to say it was mid to late afternoon." He motioned toward the counter. "If you're finished with me, Sheriff, I'll leave."

Thompson practically bowed. "Oh, that's quite all right, Dr. Shelby. Again, I appreciate your coming out here for Dr. Elliot and all. Woodbury wouldn't know what to do without a Dr. Shelby around."

Mason grinned and nodded. I felt like I was going to throw up.

As Mason walked away, Thompson turned serious again. "I asked you a question earlier, Miss Kelly. When was the last time you were in this antique store—and I want the truth."

I thought of Mason's time-of-death calculation and grimaced. "I was here this afternoon, Sheriff. I can explain, and I think you'll find it very interesting."

Thompson's eyes widened a bit. "I'm hanging on your every word. Make it good."

John sighed loudly and looked pleadingly at me.

Thompson noticed. "Dr. Donovan, if this makes you so uncomfortable, maybe I should ask these questions separately."

I thought it best to bail John out. "Sheriff, I was on my way home from Merriman Farms this afternoon, when I decided to stop here for a quick look around."

"Just a pleasant afternoon shopping," he said sarcastically.

"Yes, believe it or not. I happen to like antiques, and I frequently stop at small stores. This one looked no different than many others I've visited in the past."

"But something changed your mind, I assume."

I hesitated. "Not at first. I was just looking around, and Mr. Walenza came up to talk with me. What I think you'll find interesting is that he thought he knew me." I glanced at John. "He thought I was Karen Kelly, because we apparently have a similar appearance."

That caught Thompson's attention. "Go on," he said.

"I'm trying to," I sang. "It seems Karen and what he called a gentleman friend shopped here quite frequently. They sold him very expensive antiques. I think the antiques were stolen from the Merrimans."

Thompson frowned. "Why would you think that? What proof do you have?"

"None, unfortunately. It's just a hunch. Karen worked there every day in a house full of expensive antiques," I explained.

He shook his head. "Supposition, Miss Kelly, not proof. That means nothing to me. What about the man? Who is he supposed to be?"

This was not going well. I could tell Thompson wasn't buying my story.

"Walenza didn't know." I peeked at John and felt an unconscious tremor rumble through me. "All he kept saying was how handsome and sophisticated the guy seemed."

John's eyes met mine for a fleeting second, then he quickly looked at the sky as if he were intent on counting each star floating above us. I thought how strenuously he had tried to avoid coming here tonight. The little tremor running through me was now strong enough to register on the Richter scale.

"Miss Kelly," Thompson said, "I must confess, your story, though creative, doesn't sit well with me. One, it doesn't tell me anything; two, Karen Kelly had the right to have a boyfriend and the right to go shopping. Three, you can't assume she was stealing from the Merrimans. Try again."

I stared at the sheriff's shiny black shoes. I didn't want to tell him yet about my search of Karen's room, but I thought I'd be in a real mess if Annalee told him I'd been there. "What about the money you found around my car trunk? Don't you think that could have been money Karen had from her sales here? And what about the Merriman legend?"

"The what?" Thompson asked, clearly thrown off guard.

"Mrs. Merriman was very eager to tell me about a hidden treasure on their property. You can look it up in the 1952 papers, or ask her directly. I have reason to believe Karen was searching for the solution, I don't know, maybe financing her search by selling antiques. Who knows?"

"And how do you know she was looking for this treasure, or whatever you said," Thompson challenged.

John fidgeted like he had a bad case of chicken pox and no calamine lotion. "She doesn't know for sure. I think she should leave the investigation to you."

I figured I may as well tell it all. "I do know. I met her roommate, Annalee Chisolm. She told me Karen was looking for the treasure."

That wasn't entirely true, but I didn't want to tell Thompson that I had ransacked Karen's dorm room. "She also told me that Karen and the boyfriend were having serious problems. I understand that you know all this already. She said you'd been by to visit her."

That did it. Thompson exploded. "Miss Kelly, until you receive a diploma in law enforcement, I would suggest you quit tampering with my investigation. Leave the interviewing to me."

Following that comment, I'm sure I muddied the water further by adding, "I think you should search Karen's room. You might find something that would identify this boyfriend or give you information that confirms she was stealing antiques."

I hesitated, debating whether I should add my next thought. It bothered me enough that I went ahead with it. "And I don't know if this helps your investigation any, but as I left here this afternoon, I saw Chase Merriman pulling into the parking lot. I saw him go inside as I drove away. Maybe he saw something that could help."

Thompson and John both snapped to attention.

"You didn't tell me that," John breathed.

The sheriff rubbed his hand over his face. "Miss Kelly, your story just keeps growing and growing. Now, until you can offer any proof of this antique business, you need to drop that line and any insinuations about Chase Merriman." His frown deepened. "And it isn't any of your business, but we have a search warrant for the dorm room tomorrow."

Mason Shelby chose that moment to return and pass through the door where we were standing. His eyebrows shot up in an arch. "What's that about Chase?"

Thompson glared at me. "Nothing important, Dr. Shelby. I'll talk with you tomorrow."

Mason nodded. "Fine. Tomorrow, then." He scowled his good-byes to John and me and pushed past us on his way to his car, a dark Mercedes sedan parked a few steps away. He gunned the engine and was gone in a puff of expensive exhaust.

Thompson looked ready to cart me off to another country. I won that round. I could tell he hated to admit that he was waiting until the next day to search Karen's room.

I went for the second win. "I can prove the antique scam, Sheriff. Walenza has proof in his ledger book. He showed it to me. If you'll just let me go over there, I can prove to you that Karen was involved." I gingerly stepped past Thompson and strode toward the counter.

In a flash, Thompson was at my heels. He grabbed my elbow. "You're not going over there. Stand right here and tell me where to look."

John took hold of my other elbow. "He's right. Stay here, you don't need to see what's over there."

I nodded toward the shelf. "It's the large, brown-leather ledger book on the second or third shelf behind the cash register."

Thompson walked over to the counter.

I leaned closer and saw the top of the box holding the infamous Elvis salt and pepper shakers. "There's the box, just to your right."

He stepped gingerly around Walenza's body. It was now resting, covered, on the gurney, ready for the last trip from the store he loved. The ambulance attendants halted their conversation and focused on Thompson.

Thompson stared at the shelf, then turned to me.

I read his face instantly. My mouth went dry.

"There's no ledger book here," he said. "Just a box and a dusty, empty shelf."

Chapter 13

THE NEXT FEW MINUTES were not pleasant. Sheriff Thompson was in no mood for additional explanations from me, and despite my good intentions, I knew he didn't believe me.

For my part, I was furious. The killer had beaten me to the book. I lunged toward the counter but was stopped short by John's strong arms, which wrapped around me in a near choke hold and kept me firmly in place.

"What are you doing?" I demanded. "Let go of me, I need to see that shelf."

"No, Kate," he replied. Given the worried frown spreading across his face, I think he doubted my story as well.

Thompson intervened. "Miss Kelly, I told you once before, you are not to come over here."

I wrenched myself free from John's arms. "I know the book was there, Sheriff. I saw it this afternoon. It's obvious the killer wanted to make it scarce. That proves Walenza's death is related to Karen's."

My outburst created quite a spectacle. Every officer in the store migrated to our spot and eyed me with a cocktail of bemusement laced with practiced skepticism. One even reached for his belt and prominently fingered his handcuffs. They all thought I was the resident nut case.

"Why won't you believe me? Why don't you ask Mrs. Walenza? I'm sure she knows the book exists. She may even remember who Karen's boyfriend was."

John gently touched my arm, but I angrily pulled it away and said, "Maybe I just solved your murder. Maybe Mrs. Walenza knows the answer. A lot of good all these detectives are doing. Why don't you send them over to talk to her?"

Thompson drummed his fingers on the countertop. He glanced at his detective and nodded briskly. Reading the cue from the sheriff, the detective grabbed his notebook and slipped out the door.

So, I had won another round.

Thompson, however, was a sore loser. He insinuated that perhaps my head injury had led to rather "fanciful thoughts" and instructed John to take me home posthaste.

John was eager to comply. He wrapped a protective arm around my shoulder and steered me toward the door.

Thompson was at our heels. "Miss Kelly, I know you're trying to help, but you're not. If I learn anything relevant to your accident, I will tell you. Otherwise, I have a great deal of work to do. Please, go home and recover from your injuries so you may return to your job in Washington. Woodbury will survive without your skills at detection."

John deposited me in the front passenger seat of his car. Thompson reached for the door handle and bent his head into the car. "Stay away from this case. Do you understand me?"

I slapped my head against the back of the seat and shut my eyes defiantly. Thompson sighed, straightened, and shut the car door with a loud thud. I heard John apologize for any inconvenience we had caused, to which Thompson merely grunted.

John slid into the driver's seat and flew out of the lot.

We drove in silence for several minutes. So much had happened in the past few hours that my head truly was swimming. I flashed through the events as quickly as I could, but nothing stuck. I shot a quick glance at John, who was concentrating on the road like he was in the middle of his driver's test. He had completely confused me all night. I didn't like how unsettled he was at the restaurant and the store, and I certainly didn't appreciate the force he used to keep me away from the counter. What was that all about?

He caught me staring at him and raised a curious eyebrow.

I grinned slightly. "Hell of a first date, aren't I?"

To my chagrin, he didn't return the smile. "Kate, are you sure you're okay? I'm going to take you straight home. We can get your car tomorrow. I think you need some serious rest."

I sat up. "No, John, I'm fine. Take me back to campus so I can get the car. I'm perfectly capable of driving home."

We argued that point for several more minutes until we ultimately reached a détente. He agreed to let me drive my car on the condition that he follow me all the way home.

We arrived on campus and John drove up alongside my car, which was still parked in front of the SG house. He killed the engine and leapt out with me. I stalked to my car and fumbled with the keyhole in the dark.

John stood very close to me, so I turned to face him, and in a flash of déjà vu, he cupped his hands around my chin and pulled me close. "I'm worried about you, Kate. Are you sure you're okay?"

No, I wasn't okay. Two people were dead, I was the sheriff's favorite suspect, and I couldn't decide whether I should trust the beautiful guy who was standing nose-to-nose with me.

I searched his eyes and found myself thinking it would be okay if he kissed me again. That would help me make a few decisions.

Obviously, our mental telepathy wasn't fully developed yet. He bypassed kissing me and, instead, let his hands fall to my shoulders. "Drive slowly. I'll be right behind you. We need to get you into bed."

He patted my shoulder, then returned to his car. The part about getting me home to bed might have been more thrilling if not for the fact that I knew he had something else in mind—like taking me to my parents' house and actually seeing to it that I got to sleep.

Story of my life. I dropped behind the wheel.

We arrived home within minutes. I pulled into the driveway and got out, expecting John to be parked and hoofing it up the sidewalk. Instead, he remained in the street with his car idling. He rolled down the window and motioned for me to come over. "Please try to get some sleep. I'll call you tomorrow. Stay home—and try to keep out of trouble, okay?"

I was going to attempt a witty reply, but before I could say anything he pulled away, leaving me on the sidewalk. I knew instinctively that I wasn't alone. I turned toward the house just in time to see the curtain in Dad's study snap shut. His concern was sweet, but I didn't need to hear his reaction to everything that had happened all day.

I took a deep breath and strode quickly to the front door, knowing that I wouldn't have to worry about a key. The minute I hit the first porch step, the door swung open like clockwork and Dad's silhouette filled the entryway. I prepared for a brisk battle.

He began before I hit the top step. "Kate, do you realize that you've been God-knows-where since early this morning? You never once called. You've been ill; anything could have happened. Then you come home with him."

Dad paused long enough to gaze down the street and gesture idly to the wind, no doubt thinking he was keeping me safe from the likes of handsome, young men like John.

I took advantage of the pause and bussed his cheek as I continued past him and straight up the staircase toward my old bedroom. "Daddy, I'm fine, but very tired. It's been a busy day; I'll tell you all about it tomorrow. Of course, you're right. I stayed out entirely too late, and I need to get some sleep. I'll see you first thing in the morning. Love ya." I knew without looking back that he was standing at the bottom of the steps with his hands anchored firmly on his khaki-chinoed hips.

I flipped on the light and shut the door quickly behind me. My room hadn't changed much over the years. It was still the same bright shade of yellow that I had painted it in college, and my antique brass bed still nestled in the alcove of a large bay window.

I dug into my open suitcase and grabbed a pair of sweats. I grinned when a voice filtered through my door.

"Since the last time you pulled this 'Oh, Daddy, I'm so tired' stunt was when you were in school and truly adding to the silver in this head of once-black hair, I will forgo inquiring about what trouble you're mired in. I, too, am old and tired, and I'm afraid whatever mischief you've caused might be detrimental to my ancient heart. Sleep well, Katherine. We'll talk in the morning."

Despite Dad's kind wishes, I didn't sleep well. I tossed and turned all night as pictures of Walenza and Karen, Chase and Constance, Sheriff Thompson and Dr. Shelby all flashed through my dreams.

Okay, so John ambled through the picture once or twice, too. I admit it, guilty as charged. I punched my pillow for lack of anything better and buried my face in the fluffy down.

The next time I awoke, it was nearly 9:15 A.M. I groaned at the clock on the bedside table. I dragged myself out of bed, a process that was more difficult than usual thanks to the stubborn aches that still lingered from the accident. I stumbled into the bathroom and looked in the mirror. I thought of the scene in the movie *Funny Girl* where Barbra Streisand looks in her mirror and vamps, "Hellooo, gorgeous," but I ruefully had to admit that no one in his right mind would say the same of me right now.

I bent over, splashed cold water on my face, and visited the mirror once more.

It didn't help. My hair was an unruly mess, and my lovely bruised forehead was now an attractive shade of muddied green flecked with yellow highlights. I made a pass at brushing my mop and swallowed a breakfast of two Tylenols.

I ventured to the kitchen, praying for the salvation of a cup of coffee. The house was serenely quiet. Dad had a lecture class at 8:00 A.M., so that saved me again from explaining everything. I made a silent promise to call his office later.

I smiled when I spied a half-full pot which, curiously, was still hot. I poured a mugful and snared a banana from a bowl of fruit near the windowsill. The only thing missing was the newspaper. Mom and Dad would read it religiously every morning, then neatly fold and place it on the end of the kitchen table, but for some reason it wasn't there. I looked under the table and on the countertop. Then, as a last resort, I poked my head in the utility closet.

As I fought off a sneeze from the noxious combination of cleaning agents stored there, I heard the thud of paper slapping the table. I jumped and yanked my head out of the closet.

Dad stood behind the kitchen table. He was dressed for work in charcoal-gray pants, the ubiquitous navy tie, and a blue-and-gray tweed blazer. His scuffed and worn briefcase rested at his feet.

"Dad, you scared me. Why aren't you at your class? Is something wrong?"

He set his jaw in a manner that made me wince. "I'm having one of the associate professors cover for me this morning. I thought perhaps I should spend some quality time—or whatever it's called—with my daughter." He reached for the paper and flipped it over to reveal the front page. "I want you to explain this headline to me."

My pulse quickened and my cheeks glowed crimson as I read the large-point headline which screamed, "MURDER AT MERRIMAN ESTATE—TWO HOMICIDES IN TWO DAYS HAVE POLICE BAFFLED."

I glanced at Dad. "Am I mentioned anywhere?"

He rolled his eyes. "Katherine, if it's notoriety you want, I'd suggest you look elsewhere." He pulled out a chair and sat down heavily. "And no, you've yet to become flavor of the month with the newspaper. Now, start at the beginning and tell me what happened yesterday."

Knowing he'd need it, I reached for another mug and filled it with coffee—black, no cream, no sugar. Then, like a dutiful child, I joined him at the table and meekly reached under the sports section for my banana. "Mind if I munch on this while I tell you?"

He pulled his glasses down the bridge of his nose and gazed over the rims in a silent but understood answer. I slowly peeled the banana with the precision of a surgeon, then began my story. I told him everything; in part because I felt obligated to, but also because I hoped for some inspiration or enlightenment.

Dad may never admit it, but he's spent the better part of thirty-odd years listening to my mother's theories on many of her investigative pieces for the paper. She will often become so involved in her story that she needs a "third eye," as she calls it, to step aside and make sense of everything. Dad is a master at that. He'll listen quietly, nodding his head or making faces to show his disagreement. Once Mom's laid the pieces on the table, he'll chew on it for a while, then ultimately come up with a question or comment that ties everything into a neat package. They're a great team.

As I related my confusing story, I kept an eye on his reactions. He frowned where appropriate, raised an eyebrow here and there, shook his head when I told about my visit to the SG house, and took his glasses off, sighed, and rubbed his eyes when I got to the part about Walenza. Through it all, he remained silent, always the wise, collegiate sphinx.

"So, that's where you came into the picture last night," I concluded. I stood and took both of our now-empty mugs back for refills.

Dad waved his hand. "No more for me, I've exceeded the legal limit for at least the next two hours. Kate, you know what I'm going to say: I don't like this. By virtue of being in the wrong place at the wrong time, you're now mixed up in something that sounds like it's been brewing for a long time. This is private stuff, kid. It's human nature, people are easily tempted by money and sex. It's how nations are born and ultimately destroyed. Just look at history, there are hundreds of examples."

Leave it to history professor Jim Kelly to integrate an historical aspect.

I leaned against the sink and stirred cream into my coffee until it was the color of melted caramel. "But they don't always end up dead," I said.

"True," he agreed. "But again, it's possible. Think of the overused phrase 'crime of passion.' It can mean many things. I know it goes against your nature, kiddo, but what you need to do is let these people work this out on their own. It's their private soap opera, with the sheriff directing. You sit back and change the channel. This isn't a show I want to see you cast in."

I sipped the coffee and bit my lip as the hot liquid burned my tongue. "But it's too late, Dad. I *am* involved, and besides, I have an article to write now about the legend. I can't let Mrs. Merriman down."

Dad was a pro. He picked up the paper and neatly folded it before he placed it back on the table in its normal late-morning spot. "Oh, no, we certainly wouldn't want to upset the elder Mrs. Merriman, who may not even remember your presence yesterday. The part about the legend is probably useless. History is full of riddles and infamous legends just like that, particularly around that time. Some of them were legitimate, I'm sure, but the majority were merely elaborate parlor games. Remember, they didn't have the joys of television and the mass media in the eighteenth and nineteenth centuries."

He shook his head. "I'm sure even if the Merriman legend is real, whatever the treasure was is long gone by now. Don't assume the treasure was money; it could have represented something that was valuable—a painting, a house, or for that matter, it could be a person."

I frowned. "A person?"

"Sure. A child perhaps, an heir, a 'treasure' to carry on the family name. Or maybe it was a mistress. You've got the part about the servants in the riddle—maybe they knew of the affair, and the only way to figure out the riddle was to know which servant to ask."

"That seems so farfetched," I grumbled as I rinsed my cup in the sink.

"It's a century-old riddle, Kate. It could mean anything. That's my point. You need to stop trying to connect it to something that's happening in today's world."

"Well, we'll see," I said slowly. "I still think it's connected in some way."

Dad picked up his briefcase. "I need to go. I'm almost afraid to ask what you have in mind for today. I'd like to think you're planning to lie on the couch, watch television, and actually try to rest, but something tells me you have no intention of doing that. Am I correct?"

"That's why you're a professor, Dad. I know you hate to hear this, but I *am* obligated to complete that article with Mrs. Merriman. Given everything that happened yesterday, I didn't get very far with it, so I thought I'd try to set up another interview with her." That was partially true, but I also planned to do a little more snooping on the side once I made it to Merriman Farms.

I hugged Dad. "Don't worry about me, I'll be fine. If I need anything, you'll be the first to know, I promise. Now, go off to school like a good professor should."

He frowned and raised his eyebrow at the same time. I wondered about the workout his facial muscles had to go through to accomplish that. He reached for the doorknob. "Be careful. Understand?"

I smiled. "Understood."

Once he was gone, I grabbed the newspaper and methodically read through the article. The reporter heavily played up the murders, with a sorority photo of Karen and a fuzzy, blurred shot of Walenza, which probably came from his driver's license. There was also a picture of Walenza's Antiques, with the crime-scene tape in evidence, and old file photos of Chase and the gates to the Merriman estate.

Upon closer inspection, the article itself didn't hold much information. The newspaper editor probably made the pictures and headlines so prominent to sell a few more papers. The story detailed the bare facts about Karen's drowning death and ominously stated that "preliminary autopsy results indicate that the girl's death was not an accident." Chase Merriman, when contacted at his office, had no comment, and calls to the Merriman estate were not returned. A press release issued later by Merriman Farms, Inc. stated that the family was "saddened by the untimely passing of a valued employee" and pledged to cooperate with officials in "tracking down the person or persons responsible."

As a reporter who's read one too many press releases, I'm sure the information provided was annoyingly bland and, no doubt, purposely avoided any official quote from Chase. The remaining length of column space detailed the history of Merriman Farms and current business facts, the usual boiler-plate stuff tacked on to stories about corporations. The reporter probably lifted it right off the bottom of the press release from the Merriman corporate office.

The details of Walenza's death rated a sidebar piece. The reporter didn't link his death at all with Karen's. His murder was described as a probable end result of an armed robbery. The clear insinuation was that a madman was running loose in Woodbury, which—as the sheriff had reminded me—hadn't had a homicide since 1989. Thompson even chipped in a quote, imploring the community not to panic and assuring readers that the police were doing everything possible to solve the murders.

I ripped the article out of the paper, took it upstairs, and shoved it deep into my purse. I glanced at the clock. It was almost 10:30. Where had the morning gone?

I took a quick shower and threw on a pair of jeans and a pink long-sleeved cotton shirt. Grabbing my notebook, I went into Dad's study. I checked my notes and placed a call to the Merriman estate.

An Hispanic voice I assumed belonged to Maria answered on the third ring. I told her my name and asked for Constance, imagining that I'd have better luck with her than with Chase. I doodled on my notepad for a couple of minutes while Maria went in search of her.

"Yeah, this is Constance. Who's this again?"

I stumbled all over myself. "It's Kate Kelly, Mrs. Merriman. I thought, uh, perhaps I, if it is convenient, um, could come by to talk some more with Mrs. Merriman, your mother-in-law."

I rolled my eyes at my lack of eloquence and whacked my forehead with my palm, momentarily forgetting the bruise, which retaliated by sending a wave of pain crashing through my head. I winced at my stupidity and listened with squinted eyes to Constance's answer.

"I know who you're talking about, I only have one mother-in-law, thank God. What do you want with her?"

Where had the proper, Southern socialite gone?

I cleared my throat and regained my composure. "I'd like to talk with her more about the article we discussed yesterday. Would it be all right for me to come by within the hour?"

Silence hung on the line. Finally, in a softened voice that sounded more like the Constance of the day before, she said, "Of course, Miss Kelly, we'd like to see you again. I'm sorry if I was abrupt earlier, but we've been inundated with calls since the paper came out with that horrid story. I'll call down to the gatehouse. Don't say you're a reporter, or you'll never get through."

A muffled noise filtered over the line, as if Constance might be drinking or eating something. "Oh, and Miss Kelly, if you're coming, come alone."

The phone went dead.

Chapter 14

EVEN THOUGH I MISSED seeing Mom, who was still in Louisiana, I had to admit it was nice to have unlimited access to her car. It made life that much simpler, particularly since my rental car was down for the count in the worst way.

The pleasant day provided a nice drive to Merriman Farms, but my thoughts didn't match the ambiance of the beautiful afternoon. The phone call with Constance had been very strange, and I was anxious to see how she acted in person.

In less than thirty minutes I drove up to the gates and spied a source of her concern. The press had descended upon the estate en masse. I paused at a traffic light near the entrance and counted heads. Trucks from two local television stations were parked on either side of the gates, antennas and signals up, ready to broadcast live shots. Engineers and technicians scurried about like mice, pulling cable across the drive.

While one neatly coifed reporter chatted animatedly into his cell phone, the other reporter was perched on a tree stump, looking undoubtedly professional as she gazed into a compact mirror, her pinkie in her mouth. She either had lipstick on her teeth—which wouldn't be a stretch given the bright purple shade I could see from across the street—or she had wolfed down an early lunch. I favored my first guess.

Their slightly scruffy-looking cameramen huddled together, looking bored, while a clump of print reporters and a couple of still photographers hovered nearby in their own chummy group.

The Merriman Market across from the estate was much more crowded today. I spotted another television crew smack in the middle of the flowers displayed in hanging pots. The reporter was busy interviewing two women who were no doubt offering their wise assumptions as to how two murders would affect the blooming potential of yellow mums.

Being a reporter myself, and knowing how the beast thinks, I quickly rummaged in my purse for my sunglasses. I popped them on and rolled up my car window as the light changed. No doubt I would be splashed across the noon newscasts as the "woman who visited the

Merrimans." I knew how it worked when reporters were denied access to a story. With their lack of anything else to talk about or take a picture of, I was apt to become important for the mere fact that I was about to drive through the gates.

Sure enough, the roaming herd perked their ears expectantly as I pulled up to the gatehouse. I rolled down my window just enough to speak to the clearly flustered guard. I managed to spit out my name and mention that Constance was expecting me, just as a camera was thrust in the open crevice of my window.

The reporter who had been on the cell phone clamped his fingers on my window. "Excuse me. Doug Butler, Action 15 News. Are you a friend of the family? Are you a relative? Are you connected with the murder investigation at Merriman Farms?"

The gates swung open, so I smiled and shot back, "Are you prepared to lose your fingers when I drive away in the next two seconds?"

He removed his hand and stood back, shocked that I hadn't wilted under his intense interrogation. Given his withered expression, I'm sure he wasn't thrilled with me or his photographer, who burst out laughing. I pressed my foot to the accelerator as he shouted, "Who are you, ma'am? Are you with the police?"

He was still going strong as the gates slammed shut behind me.

I wound my car up the hill and parked in the semicircular drive in front of the estate. I rang the bell once before a stocky, distorted form appeared behind the stained-glass front door. The door opened just a crack, and half of the maid's face peeked out. "You have appointment today?"

I pasted on a friendly smile. "Yes, I'm here to see Mrs. Merriman. She's expecting me."

A linebacker with an attitude couldn't get past Maria. Her body was squarely angled in the doorway, and a small foot in a large, sensible shoe wedged itself against the door's edge. She shook her head. "Señora Constance not well. She not feel too good. You come back another day."

What was wrong with Constance? She had looked healthy the day before, and she hadn't sounded sick over the phone. A little strange or neurotic, perhaps, but not sick. Besides, Maria had the wrong Mrs. Merriman.

"I'm sorry to hear Constance is ill, but I'm actually here to see Winifred Merriman."

"Who said I was ill?"

The door jerked open and Maria quickly stepped away. She continued to back away until she disappeared into the blue sitting room to the left. The quick patter of feet indicated she picked up a great deal of speed once she was out of sight.

Constance leaned on the wall to the right, her head tilted back, chin jutting out and blonde hair spilling over her shoulder. She wore a tunic top covered in light blue and green seashells. Her broomstick skirt was a matching seafoam green and was so long it dragged the floor. A beaded necklace, anchored in the center with a real seashell, matched her seashell bracelet; and I noticed that a large, square-cut aquamarine-and-diamond ring augmented the diamond count on her hands. On tall, thin Constance, the ensemble looked fashionable and very, very rich. On me, it would look like a little kid playing dress-up in someone's larger clothes.

A deep laugh worked its way out of her throat. "Well, Kate, you didn't waste any time getting here, did you?"

She straightened and, stepping on the hem of her skirt, tripped a few awkward steps forward. She laughed again and yanked at the skirt. "Damn thing. It's comfortable and cost an obscene amount of money. You'd think it would treat me better. Oh, well, it's probably Chase's way of getting back at me."

"I don't understand," I said.

Honestly, I didn't. Something wasn't right with Constance.

She tilted her head and slid a grin up one side of her face. "When Chase pisses me off, I go shopping. I get him where it hurts." She tapped her size-six derriere. "Right in his pocketbook. I can melt a Gold Card in a single afternoon."

She pointed a manicured finger at me. "Learn that, Kate. You can love a man all you want, but the only way to truly touch him for better or worse is to touch his money."

She snorted a decidedly lower-class giggle, repeated "for better or worse," and staggered across the hall to the sitting room. I followed and found her at the far end, clinking ice into two small glasses. She reached for a crystal decanter and swung it around toward me. "Do you like bourbon straight up or over ice?"

It wasn't even noon yet. I shook my head politely. "No thanks. I'm fine, I don't need anything to drink."

"Fine. *You* may not need anything, but *I* do." She uncorked the decanter and poured the bourbon. I expected her to stop once it splashed over the ice, but she continued to pour until it nearly reached the rim. She swished it lightly, then tilted it to the ceiling. The amount she inhaled in one gulp would have sent me under the table.

Slamming the glass onto the marble-topped buffet table, she shivered as the bourbon traveled down her throat. She coughed, shook her head, then turned to me. "Just what Mommy ordered. Are you sure you don't want a drink?"

"Uh, no, thank you," I stumbled. I stared at her. She was drunk, trashed beyond tipsy. I wondered if this was a result from the stress of the previous few days, or a natural occurrence. Maybe Maria often turned people away when "Señora Constance not well."

I patted my purse nonchalantly. I could feel my tape recorder, unfortunately buried deep in the bottom. Something told me I was about to have a very interesting conversation worth saving. However, there was no way I could stick my hand down in the purse and fish around for the RECORD button without her noticing.

"Constance, is everything okay?" I asked. "Would you like to talk about something?"

She stared at me, then turned back to the decanter. She refilled her glass and walked over to the white couch. "I'm fine, Kate. I'm just concerned about this mess. It's not my—uh, our—fault. That damn paper had to splash everything across town today. The phone has been ringing off the hook. All my dear friends, calling in a panic, anxious to offer any help they can." She grinned into her glass. "Yeah, like I don't know that they're all having lunch at the club right now, making up all kinds of horrid stories about me and Chase."

Looking back at me, she said, "And don't try to deny it to make me feel better. I know how these women think. They have nothing better to do than gossip. I know, because if this were happening to someone else, I'd be there with them at this moment, adding my two cents worth. It's the curse of being a so-called socialite."

She sipped on the bourbon. "I don't know how we'll face them. The Hursts are having a cocktail dinner on Friday. Everyone will be there. I can feel the stares already."

Even though she had warned me not to offer my sympathies, I feebly tried. "I'm sure it feels worse right now because everything is so fresh. By Friday, they may have moved on to other topics."

Constance looked me up and down. "It's obvious you don't travel in society, dear. You don't know how these witches act." She leaned against the back of the couch. Her hand slid to her side, and the bourbon sloshed dangerously close to spilling onto the couch's lily white fabric. She closed her eyes and moaned. "And oh, the press. They're simply unrelenting. I never knew there were that many reporters in this town, the vultures."

"I know," I commiserated, hoping Constance would forget for the moment that I was one of those vultures. "There were several news crews down at the gates when I arrived. Has your husband talked to them yet?"

Her head lolled in my direction. "The answer is no. He has an almost morbid fear and loathing of the press. In fact, I wouldn't put it past him to take in some target practice near the gates."

She sat up, blinked her eyes, then stared at the glass before finishing off the remaining bourbon. "We wouldn't be in this spot if Chase kept his pants on."

I struggled to say something. I wished that I had a drink—or something, anything, to do other than stare at Constance. My mind raced

— 113 —

as I searched for a reply. She was accusing Chase of infidelity, but with whom? Karen, of course, immediately sprang to mind, as did Chase's profile of being older, handsome, and wealthy.

Tears were gathering in Constance's hazel eyes, and she bit her lip to keep it from trembling. "I didn't mean to say that. Please don't repeat it." She sniffed and blinked her eyes, lightly rocking back and forth on the couch. "Kate, are you married?"

"No, I'm not."

"You're smart. Marriage isn't always what it's cracked up to be, particularly when you get to be my age. Men don't take to aging very well; they like to try and recapture their youth. They want to prove their manhood, I guess—by being strong and macho, eager to prove their prowess over women."

She stared across the room, avoiding my eyes. "I'm not that old, I think. I take care of myself, go to the best spas, and spend an enormous amount on makeup and creams. But I guess sometimes the one who's always there isn't much of a challenge. And that's what it is, a challenge, a game. You have to fight to win it, and do whatever it takes to make sure you come out on top."

Constance looked at me with cold, haunted eyes. "Whatever it takes," she repeated. She stood quickly, wavered a bit while the bourbon-induced haze cleared, then strode over to the window.

Her last comment disturbed me. I had been concentrating so hard on finding Karen's boyfriend that I hadn't considered what the jilted wife might do. Constance was refined, and delicate looking, but if you pumped a few drinks into her, I could see how she might fly off into a jealous rage. I also remembered Karen's cartoon drawing of the witch labeled "Constance" and wondered if the two women had confronted each other.

"If you're unhappy," I said, "why don't you leave Chase?"

She spun around. "Do you think it's that easy? For one thing, he'd never allow it. He'd kill me before I could leave. And what would I do? I have no skills, I've never held a job. I'm a rich man's wife. I hold parties and smile a lot, that's all."

She smiled bitterly. "And who would want to leave this? Chase is very wealthy, but his mother is unbelievably loaded. He's an only child; he'll get it all when she's gone. I'm just waiting for the old woman to die so I can take her son-of-bitch son for everything. He's humiliated me. When she's dead, it'll be my turn to get him."

Oh, boy, ain't love grand?

I joined Constance near the window and said in a soothing voice, "How can you be sure Chase is being unfaithful? Has he told you?"

She looked at me with an intoxicated mix of surprise and pity. "He doesn't have to tell me, Kate. I have eyes. I hear the gossip and I feel the stares. You know, I think I could take it better if it were just one woman, but history keeps repeating itself."

"What do you mean?"

"He's just like his father," Constance said in a tone that hinted I should have known better. "Robinson Merriman probably slept with every woman in town. I wouldn't be surprised if Chase didn't have dozens of brothers and sisters running around Woodbury. It's in the Merriman genes. The game, remember? See how many women you can charm with your looks, money, and sex. It's a fun game for them, but not so much fun for the cheerleaders on the sidelines."

What a family trait. It was probably a good thing Chase and Constance didn't have children. What would you take to school for show-and-tell when you discussed your family tree?

"Did Mrs. Merriman know about her husband's affairs?"

She shrugged and smoothed her hair with a trembling hand. "Surely she did, she's not blind. It was different back then; women just sat around and tried to ignore it. Today, women can take a stand and see that it doesn't happen again."

I wondered how she would see to that. "Have you discussed this with Chase?"

She paused. "I take care of things in my own way. He won't do this to me again; I won't let him."

A tremble rolled through Constance, and she looked at me with a frightened gaze. "You shouldn't be here today. I'm sorry to have taken your time. It would be best for you to leave, Kate. I'm sorry."

The Merrimans certainly enjoyed stringing me along like a hungry cat and then pulling the milk dish away at the last minute. I had no intention of leaving. "But, Constance, I haven't spoken to Mrs. Merriman about the article yet. I'll just go upstairs and talk with her for a few minutes, then I'll leave. If you need to rest or go somewhere, I'll be fine on my own."

I'll be wonderful on my own, I thought. I had to get a better look at the house, and I could think of all kinds of questions to ask Winifred Merriman when I saw her. My work was far from finished.

Constance realized how much she had said. Her eyes took on the guise of a frightened child, and she pulled at her bracelet nervously. "I don't know. What if Chase comes back? It wouldn't be good for you to be here." She looked around the room. "What time is it?"

I glanced at my watch. "Just about noon."

"Oh, he'll be here any time. I thought you'd be gone by now, but that's my fault for talking so long." She shifted her weight and placed the empty glass on a table. "I need to get rid of this, too. Look, if you want to see Mother Merriman, fine, but you'll have to leave for about an hour. Chase comes in for lunch about now. Why don't you take a stroll around the grounds or something? I can call one of our staff to show you where you can walk. It's a nice day, I hope you don't mind.

It would be better for everyone if you did that. You can talk with Mother Merriman later."

It was an odd request but I jumped at it anyway. I knew precisely where I wanted to walk.

A certain lake sprang to mind.

Chapter 15

CONSTANCE WALKED OVER to a phone. "Eddie, it's Mrs. Merriman. I need a favor. I have a guest who wishes to take a stroll. Please come up to the house and show her some of the garden."

She hung up and turned to me. "Go out the door and take a right. At the side of the house, you'll see a path that leads down a little hill to a walled garden. Eddie will meet you there."

Constance crossed the room, swept the empty bourbon glass off the table, and tried for one last drop of alcohol. She settled for the ice cubes, which she sucked like a teething baby. "An hour. Be gone an hour."

I followed her into the hall, then slipped out the front door and turned right as instructed. I walked down the cobblestone path toward a square, stone-walled garden that sat about fifty feet from the house.

The sun was beating down on the stone wall, casting odd miniature shadows along the grass and walkway. It was warm again, and the flowers and shrubs covering the garden attested to the string of toasty days that were fighting against the approaching cold season. Roses and wildflowers grabbing the noonday sun speckled the lush green foliage with a palette of red, white, yellow, and purple. The grass was emerald green and clipped close to the ground. Not a weed was in attendance.

A set of black wrought-iron tables and matching chairs dotted each corner of the garden, along with tall tiki torches which would bring a golden glow to evening parties. For a minute, I was lost in my imagination, picturing the elegant lawn parties that were probably held here. I shut my eyes and bent my head over a fragrant, tall, white rosebush and inhaled the sweet smell.

"Are's you the lady Mrs. M was talkin' about?"

I glanced up from the rose petals. "Eddie, right?"

"Yes, ma'am, that's me," he said. Close up, he looked to be in his late 30s, but from a distance he might be mistaken for a teenager. In a white undershirt and large, faded overalls, Eddie was bone-thin and only about five feet six. He had a sharply angled, heart-shaped face, beagle puppy eyes, and large ears which successfully held up a Red Man Tobacco baseball cap.

He doffed the hat to reveal a closely shaven blond head. "Nice to meet you, ma'am. Mrs. Merriman says you want to walk for a while. Anywhere's special you want to go? We gots lots of space out here. I'm the land manager, so's I know the entire spread like it was my own."

He wiped his brow with the back of his hand, then put the cap on again. "I guess in a way, it is my land, since I take care of it so well, but I never would say that in front of Mr. M., if you know what I mean."

I returned his smile and said, "I understand there's a nice lake nearby. Could we go there?"

Eddie blinked a couple of times, then fiddled with the brim of his cap. He took the hat off, then immediately put it back on again. "Yeah, there's a lake. Any special reason you want to go there?"

I shrugged. "I like the water and I heard it's a very nice spot."

I watched him shift his weight back and forth like a skinny metronome. "Well, it's a far piece from here."

"I have the time."

He tapped his foot on the ground. "Yeah, well, if that's what you want, ma'am." He swiveled his head around the garden. "Well, okay, then, follow me."

Eddie turned and led me down the remainder of the cobblestone path until it ended at a row of tall thin evergreens. A faded dirt path plunged through a thick growth of trees, whose heavy foliage blocked out a huge chunk of sunshine. The smell of pine, wild honeysuckle, and damp, mossy grass tickled my nose like a tantalizing potpourri. Even though we were only a few hundred feet away from the main house, already it felt like we were in the middle of nowhere.

I patted myself on the back for wearing jeans and tennis shoes. As we passed the green leafy vines snaking up trees and across the path in a jumbled pretzel maze, I was reminded I never was a great Girl Scout. I never could remember the difference between regular old ivy, poison ivy, and poison oak. I gingerly stepped over the vines, continually picturing the poison versions coming alive and attacking my ankles with a fury.

"We certainly are deep in the woods, aren't we?" I asked.

He looked back at me. "Yes, ma'am, we are. We could have taken the bridle path, which is cleaner and more open, but this is a short-cut to the lake. I hope you don't mind."

I shoved a branch away from my face. "No, I don't mind at all."

Eddie pressed on. "Good. So's are you meeting someone down at the lake?"

"No, why do you ask?"

He stopped and glanced at me. "Uh, no reason. I thought you might be meeting someone there, that's all. Sometimes people do that, you know?"

I didn't know, but I would like to. "Do they have picnics or go swimming, something like that?"

His tanned cheeks picked up a little extra color, and he laughed. "Yeah, something like that, sometimes."

We scuttled down a steep hill and came to a clearing. The lake appeared just ahead, down yet another incline. It was a large fishing lake nestled among majestic pines. A small, wooden dock jutted out a few feet from the shore, and a floating wooden platform lazily drifted in the center of the blue-brown water.

"Oh, how pretty," I said.

Eddie nodded. "Yeah, it's nice, and stocked with some pretty good catch. I come down here a lot." He shook his head. "But I don't know if I'll be able to look at it quite the same way anymore."

Bingo.

"Oh, why's that?"

He answered in short, halting sentences, as if the words were painful to say. "There was a girl, you see. She worked here. Not here, but at the house. She, uh, drowned, the other day. Here. At the lake."

"Oh, how terrible. Were you here when it happened?"

Eddie looked at me, his large brown eyes growing by the second. "No, ma'am, not when it actually happened. But I saw her go down here earlier that day, so's I told Mr. Merriman and the sheriff that when they asked."

"They asked you at the same time?" I questioned, remembering that was how Chase had described it at the hospital.

"Uh, well, kinda, I guess," Eddie said. "Mr. M., he asked me earlier if'n I'd seen her lately, then about an hour later he showed up with the sheriff, and he asked again, actin' like he'd never asked before. Next thing I know, we was callin' for an ambulance to come to the lake."

He shook his head and squinted toward the sun. "It sure was sad, I'll tell ya that."

"Was she alone here at the lake?" I asked, crossing my fingers behind my back.

Eddie's eyebrows met on the top of his nose, and he stared at me before answering. "Uh, I guess so. I just saw her head off down the azalea trail, that's all. I don't think she was meeting anyone that day. Are you kin to her?"

I ignored him. "That day? Did she usually meet someone here?"

He chuckled nervously. "I don't know, ma'am. What folks do here, well, that's their business. I try to keep my distance and be polite, you know? I don't spy on folks or nothin'." His nervous eyes twitched my way. "Not intentionally, I mean. That particular day? Don't know, she could've been alone. Hard to tell."

Eddie shoved his hands into the overall pockets. "Look, I need to tend to things, ma'am. I'm gonna head up the bridle trail straight over there. You can follow that back to the house, or if you remember the way, you can go through the woods again. I think you'd be good to take the bridle trail, okay? Nice to meet you, ma'am."

He took off in an awkward jog toward the far edge of the lake. Before he started up the trail, he paused to look back at me. He stood motionless for a moment, then tapped the brim of his baseball cap and headed up the hill.

Now that I was at the lake, I wasn't exactly sure what I should do. The police had scoured the banks already, so I doubted if any huge clues were staring at me. I dropped my purse in the grass and ambled toward the rippling water. Maybe the police missed something.

The sun was high in the sky, and the squeak of crickets and an occasional belch from an unseen frog sang in the air. A light rustle of water lapped at the shore as I walked slowly, staring down at the pebbles and muddy patches of grass which formed a crooked boundary around the water. After circling the entire lake, I found nothing more interesting than a couple of odd-shaped stones and some unknown, slimy-looking creatures slipping between the rocks.

I walked out onto the wobbly, weather-beaten dock and sat cross-legged on the edge. I reached down and let my fingers rake through the cool dark water as I tried to picture Karen in the same spot. My eyes drifted to the shore. Thompson had said her clothes were stained with mud, so that probably meant she wasn't on this dock, but in the grass. Could she have been trying to run away? Did the killer jump her from behind? I shut my eyes and tried to imagine the scene.

A voice sliced through the still air. "Get off my property now!"

My eyes flew open and I scrambled to stand. Chase Merriman was storming down the hill, heading straight for me. His face was twisted. His eyes were fiery, narrow slits as he stomped onto the dock.

I backed up a couple of steps, keenly aware that the end of the dock was inches away. Chase's broad figure crowded the dock's width and left me in a very uncomfortable spot.

"I want you off my property and away from my family—now," he growled.

I played dumb, with all the innocence I could muster. "Mr. Merriman, is there a problem?"

He exploded. "Yes, there's a problem; you're a reporter. I do not tolerate the press. You have woven your way into this family the past few days and caused nothing but trouble. All reporters are like a bad flu or an annoying itch. No matter what you do, they hang around and gnaw at the guts of their victims."

Chase's elocution was colorful, but I was tired of being the punching bag for the Woodbury press association. I enjoy my occupation. Why should I put up with his ranting?

"Mr. Merriman, I'm a feature writer here to do a nice, gentle story on your family history, that's all. You agreed to it, remember? Look at my work as educational. Or entertaining. I'm not here to do some wild exposé on your family. I'm not like the other reporters down at the gate."

"The hell you aren't," he shouted. "You're all alike, a bunch of deceiving trash-mouths who are only interested in destroying other people's lives just to make a paltry couple of bucks. I know what reporters are paid. It's pathetic. So I guess you just lower your standards to equal the measly paychecks you cash each month."

"That's not fair," I argued. The part about the measly paychecks was true, but it still wasn't fair.

"Don't tell me what's fair. I'm a successful, busy man. I have a corporation to run and several hundred employees to manage. I don't have the desire to give the time of day to the likes of your so-called profession."

I looked around the lake. We were very much alone, out of earshot of anyone except woodland creatures. Chase was furious or afraid of something, and he was taking it all out on me. Little old me, alone on a wobbly dock at a deep lake where someone had been murdered a couple of days earlier.

And me without my sunscreen or swim fins.

Chase was on a roll. "Do you know where I spent my entire morning? Do you?" he demanded. "With Sheriff Thompson, answering ridiculous questions about the murder of some store owner. And do you know why?"

I knew and Chase knew.

"Because," he said, "you, Miss Kelly, told the sheriff that I was somehow connected to the man's murder."

"No, no, I didn't say that," I quickly defended. I thought it was interesting, though, that Thompson had followed up. He must have listened to my story after all.

Chase was a man possessed. "I don't care what you said, but I am not accustomed to being accused of murder. Where do you get off spreading lies like that?"

Cut down my profession, accuse me of being a snoop, criticize how I look, for criminy's sake, but don't call me a liar.

I threw my hands on my hips. "Look, Mr. Merriman, I did not lie to anyone. I very plainly saw you pull into Walenza's Antiques yesterday afternoon. You were driving a convertible Mercedes with the top down. You passed me, parked in front of the store, and went inside."

His breaths were coming hard and fast. "What were you doing at that store, Miss Kelly? Maybe the sheriff should talk to you, not me."

I rolled my eyes. I was entirely fed up with people trying to pin the blame on me. "You know what I think, Mr. Merriman?" I challenged.

"I think you know a lot more about Karen than you're letting on. I think you have intimate knowledge of her that could prove very interesting."

Okay, so maybe I put a little too much emphasis on the word *intimate*, but it was obvious that I had struck a frayed, raw nerve.

Chase's nostrils flared, his eyes narrowed, and he lunged toward me. I knew I didn't have anywhere to go, but, instinctively, I stepped back. My left foot slid off the edge of the dock, and I felt the flesh scraping away from my ankle as it made a rough pass on the splintered, jagged wood.

My foot plunged into the cold water as I fell backwards. I took a deep breath and prepared to hit the water, but, instead, Chase grabbed my arm and wrenched it forward. He roughly pulled me back onto the dock. His grip twisted my arm at an unnatural angle and sent a crashing pain to my shoulder. I glanced at my ankle, which was cold, wet, and extremely raw. I was now effectively battered from top to bottom.

How lovely my vacation was turning out to be.

Chase spoke slowly and distinctly between heaving, angry breaths. "You are a troublemaker. I have had enough—"

"Mr. Merriman! Mr. Merriman!" Eddie ran toward us, wildly waving his hands. "No, sir, please!"

Chase relaxed his grip and hauled me to my feet. He stared hard at me, then took a breath and turned to Eddie. "Is there a problem?"

Eddie stopped just short of the dock. "Uh, I don't know sir. I, uh, well, thought there might be a problem."

Chase glanced at me, then smiled sympathetically. "Everything is fine, Eddie. Miss Kelly and I were talking, and I'm afraid she accidentally slipped off the dock. I had to catch her before she fell into the water, that's all."

Eddie looked straight at me with a curious expression. "Are you all right, ma'am?"

"Of course she is," Chase said. "I said it was fine, didn't I? What brings you here, Eddie?"

"Uh, you're needed at the house, sir." Eddie stared at me. "There's an urgent call from your office. Mrs. Merriman asked me to find you."

Chase stiffened. "What kind of urgent call?"

"Uh, I don't know, sir." He swallowed hard. "But Mrs. Merriman, she said you should come to the house right away."

Chase let go of my arm, spun a heated look at me, then stalked off the dock past Eddie. He bypassed the bridle path and headed for the woods.

Eddie stepped onto the dock and held out his hand. "You sure you're okay, ma'am? That's a scrape and a half you've got on your foot."

I nodded and took a few stinging, tender steps forward. "Oh, I'll survive. Thanks for asking."

I could walk on it if I stepped lightly and didn't mind a twinge here and there. My ankle was bright pink and stained with little polka-dots of clotted blood. I heard my mother's litany about wearing socks with tennis shoes instead of merely slipping my treasured Keds over my bare feet. I didn't think amputation would be necessary; a squirt of antiseptic and a good-sized Band-Aid would probably do the trick.

Chase stopped at the top of the hill and commanded, "Come back to the house with me, both of you."

Eddie held my elbow as he guided me off the dock. He didn't need to do that, but I appreciated the offer.

"Guess we better go, huh?" I said.

"Yes, ma'am, I think that might be wise."

We began the trek back to the house in a restless silence. Chase was clearly angry, and I didn't want to push him any further. I was quite relieved that Eddie had appeared when he did. It was not lost on me that I was standing at a murder site with a man who was furious enough to perform the act.

For the first time.

Or was it maybe for a second or third time?

The faces of Karen Kelly and Rupert Walenza flashed in my mind, sending a shiver through me that wasn't the result of an afternoon breeze. I looked at Chase as he strode purposefully up the path, crushing pebbles and weeds underneath his feet. His chin was set tightly, and beads of sweat dotted his hairline. I noticed his tall, strong physique. He had a broad chest with muscular, powerful shoulders, and big, strong hands.

All the better to strangle you with, my dear, I thought uneasily.

We reached a clearing in the woods where the house loomed in the distance. We turned onto the path that led to the driveway, which was littered with a handful of expensive cars—and my mom's measly little middle-class Corolla. It looked rather forlorn against a blue metallic Jaguar XJS, Chase's silver convertible Mercedes, and a black Mercedes sedan parked side by side.

The black Mercedes looked suspiciously like the car Mason Shelby had been driving. I wondered what he was doing at the house. Mrs. Merriman had appeared the picture of health when I saw her the day before.

The sight of the cars prompted something in Eddie's mind. He picked up his pace until he caught up with Chase. "Oh, Mr. Merriman, I forgot to tell you this earlier. The body shop in Clarksville called. That dent and other damage has been fixed on the front of your Land Rover."

Eddie snorted with approval and rubbed the back of his hand

under his narrow nose. "Shoot, that was a quick repair job, wasn't it, Mr. Merriman? Just a couple of days for all that work? If you're wanting me to, I can pick the car up from the shop for you this afternoon. You know, since it's so out of the way for you and all. If'n it was me, I would have taken it to Cooper's in Woodbury, 'stead of all the way to Clarksville. But, hey, I guess that's why you're the boss, sir. Anyhow's, they got that big dent in the front grille fixed."

Chase froze.

He slowly turned and his eyes bored into mine.

I watched the blood drain from his face.

Chapter 16

SOMETHING IN MY MIND flashed to every disaster movie I'd ever seen. Chase wore the look that all characters facing imminent danger held just before the explosion or natural disaster. All the hallmarks were there: the pale perspiring skin, the wide eyes with twitching lids, and a slightly parted mouth, sucking in air as if he were taking his last breath. If a Hollywood talent agent had been nearby, Chase would have been cast on the spot.

I admit I was a mirror image of Chase.

So, the front grille of Chase's Land Rover, a car big enough to easily send a little, rented Ford Taurus sailing off the road into a tree, had been badly damaged. What were the odds of that?

Eddie picked up on the tension, but he misread the reason. "Aw, geez, Mr. Merriman, I'm sorry. I shouldn't have second-guessed your choice of body shops. It's just that Cooper's is run by a buddy of mine, and they're much closer than goin' all the way to Clarksville. Although, they do good work down in Clarksville and all."

"That's enough, Eddie," Chase snapped. "I don't care where it was fixed. Pick up the car this afternoon. Have one of the others cover for you." His eyes were pinned on me. "Miss Kelly, follow me." He stalked toward the house.

Eddie fiddled with his baseball cap again, then nodded at me. "I'm sorry your walk was messed up, ma'am. Maybe you can do it again soon."

"Oh, it was fine," I said. "I enjoyed seeing the lake." It might not have been a conventional stroll in the woods, but it certainly had its moments.

He pointed a bony finger at my foot. "You take care of that ankle, you hear? It might hurt like a hornet for a while, if you're not careful."

I smiled. "It will be fine, Eddie, thanks for your help."

"Miss Kelly," Chase commanded, "I asked you to come to the house." He was waiting impatiently on the sidewalk near the front steps.

I had angered him more than I cared to admit, so I waved to Eddie and quickly joined Chase. He turned and marched to the front steps. I took a deep breath and followed him, unable to shake the feeling that I was being led to the principal's office.

As Chase stepped onto the porch, the front door swung open and Mason Shelby flew out the door in a blur. He was in such a hurry that he crashed chest to chest with Chase. As the startled men backed off and exchanged irate grunts, Constance stumbled onto the porch. Her face was flushed and her hair was falling out of the gold barrette anchored on the back of her head.

"Why are you here, Mason?" Chase growled. "Have a bad day at the track? Racking up another overpriced house call so you can play the ponies this afternoon?"

Mason puffed out his chest and shot a look at Constance. "Don't give me that crap, Chase. I have better things to do with my time. I was called out here today."

Chase took on a new complexion. His voice softened and he looked expectantly at his wife. "Is Mother all right? Is she sick?"

"She's fine, Chase," Constance replied. "Why does it always have to be her? I'm the one who called Mason."

"I have to go," Mason said.

Chase clamped a hand on the doctor's arm. "Why did you come out here?"

Mason angrily pulled his arm away, then looked at Constance. "Ask her." He brushed past Chase and stomped down the steps, barely pausing to acknowledge my presence. "I should have known you'd be hanging around."

"Nice to see you too, Dr. Shelby," I purred.

Chase wouldn't give up. "Why was he here, Constance?"

She jutted her chin in the air. "I had a . . . a headache."

And the dog ate my homework, I thought.

What was Constance up to? Mason was certainly in a hurry to make himself scarce. In fact, Chase missed her reply, thanks to the roar of Mason's Mercedes flying down the drive.

"You what?"

"I had a headache, Chase. I didn't feel well. Your mother isn't the only one who might need a doctor sometime."

Constance and Chase leveled aristocratic stares at each other. I had vanished into thin air.

That changed when Winifred Merriman appeared in the doorway. "Why, Kate, how good to see you. I thought I noticed an unfamiliar car." She peered down the drive. "I thought I heard Mason's voice in the hall. Is he here too?"

Constance bit her lip. "He was, until Chase came in. I wasn't feeling well, but Chase thinks everything is all right, so he told Mason to leave."

"He was leaving before I got here," Chase shot back.

Winifred cleared her throat and subtly reminded her son and

daughter-in-law of proper civility. "Now, there's no need to bother Kate with your personal matters. Constance, if you're feeling unwell, may I suggest you lie down for a while; and Chase, dear, show a little gentleness. We aren't all as hale as you are."

Like naughty children caught in the act, Constance crossed her arms and turned away, while Chase dropped his head and studied the porch floor. It was amazing to watch the quiet power of this diminutive octogenarian. Where had she been when Chase was ready to tango with me on the dock?

Winifred stepped onto the porch but stopped abruptly and pointed her cane at my feet. "My goodness, dear, your slacks are wet. Did you slip and fall somewhere?"

Constance spun around, and Chase's head popped up like he'd been slapped.

Watching Chase, I answered, "Yes. I'm a bit of a klutz, I'm afraid. I was walking by the lake and lost my footing."

Chase took a deep breath. Constance fired a look at him, gurgled her anger deep in her throat, and stormed into the house. Winifred ignored both of them.

It was time to change the subject before Chase truly kicked me off the farm. "I'm fine, though," I continued. "But, Mrs. Merriman, I'm actually here to visit with you. Would you mind if we chatted some more about the family history? If you'd like, we could sit out here."

Chase's eyes burned a hole into my skin. "It's too warm out here," he said. "You can talk upstairs in Mother's dressing room for a few minutes; then Mother will need to rest."

"We can visit as long as it takes, Chase. I don't need to rest. Come, Kate, I'll show you upstairs." She extended her hand toward me, but Chase reached for it instead and led her inside.

Winifred looked over her shoulder and smiled politely. "Follow us, dear."

I did as instructed and followed the pair up the grand staircase. It was a slow process for Winifred, but she climbed the steps with determination and nary a wasted breath. We reached the top and turned left down a gold-carpeted hallway which led to another wing of the mansion.

The walls were ivory and flecked with elaborate, scrolled crown molding. Vases full of fresh flowers dominated the polished tables lining the hallway, and a massive oil painting of the house stretched down a major portion of the wall. The maid met us coming down the hallway.

"Do bring us some tea, Maria," Winifred said. To her son's disapproving glance, she repeated, "We'll visit as long as I like, Chase."

He stopped at a heavy, inlaid wooden door and turned the porcelain handle. The door swung open with a creak, and we stepped into

Winifred's dressing room.

Pink roses, tightly stretched on silk damask fabric, stood in for wallpaper. A tall oriental screen, decorated in silver and pale shades of rose, sat diagonally in the corner. In the center of the room was a claw-footed, silver-cushioned, S-shaped lover's couch with opposing seats. Two small glass tables holding three fresh pink roses in slender silver vases anchored each end of the couch. A triple-mirrored antique dressing table laden with old photographs and a pair of crisp, white ladies' gloves lined one wall; a carved dresser holding more photographs sat opposite.

"I'll leave you here," Chase said curtly before stepping into the hallway and pulling the door shut. Or nearly shut. He left it ajar, enough that I could plainly see his shadow hovering outside.

It was so nice to see how much he trusted me.

"What a lovely room," I said as Winifred settled on one end of the couch. I took a seat on the other end, reached into my purse for my notebook and tape recorder, and kept an eye on the door. The shadow didn't move.

"Yes," she replied. "This may not be one of the fanciest rooms in the house, but I feel most comfortable in here. Many of my memories are here."

I glanced at the door again. "Why don't you tell me about some of those memories?"

Winifred was only too happy to oblige. She delved into her memory bank and began to spin family tales—which didn't help me solve the mystery of Karen's death, but they were compelling nonetheless. I even put Chase out of my mind, until I heard a creak in the hallway. The shadow moved on, apparently satisfied that I was innocently questioning his mother as I had promised. Winifred snapped her gaze toward the door, paused in her story, and watched the door.

She turned toward me again. "I must apologize for Chase and Constance's behavior. I don't know what's come over them lately. I'd attribute it to the tragedy with poor Karen, but it's been going on much longer. Now, dear, let's talk about something more substantial, since Chase has moved on."

I smiled with a whole new respect for this feisty matriarch. "Tell me about Karen," I said.

Winifred crossed her hands over her lap and stared into the distance. A warm but sad smile spread across her face. Looking at me with clear blue eyes that belied her age, she said, "You do resemble her, you know? It's such a shame you never knew Karen. What a sweet child she was."

"How did she come to work for your family?" I asked as I nonchalantly nudged my tape recorder closer.

"Oh, I suppose Chase sent an advertisement around. 'Care for ancient old lady, easy to get along with, doesn't drool yet.' Something like that."

Winifred grinned. "They mean well, and I admit I enjoy the company, but I don't need a keeper. I guess that's what children do when they don't know how to occupy their elderly parents' time. It's a reversal of the aging process. I used to be the one looking for help to care for Chase, and now he's looking for someone to care for me. I was against the idea at first, but I came to look forward to Karen's visits."

The sad smile returned. "It was almost like having a grandchild, I suppose. I was never blessed with one. Karen worked here nearly a year, in between her studies. She'd visit with me, have lunch or tea, and in the spring and summer we worked in the garden.

"There are many sights to see on the grounds," she continued. "It's like a new adventure every day. Karen liked to go exploring when I would rest in the afternoon. I wish she hadn't gone out that day, that awful day. I told her to stay inside, but she went out anyway."

I leaned in closer. "Why did you want her to stay inside? Was she sick?"

Winifred tapped her chest. "She was sick in here, the poor child. Affairs of the heart can be terrible when things go badly."

"How could you tell?" My heart began to race.

"Oh, just things she would say. Karen was a lovely young lady. She deserved to have throngs of boys sending her flowers, but she was deeply committed to someone who upset her a great deal."

"Did she talk to you about him?" I asked a little too eagerly.

She nodded. "Karen never openly talked about him. She only said that she was in love, but it would never work out. I'm sure she thought I was much too old to understand about modern love, but I could see that she was very unhappy." Winifred looked away, then lowered her voice. "I shouldn't speak ill of the departed, but she spent a great deal of time here, and often she would be out on the farm for hours. I'm not sure, but I sometimes thought she might have been part of an illicit affair." She flicked a questioning look my way, as if I should understand something unsaid.

Good lord. Did Winifred suspect her son?

She frowned. "Love works in strange ways, Kate. Many of us fall in love with the wrong people, for all the wrong reasons and at the worst times. Maybe someone treats you kindly, or is dashing, a hero to you. Or maybe you react to a deep hurt, and strike back at the one you truly love. . . ." Her voice trailed off as tears filled her eyes. She fumbled in her pocket for a lace handkerchief.

I reached for her hand. "I guess we all make mistakes at times."

She tucked the handkerchief back into her pocket. "Yes, but Karen didn't deserve to die," she said bluntly.

"Mrs. Merriman, what do you think happened?"

She stared at me, her lip trembling. In a barely audible whisper, she said, "I don't know. Can we talk about something else, please?"

I searched her face for whatever was troubling her deep within. I wanted to continue questioning her, but on the other hand, the last thing I wanted to do was upset her too much. I couldn't think of a thing to talk about other than Karen.

I glanced over Winifred's shoulder and spied a black-and-white photo of two little boys. The picture, which appeared to be from the early 1950s, showed two fresh-faced, dark-haired boys looking horribly uneasy in their Sunday-best summer suits. Their expressions screamed discomfort, and they looked as though they would gladly exchange their starched white suits for dungarees, muddy T-shirts, and fishing poles.

I stood and walked over to the dresser. "Who are these cute kids?"

She smiled slightly. "I'm surprised you couldn't guess. It's Chase and Mason."

"As in Mason Shelby?"

Winifred chuckled. "Well, yes. Who else would be named Mason?"

I stared closely at the picture. The boys' features slowly evolved in my mind into miniature versions of the two adults I knew. Perhaps it was my imagination working overtime, but I also noticed that the boys were physically spaced from each other, in a tightly posed stance. They certainly didn't look like bosom buddies, even at that tender age. Maybe their scowls didn't come from their constricting suits, but from a lifelong dislike of each other.

"I guess I never pictured them as childhood friends," I said.

She nodded. "My husband and I had close ties with Mason and Evelyn Shelby; but, unfortunately, things changed."

I carefully placed the photo back on the dresser. "Oh, may I ask what happened?"

Winifred's cheeks flushed with color. "Evelyn . . . she, um, died when her son was quite small. We felt it was important to make little Mason feel like he had a family, but he and Chase never got along very well."

I glanced at the picture again and calculated that Mason appeared to be a bit older than Chase. I wondered if the arrival of the motherless Mason caused Chase to be jealous of this new kid who was stealing from his treasured only-child status. Maybe as a young boy he resented having to share his mother. Feelings like that can be hard to shake, even for adults.

Winifred and Robinson Merriman were probably doing the most charitable thing, but given Mason's current personality, he probably had been a royal brat as a child. I suddenly felt sorry for Chase. Who'd want to play with a nasty bully all day?

"How did Mrs. Shelby die?"

A tinny bell rang outside the door, and Winifred stood, relieved that something had interrupted our conversation. She reached for her cane and completely ignored my question. "Well, there's our tea. I was beginning to think Maria forgot about us. Come over here, Kate. Let me show you something you'll like."

I thought I'd like to have an answer to my question, but I followed her into the hallway. She walked a few steps and reached to touch a section of molding on the wall. It took my eyes a second to focus, but I noticed the barely perceptible outline of a small door. The piece of molding that Winifred handled was actually a knob. She pulled open the small door to reveal a wooden cabinet suspended on a pulley threaded with thick, braided ropes. A tray holding two tall glasses of iced tea and a plate of sugar cookies sat on a narrow shelf inside the cabinet.

Winifred smiled. "One of the pleasures of owning an historical home. This dumbwaiter is so handy. I can't figure why they don't have these in modern homes nowadays. Could you do the honors, Kate? I'm afraid I'm too wobbly to carry a tray that size."

I stood there, mesmerized by the sight of the dumbwaiter. I'd seen them many times before, but something stuck in my mind.

I thought of Winifred's comment: "This dumbwaiter is so handy."

Dumbwaiter, dumbwaiter, dumbwaiter.

Dumb waiter.

The location you'll find, not from a wise old maid or a young dumb waiter. . . .

It couldn't be.

Or could it?

Chapter 17

I MOVED SLOWLY, in a trancelike state, toward the dumbwaiter. It had been here, all these years, so obvious. Hadn't anyone thought to put the words together? Was it such a normal part of everyone's day that no one ever bothered to equate it with the riddle? Or was I going a little over the edge, consumed by the thought of buried treasure?

Quite frankly, it was just what you'd expect—five thick, aged panels of wood bolted together and suspended on a rusting pulley. I ran my fingers along the thick braid of rope that held the dumbwaiter in place. The rough, knotted fibers did nothing more than tickle my fingers' nerve endings. Only a few inches were open between the dumbwaiter and the walls on each side. Musty smelling, it was dark, with the exception of a faint glimmer of light from what I guessed to be the kitchen below.

"Kate, haven't you seen a dumbwaiter before?" Winifred asked in a puzzled voice.

I turned around with a sheepish grin. "Oh, yes, of course. I just think they are so interesting and, like you said, convenient."

"I like to think a dumbwaiter would be low on the list of architectural curiosities for someone of your intelligence. You've something else on your mind. What is it that's so fascinating?"

I reached inside and extracted the tray of tea and cookies. I spied a table sitting against the wall and placed the tray there. "I have to confess, since you told me about the legend, it's been playing in my mind. When I saw this dumbwaiter, a line from the riddle popped into my head. It says something about a 'wise old maid or a young dumb waiter.'"

She blinked a couple of times. "Oh, really? That's very clever of you. What does it mean?"

Winifred knew something. There was just a little too much "gee-whizness" to her comment for my liking.

"Do you mind if I take a closer look?" I asked, watching carefully for her reaction.

She raised her chin. "Go ahead, be my guest, dear. I doubt you'll find anything substantial. That dumbwaiter is used several times each day. I'm sure someone would have noticed a hidden treasure, don't you think?"

"Well, probably so, but it will satisfy my curiosity. I have too wild an imagination to let this slip past."

She took a couple of steps closer and peered inside. "When Chase and Mason were little, they used to take rides in this. It always made me nervous. My imagination saw them getting stuck halfway down. But you know what little fear children have. It was all a grand adventure to them." She stepped away and gestured toward the opening. "Have a look, dear, just don't climb in."

I laughed. "Don't worry, I think I'm way past the age of fitting inside for a ride."

I stuck my head into the opening and squinted to adjust my eyes to the sudden darkness. It was difficult to see anything, particularly since I didn't know what I was searching for. I ran my hand along the walls and hoped that I wouldn't pick up a big splinter to go with the rest of my walking-wounded body.

In the top corner of a side wall, I spotted a crudely scratched "C.R.M." and, just below it, a bigger, deeper carved "M.S." Chase and Mason. It was intriguing to think of them as little boys, locked in a perpetual competition with each other. I peered at the "M.S." and wondered if it was so much larger in order to make a point.

"Did you find something?" Winifred asked. "What are you looking at so closely?"

I pulled my head out of the dumbwaiter and pointed to the spot. "It looks like your son and Dr. Shelby carved their initials in here during one of their rides."

Winifred bent her head toward the opening. "Oh, yes, I do remember that. I can't see it, though. My eyes aren't what they used to be."

Perhaps her eyes weren't the greatest, but her mind was as sharp as a knife. Enough of the old chitchat, it was time to ask Winifred what was really on my mind. Chase and Mason's childhood escapades could wait.

"Was Karen searching for the answer to the riddle, Mrs. Merriman?"

I knew the answer, of course, but I wondered if Karen had pumped her employer for information. I thought of Karen's handwritten notes where she had emphasized "dumb waiter" and "flowers wilting from the heat." She must have figured something out about the dumbwaiter, but what?

Winifred nodded. "Well, now that you mention it, I think she was interested in the legend. We talked about it once in a while; joked about what to do with the loot, as she called it. I don't think she ever got very far with it, though. It's stumped too many people in the past."

"Karen never mentioned this dumbwaiter?" I asked.

She shrugged her slender shoulders. "No, not to me. We only talked about the mystery of the words. I don't think she was actually scouring the house for the answer. In fact, she was more interested in our antiques. That was our favorite topic."

I bet it was a popular topic.

"Well, I guess the mystery will have to continue." I ran my hand across the top of the dumbwaiter and reached behind it as far as I could. "I thought I had finally solved the riddle, but I guess I'm not that smart after all."

"You won't be the first person to fail, that's for sure," Winifred said. "You know, the treasure probably never existed to begin with. I imagine it was just a good story that got out of hand."

I rubbed my hand along the back side of the dumbwaiter, uneasily conscious of the gook I was accumulating on my fingers. Whatever it was, it was thick and somewhat sticky. I made a face and tried to put that out of my mind. Was I sticking my hand back here for a good story? I hoped it was worth more than that.

"I guess you're right," I sighed. "So much for buried treasure."

In one final attempt, I stretched my arm a few more inches and waved my hand back and forth with a quick swish. Then I slowly pressed my fingers to the wood. Something was taped on the back of the dumbwaiter. I ran my hand past it again, ignoring the protests from my aching arm muscles.

"There's something here, Mrs. Merriman," I grunted. "I think it's an envelope."

I tugged at the edge of the object as she moved closer.

"An envelope?" she said. "What is it, Kate?"

Whatever it was, it wasn't giving up gently. It was terribly difficult to get a grip on, thanks to its well-hidden spot and the awkward position of my arm dangling behind the dumbwaiter. There have been many times in my life when I've gazed at pictures of models in magazines and wished I had their willowy long arms and legs. Where was Cindy Crawford when you needed her? I doubted that she would be much help, either. Cindy Crawford wouldn't be stupid enough to stick her arm behind a dumbwaiter. She might break a million-dollar fingernail.

I gave the object a quick, hard yank and felt it pop free. I heard paper rip in the process. I bit my lip, hoping I hadn't destroyed something important, and pulled the object from behind the dumbwaiter. It was an envelope, yellowed by accumulating dirt and the passage of years—and torn in the corner, thanks to me. A strip of yellowed, hardened tape sliced across its center.

Winifred put her hand to her throat and absentmindedly fingered the pearl brooch that rested on the collar of her blouse. "What do you think it is? Why was it back there?"

I stared at the dusty envelope. "I don't know, but there's only one way to find out." I turned it over and gently slid my finger into the torn place. I opened it and peeked inside like I was expecting to find a winning lottery ticket. Instead, there was a folded sheet of expensive parchment stationery. I was relieved to see that the note had survived intact and that only the outer envelope had been ripped when I pulled it off the dumbwaiter.

I extracted the note and carefully unfolded it. There was no letterhead or identifying mark on the paper, but there was a handwritten message penned in a thick, black ink that had leaked through the paper fibers and blended a few letters together. The handwriting was bold and masculine, with sharp downstrokes and an angular slant to the right. That much was easy to determine; the difficult part was interpreting the meaning of the message.

It read simply: "The fire has been put out, but for children, the history of the world will always be critical."

What was that supposed to mean? It was obviously a continuation of the riddle, but it certainly didn't give the solution. I stared at the sentence and ran it through my mind again. Nothing, absolutely nothing. I turned the note over, hoping that some explanation would be waiting on the other side.

Call me a dreamer. Better yet, call an interpreter for me.

"What does it say, Kate? Read it to me, please," Winifred said.

I glanced at her eager face, then read the sentence aloud. She had the same reaction I did. Her face clouded and she shook her head. "I don't understand. What could that mean?"

"I'm not sure," I answered. "But one thing is certain. This can't be from Carter Merriman's day because the envelope was taped on the back of the dumbwaiter. I don't think they had adhesive tape like this in the 1800s. Someone obviously got past this part of the riddle. I wonder if they actually solved it and just left this here to tease whoever found it?"

"How old do you think it is?" Winifred asked.

I turned the envelope over and held it up to the light. The edges of the tape were a cocoa color, and the paper under the tape had turned to a hardened, mottled gold. Cocoa-colored cracks and fine lines were woven through the tape like a miniature highway system.

"Well, it wasn't put here recently," I mused. "I would guess it's been decades, but I'm certainly not an expert."

"Isn't that something?" She shook her head again and reached her hand out. "May I look at the note?"

"Of course, Mrs. Merriman. See if it lights any fires for you."

She smiled. "Oh, I doubt that." Squinting her eyes, she stared at the paper for a split second before her mouth dropped open. Drawing the note closer to her face, she read it again, then dropped her hand to her side. She stared into the distance as if she'd seen a ghost.

"Robinson," she said in a choked whisper, her eyes glassy with tears. She walked slowly to the banister and leaned against it for support. She stared out over the staircase in silence, then with a wrinkled, trembling hand, brushed away a tear. "This is my husband's handwriting. I haven't seen it in years. Despite everything, I loved him dearly, and it startled me to see a part of him come alive again after all this time."

Despite everything? Despite what?

I stared at her and heard Constance's voice in my head: *Surely she knew, she wasn't blind.* Winifred must have known about Robinson's affairs. Why else would she have said that?

I joined her at the banister, conscious of the sadness in her eyes but also curious about the fact that it was her husband who knew the next part of the riddle. What was the part in marriage lore about sharing everything? Wouldn't that include, quite literally, "sharing the wealth"? I wondered if Winifred was being straight with me.

I gently reached for the note. It fell from her hands with the ease of a skate on ice. She stared over the banister at nothing in particular.

"Mrs. Merriman," I said quietly, "did your husband follow the legend? You said he burned the original copy of the riddle, but do you think he may have solved it?"

"No," she said quickly. "No, Robinson wasn't interested in things like that. This would have been a complete waste of his time."

"But the note is in his handwriting," I pointed out.

"I see that," she replied, sneaking a look my way. "I don't know where that came from, or why he put it there." Her gaze shifted out over the banister again. "Maybe it was part of a game, with Chase, or maybe. . . ."

Her voice trailed off for a moment, but then she let out a gasp, and her voice changed to a deeper, urgent tone. "You must stop pursuing this legend, Kate. Don't try to do anything else with it. Forget about it; it has no meaning or application to events today." Her words were strung together like cars on a speedway.

She snatched the letter from my hand. "Let me have that. This belonged to my husband; I'll keep it. Go on about your business, dear. If you would be so kind, I'd like you to leave this note out of your article. It won't add any meaning to your story. Know that the riddle will remain unsolved. Mysteries are meant to be that way."

"Mrs. Merriman, what's wrong? What has upset you so much?"

I didn't like the way she looked. Her face was flushed and her breathing was irregular. I swung a look down the hallway, halfway hoping and halfway fearing that Chase would be near.

Winifred stepped past me down the hallway. "Kate, you're a very nice young lady, and I appreciate how you've kept me company during this time without Karen. But, please, abide by my wishes. Give up your search. The legend means nothing. Nothing at all."

That was one *nothing* too many for my taste.

"Perhaps I should rest for a while," she said haltingly. "Like my son suggested. I've had too much excitement this afternoon. I'm sorry about the tea and cookies, Kate. Maybe we can have them another day."

I looked closely at Winifred. As she had in the past when things looked dicey, she politely changed the subject.

I tried again. "Why are you so upset, Mrs. Merriman? Is there something I can do to help?"

"No, there's nothing you can do, nothing anyone can do." She stretched out a weak smile. "I'm sorry to cut our visit short, but I think I will go rest now. Please call on me again, dear."

After squeezing my arm lightly, she stiffly walked away, plunging the letter deep into the pocket of her navy cardigan. She passed the door to the dressing room and paused at the next doorway down the hall. She turned the handle and looked back at me before she stepped inside. "Let's keep this between you and me. There's no need to bother anyone else with this matter."

Her polite edict delivered, Winifred shut the heavy door behind her with a resounding thud.

This was a pretty picture. What would I do now?

Obviously the note had struck a chord with her. Could it simply be a painful reminder of a not-so-perfect marriage, or was there more to it? Did she know all along that the envelope was there? On the surface, the note looked harmless enough, but something had jogged her memory—and that memory wasn't pleasant.

And here I was, alone in the hall on the upper level of the Merriman mansion. I was desperate to explore the house, but, knowing my luck, I'd probably stick my nose inside a doorway and run smack into Chase or Constance.

I decided to stroll down the hallway, and if I just happened to pass an open door, what was the harm in peeking inside? If I got caught, I'd say I was looking for Winifred to say good-bye. It sounded plausible enough.

I walked slowly, taking in the enormity of the soaring ceilings, massive oil landscapes on the walls, and the aroma of vase after vase of fresh flowers covering tables along the wall. I felt like I was in a well-preserved museum or resort hotel, where you feel the need to whisper and, above all, never, ever touch anything. I couldn't help myself, though. I was drawn to one oval table that held an artful arrangement of five odd-sized vases, holding various shades of red and yellow flowers.

What I found interesting wasn't the flowers, but the vases. One in particular looked strangely familiar to me. I stared at it and swiveled it around to check out all sides of the crystal. Then it hit me. It was just like the one Rupert Walenza had picked up to polish when I was talking to him in his store. My eyes zeroed in on the other four and confirmed my hunch. There were two sets of matching vases, then the one lone crystal vase.

I carefully placed it back on the table, hustled down the hall to Winifred's dressing room, and slipped inside to gather my purse and tape recorder. I frowned as I returned to the hallway and dropped the recorder into my purse. I should have carried that with me when we went to the dumbwaiter, but how was I to know it would have come in handy?

The thunderous crash of a door slamming shut shattered the quiet as I reached the stairway. I stopped on the steps and tried to figure out the noise's origin. It didn't take long, because the sound of two angry, heated voices drifted up the stairs from below. Chase and Constance were somewhere behind the staircase on the first floor, and they weren't exactly discussing what to have for dinner.

Decision time. Should I freeze and eavesdrop, or should I noisily bound down the stairs and interrupt their domestic dispute? Either way, I was living dangerously. Being a journalist, I decided to stay put. I might learn something useful.

Did I ever.

"Don't be irrational," Chase shouted. "How can you think I'd do anything with that reporter? What do you think we were doing outside in broad daylight? Give me a break, Constance."

I blinked. Chase and me? Oh, no, it wasn't like that at all. In fact, it was very much the opposite. I glanced at my chopped-up ankle.

"She was snooping all around the lake," Chase continued. "Did you send her there? What could you have been thinking?"

I reached into my purse for the tape recorder, but it had fallen to the bottom. I contemplated fishing around for it, then chickened out. I didn't want to risk making a noise and revealing my presence.

"I'm not stupid, Chase," Constance retorted. "If it's not her, it's a dozen others. Is this some kind of midlife crisis? You didn't get enough before we got married, so now you've got to get your fill again? You know what, dear? You're not that great to start with; don't kid yourself."

Oh, my. Low blow, Constance.

"Oh, please, Constance, is that another one of your alcoholic fantasies?" he retaliated. "What about Mason? You never have said why he was here. You're just his type. Maybe I should ask you why he was in such a hurry to leave."

Touché, Chase. Good point.

"Wouldn't you like to know?" she replied, slowly and pointedly enunciating each word.

Chase slammed his hand on a table, or maybe the wall. He was not a happy husband. "You should be glad you've been around this long. It's time you went away for a few months. Pick anywhere you like, just go there, dry out, and get your sanity back."

"You can't send me away," she hissed. "I know too much, and what's done is done. There's no going back now. You can't change the past, it will only hang around and hit you when you least expect it. No, I'm the perfect wife, remember? I'm going to stay right here, lovingly by your side, grinning and pandering to all your friends until I throw up. I want you to always remember that I'm here, watching, and willing to take you down in a heartbeat."

"I loved you a great deal, once," Chase growled. "Before you became such a bitch."

Yikes. Cue the commercial. We'll return to "As the Stomach Churns" right after a word from our sponsors.

I snapped to attention as I heard Chase's footsteps angrily click on the marble floor. Trying to look as innocent as possible, but knowing I probably looked like a cat with several canaries stuck in its mouth, I started down the staircase.

I made it down three steps before Chase emerged from under the staircase and came to a complete, white-faced halt upon seeing me. Constance nearly stumbled over him. They both stared at me as if I were the Grim Reaper.

I brightly feigned innocence. "Oh, hello. I just finished visiting with Mrs. Merriman. She gave me some very interesting information for the article." I was speaking too quickly and in a squeak that would have sent a lie detector off the scale. "I think things are coming along nicely with my story, thanks to Mrs. Merriman. I appreciate the chance to talk with her. She's such a fascinating woman."

Chase and Constance exchanged glances, then he cleared his throat. "I'm going back to the office. Miss Kelly, follow me down the hill. Your visit is complete." He turned on his heel and stalked out the door.

What, no good-bye smooch for his wife?

Constance stopped me at the foot of the staircase. Her skin was chalky and her eyes were wild. She clamped a manicured hand on my arm. "When did you come down the steps? Did you hear anything?"

"Why, no, I came down just this instant." I hoped she would buy it. "Should I have heard something?"

She blinked several times in rapid succession. "Um, no. You shouldn't have. Um, Chase and I were just discussing a, um, staff matter, that's all."

"Oh, I see," I said wisely. I thought it was best for me to get out of Dodge. "Thank you for your hospitality today. I should be going."

Oh, yeah, and don't forget to thank your husband for attacking me on the dock.

I smiled and walked past Constance.

She raced in front of me and leaned against the front door. The seashells on her necklace rose and fell with each heavy breath as if they were washing in with the tide. "You're a woman, Kate. Have you ever been badly hurt by someone you love?"

I stared at her. "Well, I, uh. . . ."

"It's horrible, but you can fix things, you know? When things get out of hand, you just take it under your control. It's the only way to survive. You do what you have to do. You can make the problem disappear. Permanently. And no one in their right mind would blame you, would they? They'd understand."

Tears filled her eyes. "Wouldn't they?"

Chapter 18

NOW WHAT WAS I SUPPOSED TO SAY? I stared at Constance, not sure how to answer her question. The Merrimans had quite the selection of secrets stewing in the pot. What did she mean when she mentioned getting rid of problems permanently?

One hemisphere of my brain was struggling to come up with an answer, and the other hemisphere was hollering to pay attention to the great shadow approaching outside the door.

Before I could say anything, the shadow loomed like a menacing blob over the beveled glass, and the door swung inward, slapping Constance on the back and sending her stumbling in my direction. I reached out to catch her, but she recovered after a few lurching steps. Her face was contorted, and she reached to rub the small of her back, which no doubt was protesting Chase's forceful entrance. She swung around to meet his equally disgusted gaze.

"You hurt me!" she screeched.

He filled the doorway, his big hand still gripping the doorknob. "You were in the way."

He turned to me and reissued his earlier order. "Miss Kelly, I asked you once to follow me off the property. I want you to leave now, with me." The command was repeated in a highly intimidating, raised voice. Menacing would be another good word.

I leveled a steely look his way and hoped he concentrated on that and not the quiver that was wrapping itself around my vocal chords like a large vise. "I was on my way out the door, Mr. Merriman. I'm sorry it wasn't quick enough for you."

Constance rubbed her back. "I had something to discuss with Kate. Go on about your business, Chase, she'll leave when we're finished talking."

He zeroed in on his wife's mascara-smeared, glassy eyes. "You're upset and in no condition to be discussing anything with her. She'll leave now."

I didn't want to be in the middle of another battle between the merry Merrimans. I walked to the door and hoped Chase would let me through. He stood a bit straighter and took a step back, leaving enough room for me to shimmy past him sideways. I didn't miss the significance of his body language, which threw his power over my meek, little body sneaking past him. If he was trying to make a point, he was doing a great job. I'd hate to see what he was like when he fired an employee.

"I'll be going now," I said, stating the obvious. "It's been an interesting afternoon. I hope to see you both again soon."

Chase flew around my car and met me as I opened the door and slid into the front seat. His hand descended on the top of my window and kept me from closing the door. I glanced at his hand and momentarily contemplated pulling the door shut and crunching his fingers in the process.

That's what happens when I'm angry. I get just as mean and nasty as the next person. Friends have often told me that when I'm angry, I am as silent as a monk but my eyes speak volumes.

Chase looked first at me, then at his hand. Reading the fury in my eyes, he removed his hand and let me pull the door shut.

He changed his mind. He immediately yanked the door open again. This time he had a firm grip on the door. "I don't know what you're trying to prove, but whatever it is, I want you to stop. This situation is none of your business, do you understand? I want you to leave my family alone. We will deal with things on our own. We don't need your meddling assistance. Your article is finished, Miss Kelly. There will be no need to return to Merriman Farms. Do I make myself clear?"

"Crystal," I replied. "You've made your feelings quite clear, Mr. Merriman, particularly at the lake this afternoon."

He flinched. Color rose in his cheeks and spread to the collar of his starched white dress shirt. He raised his free hand in a threatening manner, but, instead of sending it my way, he pulled at his collar to loosen his tie a notch.

I tugged at my car door. "I'm not trying to prove a thing, Mr. Merriman. Your marital problems may be great fodder for the country club, but I couldn't care less."

That was a lie, and he probably knew it. His marital problems were very interesting to me and just might be titillating for a certain curious sheriff we both knew.

"As for my article," I continued, "I'm writing that with your mother's assistance. I answer to her. If she doesn't wish to continue with it, she can tell me herself. Now, if you'll be kind enough to let go of my door, I'll leave like you've insisted—but I can't do that, can I, with you right there?"

I tilted my chin defiantly. I wasn't endearing myself to Chase Merriman by any stretch of the imagination. I probably would have kicked myself off the farm for being so nasty.

He straightened. "Tread lightly, Miss Kelly, for your own sake." He shoved my door shut with such force that a breeze slapped my face.

Chase stalked to his convertible, gunned the engine, and backed out into the drive, leaving enough room for me to pull in front of him. I glanced at him, and he impatiently gestured for me to lead the way.

I pulled out and slowly drove toward the gate, my angry escort right on my bumper. We were almost to the bottom of the winding hill when Chase kicked the Mercedes into low gear and sped around me, his tires screeching and kicking up a hail of gravel and dirt in its wake. Offering me no acknowledgment, he continued down the hill and through the media maze at the entrance gate at a speed that was probably considered a tad excessive.

His quick departure was enough to send the gathered press into such a frenzy that I slipped through the gate largely unnoticed. Chase sped off to the right, as reporters scrambled to hop into their cars. They followed him, leaving behind the echoes of squealing tires and gearshifts that were yanked so hard that I wouldn't be surprised if crucial parts of the cars were now dragging behind them like tin cans on a newlywed's limousine.

I wasn't interested in trailing after the parade, so I peeled off to the left and pulled into the parking lot at the Merriman Farms outdoor flower and garden shop. I needed to be alone for a while. Things were moving so fast, and so many accusations were flying around, that I wanted a few minutes to sort everything out in my mind.

Always conscious of my stomach, I realized I'd missed lunch.

I keep in relatively good shape, but I work at it, because food is one of my great loves. I'm not a pleasant person when I'm hungry. The beast in me is usually calmed by dangling chocolate in my face, or something of an equally dubious nutritional value.

Prospects for munchies, though, didn't look too promising in this patch of Woodbury. My best bet was a fruit stand next to the Merriman Market. I got out of the car, walked over to the stand, and bought a bottle of water, an apple, and a bag of cherries. I'd have to hit a fast-food joint on the way home.

I decided to explore the area while I ate, so I set off down Tyler Street. If I walked slowly and didn't dwell on it, my ankle didn't bother me that much. The worst part was the scrape scratching against the top of my tennis shoe. Once I got home and slapped a bandage on it, my survival would be assured.

Besides, I needed to clear my mind with a walk, and Woodbury's Victorian architecture was too inviting. I passed the library and slowly walked down the tree-lined sidewalk. I devoured my apple and began to work on the bag of cherries as I took in the sights and concentrated on my suspects.

Foremost in my mind was Chase Merriman. He had the most to lose and, apparently, was quite the ladies' man. If he was the killer, he controlled the show. First, he tried to kill Karen on a nearly deserted highway outside of town. When that didn't work, he lured her to the far reaches of his property, where no one could see them, and finished the job.

But why would a successful multimillionaire risk his future on an affair with a college student? And what would he have to gain from stealing and selling off his own antiques? Even if Walenza could identify him as a customer, why kill the man? Of course, Chase had a power complex. I could see where he'd want to eliminate every possible tie to his guilt. Since he was so wealthy and powerful, he probably didn't see much harm in ridding the world of a couple of lower-class nobodies who could only cause trouble for him.

I turned a corner and found myself on a residential street filled with Victorian homes of all colors and gingerbread shapes. A slender, blonde-haired woman in jeans and a bright purple T-shirt clipped her hedges along the sidewalk in front of a pink-and-white, gabled, two-story house. Snipped branches fell to the ground around her, and she smiled as I passed.

She couldn't have known that her appearance brought to my mind the face of a possible murderer, namely Constance. I hadn't thought of her at first, but the afternoon's events had turned my thinking around.

Constance was one bitter wife, and we all know what Shakespeare said about the "woman scorned."

Sure, she had been genuinely upset at the hospital, but she also had a lifetime degree in social politeness. She could pour on the sugar with the best of them, all for the sake of being socially correct. Get her drunk enough and she could be as mean as the portly old farm woman who routinely snapped chickens' necks without blinking an eye.

I was so lost in my thoughts that I almost bumped into a couple coming out of a small bakery sandwiched between the residences. They were clearly enamored of one another, giggling playfully as they stumbled out the door. I stopped and let them pass as they diligently tried to split a large cinnamon pastry in half without unlocking their intertwined arms.

Isn't love grand?

But then, it's not so grand when one partner is fooling around on the other.

I watched the couple disappear around the corner and thought perhaps Constance had followed her husband on his rendezvous with Karen, then tried to run her off the road. *You do what you have to do* rang in my brain, as did Eddie's comment about the damage to the grille of the Land Rover. Maybe Chase hadn't been driving. Maybe it was Constance all along. Besides, I'd always seen Chase driving the Mercedes. The Land Rover could easily belong to his wife.

And didn't she say that she was "almost always" at the house? She would have the perfect opportunity to follow Karen on her walk to the lake and kill her. I couldn't help thinking about Mason Shelby's comment that women tend to commit messier murders than men. I could almost picture the catfight between Constance and Karen. Maybe they had been on the dock after all and Karen had slipped on the slick wood planks like I did. If she had fallen, that would have given Constance the upper hand to attack her.

Perhaps once she'd killed Karen in a fit of rage, Constance realized what she had done and, in a panic, had tried to make it look like a drowning by removing Karen's T-shirt and shorts. In a strange way, it made sense that a woman, particularly someone as stylish as Constance, would pay attention to what her victim was wearing.

Constance also seemed intent on taking her husband for everything he was worth. She couldn't be too happy that Karen was selling off parts of her future divorce settlement. And again, there was the messy way Walenza was killed. Maybe she was trying to retrieve some of the stolen antiques and whacked the poor man across the head with the lamp.

Good grief, did I agree with Mason Shelby's logic?

And what about dear Mason? He hated Chase, so why not get back at him by killing his perky young lover? Given Mason's mean-spirited personality, it wouldn't be a stretch to picture him becoming violent. But why Karen?

I stopped in my tracks. Why not? He could have been dating Karen. Maybe both he and Chase were secretly dating her, and Mason found out and killed her in a jealous rage. But what would he have to gain from all of this? It just didn't make sense.

Another unlikely suspect would be Annalee. Sure, she said they were best friends, but she got awfully nervous when I asked if the police had searched their dorm room. Was she trying to hide something? Did she know something that would harm the sorority's reputation, so she ousted the "bad seed," in a warped sense of duty to sisterhood? Was Annalee afraid that Karen's affairs and kleptomania would irrevocably tarnish the Sigma Gamma name? As distasteful as the thought was, it was possible.

What I had trouble finding plausible was that she really didn't know more about Karen's boyfriends; telling your best friend about your boyfriend is a time-honored ritual. Annalee had motive and—by admitting that she was the last person to see Karen before she left for the Merriman estate—opportunity. Maybe she followed Karen out there and killed her, hoping it would look like an accident.

Annalee's involvement didn't quite explain Walenza's death, but maybe that actually was a separate incident that had unfortunately come close on the heels of Karen's death. Or for that matter, maybe we were dealing with two murderers: Annalee, and Karen's boyfriend. Was it possible that Annalee killed Karen, and the elusive boyfriend saw an opportunity to wipe out any trace of Karen's stolen antiques by killing the unsuspecting Walenza? Or was there something going on between Annalee and Karen's boyfriend that I hadn't considered? Could they have planned it all together?

I arrived at another intersection and spotted a small park bench at the corner bus stop. I sank onto the bench and sipped my bottled water.

Annalee and the boyfriend. Why hadn't I thought of that earlier? I suppose Annalee did such a good job of convincing me she was innocent that the possibility of her guilt never entered my mind. But I still had the problem of identifying the missing boyfriend.

Maybe I was completely off base with Chase. If Constance was prone to drunken rambling, maybe she made up the whole affair with Karen. Geez, she accused the man of having a fling with me at the lake.

I let my frustrations seep out in a loud, prolonged sigh.

Chase had a point. Just what was I trying to prove? I had a bowlful of suspects, with no spoon to scoop out the killer, and the broth was growing thicker by the minute. I took another drink of water and looked across the street in an attempt to wipe my mind clean of all those thoughts.

I should have known something so simple wouldn't work.

Chapter 19

THE HOUSE ACROSS THE STREET was surrounded by tall hedges, which camouflaged a chest-high stone wall that wrapped around the property. Black wrought-iron gates blocked the entrance to a long, narrow drive leading to a detached garage. The house itself sat far back from the road and was out of symmetry with the other houses nearby, giving the impression that it had been here a lot longer than the neighboring homes.

It was a large, two-story English Tudor, with yellowed stone and black gables which soared into sharp, intimidating peaks. The crisscross-paned windows were shrouded with heavy curtains. At one time the house would have been grand and inviting, but age and studied neglect had transformed it into a dark, brooding fortress.

In reality, it might not have actually looked so dark and brooding, but my mind pictured it that way thanks to the lettering on the mailbox outside the gate: SHELBY. I swung my eyes to the street sign above my bench and confirmed my location. Sure enough, I was at a corner on Clover Street. So, this was the famous Shelby residence. I gazed at the huge house and wondered how just one person could live in a place so large.

I crossed the street and peered through the gates. Some terrible, hidden snoop inside of me was desperate to get a closer look. Sometimes I worry about this streak in my character. I must have watched one too many "Columbo" or "Hart to Hart" episodes when I was little. The problem is that whenever things got ticklish, you knew the safety of a commercial was coming soon; in real life, what I was contemplating was called breaking and entering and was definitely against the law.

Still, I rationalized, what would it hurt just to walk around outside? At best, I was just being nosy. I glanced furtively up and down the street. No one was in sight, and I couldn't see any neighbors staring at me from their windows. It was the middle of the afternoon. Most people would still be at work or deeply involved in the soaps.

I tried the gate but it wouldn't budge. Closer inspection revealed an electric latch that most likely was attached to a remote button in Mason's Mercedes. I ran my eyes along the inside of the stone wall and spotted another small gate near the garage. I checked the street again, saw I was still alone, and sprinted down the sidewalk. At the left corner, I discovered a footpath that ran between Mason's house and the mature trees in his neighbor's yard. I walked through high grass and weeds and tried the back gate, which swung open with ease.

I slipped inside and positioned myself behind the trunk of a maple. I studied the windows on each floor for any sign of movement, but most of them were shrouded by thick curtains. Mason treasured his privacy.

Spotting a window on the side of the large double garage, I snuck over to it and peered inside. To my great relief, the car was gone. Mason wasn't home. How fortunate.

Feeling much more confident, I strode through the yard and headed for the house. I spotted a small porch and side entrance near the back. I glanced around to make sure I was alone, then climbed the four steps to the door. The porch was big enough for only one or two people and had no side rails. I stepped to the edge and stood on my toes to reach the windowsill on the side. I could see into a narrow hallway leading into what looked like a dining or living room, but it was too dark inside to see clearly. The door, however, did have four windowpanes which invited me to peer inside. I cupped my hands to the window and leaned against the door.

I heard a click, and the door swung open. I stumbled inside, not sure what to say to the person on the other side. But thankfully I was alone, standing in Mason's kitchen, heart racing and ears primed for the squeal of an alarm. I heard my heart thumping and my anxious breaths, but no security alarm.

Turn around and run for your car, my good angel commanded.

You're in this far, why not take a look around? my bad angel prodded.

I shut my eyes, as if that would help, and clenched my fists. I knew what I wanted to do, and I also knew what I *should* do. Yes, it was very, very wrong to be standing inside Mason Shelby's house uninvited, but it was also very, very tempting to take a quick look around. If I left, I'd be mad that I didn't have the guts to snoop around; but if I stayed, I knew I'd feel guilty.

I've never willingly broken the law—if you don't count ignoring the odd stop sign here or there after midnight—and the thought of being arrested didn't sit well. When I worked at the newspaper, I saw the inside of jails and sat in a number of arraignment courts. It wasn't like registering for a night in a Hilton.

I particularly didn't relish the thought of spending any time in Sheriff Bowman Thompson's jail. That was not an experience I wanted to add to my résumé. But I was inside Mason's house. The temptation was too great.

I'm sure I could name any number of people who would equate my lack of morals with my journalistic profession—which, I think I've made clear, is something of a family legacy. For that matter, Mom would probably be proud of my moxie. I rolled my eyes. I was really stretching things if I was wrangling it around to make my mom proud of her only child becoming a criminal.

Oh, what the hell, I thought. *Mason should have been more careful about locking his back door.*

I quickly glanced around the kitchen. The floor was covered in large black and white tiles, and the walls were painted black with white trim. Stark white appliances filled the kitchen. A tall, narrow, silver table with a glass top and matching silver bar stools sat opposite the sink. The chairs didn't invite you to sit down and enjoy a long, leisurely meal. My eyes rose to see an artful arrangement of copper pots and pans dangling from the ceiling. Either Mason was a gourmet chef in his spare time or he had an overly excited decorator.

I took a deep breath and turned down the small hall to the right. The narrow passageway looked as if it had once been a pantry. Inset shelves, painted gold, lined either side of the wall. Oddly shaped objets d'art were housed on each shelf. Most were abstract sculptures that I'm sure represented something deep and meaningful, but to my unappreciative eye they looked like globs of Play-Doh or pipe cleaners twisted together.

The hallway led into a dark orange dining room with a black dining room table that could have easily seated twelve. The centerpiece—a silk floral arrangement of bird-of-paradise flowers, sticky cattails, dried leaves, and an assortment of artfully arranged sticks—was so enormous I was afraid a diner would need a tetanus shot to reach across the table for a salt shaker. While Mason's decorating tastes were, at best, debatable, my attention was drawn to what covered the table and a good portion of the black-and-orange Oriental rug.

Stacks of black-and-white photos, manila files, and sheaths of paper were scattered across the table, and heavy, cardboard file boxes lined the floor. The boxes were labeled with dates from the late 1940s to the mid-1960s. One large box was labeled simply "Evelyn." A quick glance in the top of the boxes showed them filled with large brown envelopes and yellowed file folders.

My eyes scanned the pictures on the table, and I recognized several which included a young Winifred and Robinson Merriman and another couple who I assumed were Mason's parents. There were several photos of a young, dark-haired woman with high cheekbones and small, somewhat sad-looking eyes. I matched her face to the other photos and decided that it was Evelyn Shelby. If I squinted, I could make out the resemblance to Mason.

Placed on top of one of the pictures were two yellowed newspaper

— 149 —

clippings announcing Chase's and Mason's births. Happy photos of the respective new parents holding their newborn sons topped each article. I glanced at the dates; Mason had been born January 4, 1948, and Chase on May 28, 1948. I hadn't realized they were that close in age. A quick finger count told me that Winifred had been pregnant with Chase at the same time Evelyn was pregnant with Mason.

Next to those articles were two more clippings. The first one that caught my eye was dated February 16, 1951, and featured a portrait of Evelyn and a bold black headline that screamed, EVELYN SHELBY DIES IN FALL AT HOME. I picked up the article and read her glowing obituary. Evelyn, the "beloved wife of Woodbury's own Dr. Mason Shelby, and young mother of the toddler Mason Jr., died in a tragic, shocking fall at the Shelby mansion on Clover Street."

The Shelbys were entertaining their good friends the Merrimans when Evelyn apparently slipped and fell, striking her head in a fatal blow. "The utterly distraught Dr. Shelby fought to resuscitate his dear wife and mother of his child," but could not save her. Robinson Merriman, it said, had to restrain his anguished friend Mason when the coroner and police arrived on the scene. Winifred Merriman was sent "home to rest and will be leaving Woodbury for an extended time to recover from the shock of this accident." Three-year-old Mason Jr. was being "sent to the care of grandparents in Roanoke."

The article went on to list the many social groups and charities the 34-year-old Evelyn belonged to, and bemoaned the loss of one of Woodbury's "most treasured citizens." What struck me was the fact that Winifred and Robinson were present that day. No wonder Winifred had changed the subject so abruptly when I asked how Evelyn had died.

I read through the article again and noticed that it never clearly stated exactly how Evelyn had fallen. Was it indoors, outdoors, on a staircase, where? A person doesn't normally just fall down and go boom. I wondered why the newspaper didn't elaborate.

I put the obituary back on the table and picked up the next article. It was a social column from Christmas 1947 that detailed several parties given by the area's well-to-do families. I couldn't see its significance at first, but as I finished one country club report, my eye zoomed to the chatty final paragraph.

Someone named Webster Tierney had hosted a very successful party which was marred at the end of the evening by a very public spat between "the inseparable Shelbys and Merrimans of Woodbury. Apparently the respected Dr. Mason Shelby and the industrialist Robinson Merriman became engaged in an altercation that included many heated insults and unbecoming physical scuffling."

The article went on to say, "The visibly shaken Mrs. Shelby, who is due to give birth shortly, had to be helped from the party, and Mrs.

Merriman, who is also expecting, was seen weeping uncontrollably in the ladies' lounge." Though the report was titillating, it was not gossipy enough to spill the topic of the argument.

I carefully replaced the article as I had found it and moved on to the next stack of papers on the table. It was actually two wrapped stacks of old canceled checks which dated from 1948 until the late 1960s. I quickly thumbed through both stacks and discovered that all the checks were fairly substantial sums from Merriman Farms, Inc. to the account of Dr. Mason Shelby Sr.

That was odd. The Shelbys were wealthy in their own right. Why would they receive regular checks, each written for at least five figures, from Merriman Farms, Inc.? I thumbed through the checks again. They were all personally signed by Robinson Merriman, and the reference lines all read, "Per Agreement."

Why did Mason have all this stuff sitting out? Why was he suddenly so concerned about his family history? Hadn't John said that Dr. Shelby died over a decade ago? Surely Mason wasn't just getting around to going through his father's personal belongings. There had to be a reason for the sudden urge to get in touch with his roots. If this was the first room that I'd looked in, what could the rest of the house hold?

At the far end of the dining room table sat a lock box. I bit my lip and stared at the handle. A lock box meant business—and certainly not mine. This was bad, really appalling. I was a terrible, horrible, no-good, breaking-and-entering, shuffling-through-private-stuff, nasty criminal. Once again, my good angel was screaming in my ear to hoist anchor and run.

I took a step toward the lock box and heard my heart lunge against my chest as a high-pitched screech sounded outside. I froze for a second, then forced myself to move the curtain a hair to the right. My heart quit pounding in my chest and instead lodged itself firmly in my throat.

Oh, no.

The front gates were opening.

Oh, no.

A black Mercedes sedan with tinted windows was slowly turning into the drive.

Oh, no. Oh, no. Oh, no. Oh, no.

The only exit I knew of was the kitchen door, which was in full view of the garage. I felt doomed, but I knew I had to get out of the house. I danced back and forth on my toes and began to hyperventilate.

I peeked out the curtain again. Mason had paused to check his mailbox and was getting back into the car, ready to continue up the driveway.

I did the only thing I could do.

I made a run for it.

I ran to the kitchen and reached for the doorknob. I was shaking so hard that I had to use both hands to turn the knob. I opened the door and slid out sideways, flattening myself against the stone exterior. I pulled the door shut without a sound and dove off the small side porch into the soft, moist mulch anchoring the house's overgrown landscaping. Two enormous evergreens successfully hid me from view as I landed on my knees and curled into a tight ball. I desperately tried to slow my breathing and calm down as I watched the Mercedes wind its way up the narrow driveway.

On one hand, I was extremely glad Mason hadn't paid much attention to his gardening duties, since the thick overgrowth hid me so well. On the other hand, I stifled a sneeze and tried to ignore the moldy mulch odor, cobwebs, and prickly branches sticking me as I crouched close to the ground. The desire to sneeze and the remnants of my hyperventilation resulted in a furious, painful protest from my lungs. I held one hand over my nose and the other over my chest as I watched Mason park in front of the house. I closed my eyes quickly in silent thanks that he didn't choose to park near the garage.

I peered between the branches and watched both front car doors swing open, revealing the occupants behind the darkly tinted windows. Mason wasn't alone. I forgot the sneeze entirely and cupped my hand to my mouth to squelch the gasp struggling to spill out.

In all my ruminations about the murders, I'd purposely avoided considering one person as a suspect. Now I watched him get out of the car with Mason and follow him to the front door.

John.

Chapter 20

MANY THINGS BOTHERED ME as I tried to remain hidden. I was terribly allergic to something in the bushes, I had almost been caught red-handed breaking into the house—and oh, yeah, what in the world was John doing with Mason?

Not only had John followed him inside the house, but the two of them were talking like old friends. Mason actually looked halfway pleasant. He had been nasty to John every time we'd seen him except that first day in the hospital parking lot. Why the sudden change?

I didn't know what to think. I also didn't know what to do once they disappeared inside. What if they glanced out a window and saw me? Where was John's car? How long would they be inside? And what on earth were they doing in there?

I held my breath and strained my ears to hear anything inside, but it was useless. Mason's house was quite literally rock solid. The only way I could hear anything would be if they threw open the window above me or decided to move their chummy conversation out onto the side porch. I certainly didn't want that.

My eyes moved across the lawn to the gate near the garage. It had taken me only a couple of seconds to cross the yard earlier, but now the gate looked like it sat in the next state. It would be one awful sprint, with nothing to hide me. Still, I knew I couldn't stay in the bushes much longer. But what would happen if they left the house just as I was making like a bread truck and hauling my buns across the yard?

It was all like a bad flashback to playing hide-and-seek when I was little. I never had the patience to hide very long. Everyone knew how I was, so whoever was "it" would simply stand there and wait for me to come out of hiding. I was terrible at the game then, so I had a feeling I'd be just as rotten at it as an adult.

I didn't have to wait too long. I was ready to make a run for it, when I heard voices and a door shut. I hunkered down as close to the ground as I could and watched John and Mason walk toward the car. John had several large yellow file folders in his hands, and Mason was now carrying a briefcase. He aimed a remote on his key chain at the Mercedes and unlocked the doors. He tossed the briefcase onto the backseat before settling behind the wheel.

As John walked over to the passenger side, one of the file folders slipped from the stack in his hands. The folder fell to the ground in front of the car, and several papers scattered across the driveway. He dropped to the ground, scooped up the loose sheets, and stuffed them into the folder. The breeze picked up one paper and sent it a few feet in my direction. John duckwalked over to the grass and reached for the errant piece of paper. As he shoved it into the folder, he stood, then suddenly stopped.

He was staring at the bush I was hiding behind.

I froze every muscle in my body.

John's eyes narrowed before he quickly turned and got into the car. Mason started the car and drove out, and John's head turned to stare again in my direction. Did he see me?

I watched the Mercedes disappear down the street and listened until the hum of its engine was replaced with the twitter of birds in the trees overhead. If I had kept with my daredevil attitude, I would have climbed out of the bushes and marched right back inside Mason's house. Instead, I did what I should have done at the beginning.

I got out of there as fast as humanly possible.

I raced to the gate and didn't look back as I flew toward the sidewalk. I froze for a moment when I realized that it was possible that John might have told Mason I was in the bushes. What if they turned around and drove back immediately? It wouldn't look very innocent for me to be strolling nonchalantly down Clover Street. Instead, I took a left and headed around the opposite corner, figuring I'd take the next street over as my route back to the car.

For once, my strategy seemed to work. The faster I walked, the more my ankle hurt, but I didn't have time to dwell on it. I was much too busy scanning for friendly bushes to dive into in case a certain black car came in my direction.

That never happened, and two sneezes and a few minutes later, I rounded a turn and had the Merriman Market in sight. The subtle transformation from neighborhood street to main thoroughfare gave birth to a concentration of cars and people that toyed with my growing paranoia. *Every black car in the city must be on this street today,* I thought.

I spotted my car and, relieved, broke into a run. I jumped inside and sped out of the parking lot in a desperate search for the highway. Forget the scenic drive into Williamsburg on Higgins Pass. I wanted to get out of Woodbury. I wanted to be home, safe and sound. I wanted to forget about all this murder business. I wanted to forget about all my aches and pains. I wanted to forget about the possibility that John might be more involved in this mess than I wanted him to be.

I flew down the highway at near-warp speed, my eye on the rear-view mirror in case a black Mercedes decided to whiz past. The road ahead of me was replaced with one haunting vision: John's face. What was he doing? I had convinced myself the previous night that all was well, but now I couldn't be sure.

As much as I hated it, he had lied to me. He didn't tell me about Karen from the start, and who knew if the story he concocted at the restaurant was true? He'd even aroused Sheriff Thompson's suspicions when we were at the antique store. Granted, stumbling over a murder scene can upset the calmest person, but it didn't take an idiot to see how uncomfortable John was while we were at the store. He hadn't wanted to go to Walenza's to begin with, and then he had grabbed me so forcefully when I tried to get closer to the scene. His arms were strong. But strong enough to do what?

I snapped back to reality and discovered I was driving with one hand on the wheel and the other rubbing the front of my neck. I shook my head and gripped the wheel with both hands. No, I couldn't let myself believe that.

I thought again about my childhood hide-and-seek handicap. I was always so gullible, just blindly walking out into the open where I'd be tagged immediately.

John could charm the honey from the bee as far as I was concerned. He knew everything I knew, so he could easily stay one step ahead of the game. Was he patiently waiting for me to fill him in on everything I was learning, so he could seal his alibi and quite literally get away with murder?

If anyone could help me sort this out, it would be Dad.

I swung into the driveway, popped open the front door, and called out, "Daddy? Where are you? I'm home, alone, in one piece, no police along for dinner."

I thought that would at least elicit a grunt, but I was answered by silence. I walked down the hall and peeked in his office, the study, and the kitchen. He was nowhere to be found. I dropped my purse on the kitchen table and noticed the blinking little red light on the answering machine.

I punched PLAY and heard Dad's voice. He spent the first half of the message telling me how many times he'd called all afternoon with the expectation that I'd be home. Once he'd expressed his hope that I wasn't "getting into more trouble," he told me he'd forgotten about a dinner meeting that would keep him out past the time "someone in your condition should be fast asleep."

As the message continued, I smiled and walked over to the refrigerator to get a drink. It was nice to have someone worry about me so much. Since it looked like I'd be on my own for the night, I'd just have to mull it over alone and wait up for Dad to come home. I pulled a Coke out of the refrigerator, popped it open, and proceeded to satisfy my afternoon caffeine fix.

The machine beeped to signal the end of Dad's message, so, drink in hand, I headed into the hallway. A loud, prolonged beep stopped me as a second message began.

"Kate—it's John. I just wanted to call and see how you're feeling today. I, uh, hope you spent the day resting at home."

I stared at the machine. That could mean two things. Either he hadn't seen me in the bushes or he was testing me to see how I'd respond.

Please be the first one.

There was a burst of static on the line, then John continued. "I'd like to talk with you tonight, Kate. Give me a call, okay? Take care and, um, please call soon." There was more static, then the machine beeped a final time.

I sat the Coke on the counter and returned to the machine. I pushed PLAY again and listened to John's message more closely. His voice was muffled, like he was on a cell phone or in a phone booth. I opted for the cell phone, because the only background noise I could make out was an even-toned hum, like a car engine. "I hope it's not Mason's car," I said aloud.

I pushed the button again and listened for a third time. John's voice at first sounded forced, too cheery, and then it slipped into a more apprehensive, all-in-one-breath message. Maybe he was just tired after a long day. A day of what, I wasn't sure, but a simple, innocent, long day, nonetheless.

I'm nothing if not hopeful.

Or just easily fooled.

I headed upstairs and sank into a steaming, hot bath. Trying to clear my mind, I soaked until my skin wrinkled into little prune patches. But instead of floating away to some aromatherapy-induced nirvana, I literally stewed over the day's events.

Everyone could be guilty, even John. The more I thought about it, the more frustrated I got. As I went over the list in my mind, one unlikely person kept floating to the surface: Annalee.

Her story—or convenient lack of memory—just didn't settle well with me. So much had happened since I last talked with her that I couldn't help but wonder if she'd still say the same thing. Now that I could wing my own questions her way, I thought it might be interesting to see if she stumbled over her previous account—or displayed further evidence of the premature onset of Alzheimer's disease.

I needed to visit the sorority again. Soon.

After I'd tended to my ankle and other assorted bumps and bruises, I threw on a clean pair of jeans and an old William & Mary sweatshirt I found hibernating in a hall closet. I rummaged around the kitchen cabinets until I came up with the fixings for a sandwich that would make Dagwood Bumstead proud, and considered my next move.

I'd call John, but not immediately. I wasn't sure what I'd tell him, and if my hunch was correct, the longer I'd wait to call him, the more curious he'd be about my whereabouts.

My first priority was Annalee. I snagged the phone book from a drawer and dragged the phone over to the kitchen table. What if she had figured out that I really wasn't related to Karen? It wasn't very ethical of me to keep pretending to be her cousin, but when had my ethics held me up in the previous few days? I was sinking pretty low, I admit, but in my view, the gloves were off. Everyone else was keeping secrets, so why shouldn't I jump in the game?

I dialed the sorority's number and asked the perky, Minnie Mouse voice that answered if Annalee was home.

There was a short pause. "No, Annalee can't come to the phone right now. Who's calling?"

"Is she there, or is she out for the evening?"

Minnie's voice rose an octave. "She is not here. Who's calling?"

"Do you expect her back soon?"

There was a long pause. "I expect her back when she arrives home, that's when." Minnie had an attitude; Mickey and Goofy better beware.

I cleared my throat. "Could you please make sure you leave her a message?" I purred. "It's important. This is Kate Kelly, and I'm calling about—"

"Oh, my, it's about Karen," Minnie interrupted. "I am so sorry, ma'am, I didn't realize it was you."

Ma'am, my behind. I pulled the phone away from my ear and made a face at the receiver. "Please have her call me as soon as possible, okay?"

Minnie was anxious to make amends. "Oh, yes, ma'am, by all means. I'll have her call you as soon as she gets home. Now, it won't be too late for you, will it?" She had started off so well, but then had to add the last comment.

"No, it won't be too late, I assure you. Just have Annalee call me." I gave her the number, then hung up the phone and successfully chomped into my sandwich without losing any of my geriatric teeth. It wasn't even time for my ten-year college reunion. I was not old and out of touch at all. Far from it. I could party and stay out until the dawn broke through the clouds if I wanted to.

I glanced at the clock and silently hoped Annalee would come home soon. So sue me, I was tired. It's not every day you try to solve a murder and almost end up swimming with the fishes in a lake or become trapped in a house you were busy breaking into. These things can wear you out, take it from ancient old me.

I grumpily finished my sandwich, and, as I turned on the water to rinse the dishes, the phone rang. I quickly wiped my wet hands on my jeans and answered, hoping to hear Annalee's voice.

"Kate, it's John. How are you? I'm glad you're home."

And just where did he think I'd be, in Mason's bushes?

I ran my hand through my hair and took a deep breath. "Yeah, I'm home. Where should I be?"

"Kate, I'm sorry. I didn't mean it that way. Is everything all right?"

Oh, sure, Wally, Beaver would say. *Everything is just dandy.* "Everything's fine, John. How was your day?" *That's it,* I thought proudly, *go straight for the jugular.*

He hesitated. "Well, it was normal, pretty uneventful. I called you earlier and you weren't home. I thought you were going to stay home today and rest. Did you go somewhere?"

He knew how to play the game, too. I stared ahead, studying the flowers snaking up a vine on the wallpaper, and decided on an edited version of my day. "I actually had a pretty busy day. I visited the Merrimans, saw the whole family."

John sounded startled. "You did? How did you get up there? Did you learn anything about Karen or her murder? Kate, I hope you were careful. I don't know if it's very wise of you to visit them like that. It could be dangerous."

Dangerous for whom? I thought glumly. "Why would it be dangerous?" I asked. "I was just interviewing Mrs. Merriman for the article I'm writing."

"Oh, I see," he said. From the less-than-enthusiastic way he spoke, I could see him tap-dancing around what subject to try next. He cleared his throat. "You didn't learn anything more about the legend? No more clues about Karen's stolen antiques?"

"Not really," I lied.

"Hmm, interesting. So, did you go anywhere else?"

I stood a little straighter and focused intently on one flower on the wallpaper. He knew. I could tell from the way he asked it that he'd seen more than green leaves when he looked at Mason's bushes. "Why do you ask?"

"Well, I called you pretty late in the day and you weren't home. I just assumed that you probably did some exploring or something. Knowing you, I thought you might be snooping around somewhere you shouldn't be. What time did you leave Merriman Farms?"

He knew. Why didn't he just come out and ask me what brand of fertilizer Mason uses? If he could ask point-blank questions, so could I. "Were you out and about this afternoon?"

"What? I, uh, well, yeah, I had a few errands to run. How did you know that?"

Because I have eyes, too. We stared at each other this afternoon, remember? "Your message sounded like a cell phone, but, come to think of it, I didn't remember seeing one in your car the other night."

Much to my dismay, he didn't answer my question. Instead, he lost his temper. "Kate, what's with all the questions? I had stuff to do today, as you did, too. I'm just afraid that your stuff was a little more risky than what I did."

That was debatable.

He waited for me to confess, and when I didn't, he sighed and continued. "Kate, we've had this conversation before; let the sheriff work on Karen's murder. I'm afraid you're learning too much. You might cross the wrong person. I don't think I have to tell you that would be a very bad idea. Back away from all of this, before someone else gets hurt."

In another setting, his last comment would have warmed my mushy heart with thoughts of his concern, but all I heard at this juncture was not a request, but an ultimatum.

I frowned into the phone. "John, I think—"

"Kate," he interrupted. "Give it up. Don't try to do anything else with this. I'll call you tomorrow morning, and I hope that this time you'll be home. Stay away from Merriman Farms." He hung up before I could reply.

I started to punch in his number, then hesitated. What a mess. I wanted more than anything to tell him everything that had happened to me, but at the same time, I was more than a little nervous that I might tell him too much. I threw the receiver into the cradle and watched it furiously bounce onto the floor. *That was supremely mature, Kate.* I scooped the receiver off the floor and gently put it in its place.

It was late. I was tired, confused, and extremely grumpy. I took out my frustrations on the kitchen as I cleaned the dishes and straightened up the table.

After my hands began taking on the perfume of Comet cleanser, I wrapped up my domestic spurt and tore a piece of paper from the pad by the phone. I scribbled a note to Dad: "I am in bed like you requested, but please nudge me when you get home. Sorry I didn't leave you a message earlier, but it's been a busy day. I have a lot to tell you."

I glanced at the note and considered crossing out the last part. Dad would have a stroke for sure if I told him about my visit to Mason's house, and I could easily picture the veins swelling under the skin on his forehead when I told him about my encounter with Chase at the lake.

I left the sentence there, then continued: "I'm going by the Sigma Gamma house tomorrow, so how about meeting me for lunch? I'll come by your office by noon. Night, Daddy." I placed the note in the center of the kitchen table and wearily headed upstairs.

I had to see Annalee, and since she hadn't returned my phone call, I'd just have to show up on the SG doorstep and hope she'd be there. I also decided to drop by Merriman Farms again, Chase or no Chase. I wanted to talk to Winifred to see if I could find out more about how Evelyn Shelby died. Hopefully, with luck, the same guard would recognize me and let me go through without checking up at the house.

That would be the plan, even if everyone had warned me to stay away from the Merrimans. I ticked off the list like I was counting sheep: Dad, John, Sheriff Thompson, Mason, even Winifred and Constance, in their own ways. And don't forget Chase.

What was it he'd said? "Tread lightly, Miss Kelly, for your own sake."

I rolled over in bed and pulled the comforter up to my chin.

Since when had I ever listened to anyone's advice?

Chapter 21

ONE OF THE THINGS I've learned as a frequent flyer is that sleeping in an unfamiliar bed can have two results. Either you toss and turn all night on a lumpy mattress with scratchy sheets and an odd odor you're not too sure you want to decipher, or the bed is like a toasty cocoon and you slumber like you've been drugged with some serious narcotics. Of course, a great deal of your comfort level also rests on who, if anyone, wakes up beside you, but that's another story entirely.

I guess my old bed conjured up good memories, because I slept like a log—so soundly, in fact, that I once again succeeded in missing Dad's morning departure. I woke up with a start around 8:30. Something must have triggered that, because it usually takes a very loud alarm clock and two or three passes on the snooze button to get me moving. I growled an inhuman gurgle as I rolled into a sitting position and rubbed my eyes free of any night critters.

I'm definitely a night person. I've always been highly suspicious of those eternally energetic people who rise as early as 5:00 A.M. and can accomplish more by 7:00 than I can by noon. I truly believe they may be members of some secret cult or group of aliens living among the rest of us sleep-deprived slugs. Mornings are lovely, fresh, and new, but I just wish they started later. Like maybe noon.

Since that wasn't possible, I took care of my new morning routine—I inspected my various bumps and bruises. The bruise on my forehead was finally fading into oblivion, and I could successfully stretch without muttering words my mother wouldn't approve of. Although I was still stiff, the painful jabs had disappeared. My ankle left a little to be desired, but that was a minor nuisance.

My version of a sultry red satin robe and matching fuzzy high-heel slippers is a pair of old sweats and my feet au naturel. Someday, I hope to lounge all day in such a fancy getup, propped up by fluffy, white satin pillows on a king-size bed while I munch French chocolates and read glossy magazines. But for now, I just pulled on a pair of gray, wrinkled sweats and headed downstairs.

Next to the newspaper neatly folded on the kitchen table, Dad had left half a pot of warm coffee and a small box of pastries. I peeked under the lid and grinned as I saw my favorite—chocolate cake doughnuts.

Good old Dad—he sure deserved a good Father's Day present next June.

I spotted the note I had written before going to bed, with an addition at the bottom. Dad had scribbled, "By the time I got home, you were fast asleep. Proud of you, kid, it's about time you got some rest. Would love to have lunch—come by my office at noon. I'm almost afraid to hear about your 'busy day,' but I think it mustn't be that bad, because I didn't see any front-page headlines about you in today's paper. Call if you need anything."

I nabbed a couple of doughnuts from the box. Dad may not have seen any headlines about me, but something told me the stories I'd gathered the day before were quite newsworthy. I emptied the remaining coffee into a mug and doctored the brew with an overdose of milk and sugar. Satisfied with my concoction, I settled onto a kitchen chair and surveyed my breakfast of champions: caffeine, sugar, chocolate, and more sugar. It was enough to give a nutritionist a coronary, but I'd successfully survived on similar daily morning combinations since college. Besides, there was milk in the coffee—that was healthy, wasn't it?

I munched on the doughnuts and scanned the paper quickly, pausing only to brush crumbs off the pages as I turned them. The only reference I found to the murders was a small side note toward the bottom of the Metro section's inside page. The headline announced, STILL NO ARRESTS IN WOODBURY MURDER SPREE.

Maybe I've lived in D.C. too long, but I'd hardly classify two murders as a *spree*. Perhaps *puzzle* or even *double homicide*, but definitely not a spree. A spree sounded more like a madman on the loose emptying out an automatic weapon on a busload of nuns holding babies.

The article blandly stated that there had been "no progress" in solving the two deaths. Thompson interjected some typical police mumbo jumbo about "searching out the perpetrator," but he didn't allude to how close he was to nabbing said perp. Chase Merriman, according to the reporter, was not cooperating with the media.

I licked chocolate off my fingers and grunted. Imagine, Chase being uncooperative. Stop the presses, there's a story.

The reporter was finally beginning to hint at the possibility that Karen's and Walenza's deaths were connected, because after the article noted Chase's refusal to comment on Karen's murder, it moved on to talk about Walenza's Antiques, which, it pointed out, is "in close proximity to the Merriman estate." I found that interesting and wondered if it would turn up the pressure on Chase.

I could ponder it later. A quick glance at the clock told me to get busy. I put my mug in the sink, then bolted upstairs for a quick shower. Once I was squeaky clean, I discovered I was running short of clean clothes, so I rummaged in Mom's closet until I came up with a long-sleeved white cotton blouse and a navy blazer. That would work fine with my jeans, which could stand one more day of adventure before visiting the washing machine. I slapped on a little bit of makeup and dried my hair quickly, using the idle blow-drying time to plan my next move.

I wanted to show up on the doorstep of Merriman Farms, but I didn't want to risk running into Chase. Constance said he usually came home for lunch, so that gave me a couple of hours to play with.

I placed a call to the Merriman Farms corporate office, knowing that I'd probably have to leapfrog my way past a battalion of secretaries and voice mail in order to reach Chase. I wasn't too far off course.

The switchboard operator transferred me to a secretary, who answered, "Corporate suite, how may I direct your call?" I had a feeling she'd block my progress, but to my surprise, she sent me through to Chase's personal assistant, Miss Georgehead.

My goal was to hear his voice so I could prove he was in the office. I've been a reporter long enough to know all the polite ways of lying about the whereabouts of your boss. There's the modern "on a conference call," along with the old standby "out to lunch" or the useless "in a meeting." While "out to lunch" could be true in more ways than one, if it's a nice, sunny day, "in a meeting" probably translates to a meeting on the golf links.

After I asked for Chase, Miss Georgehead paused and rattled off in a practiced manner, "Mr. Merriman is not available at this time. If you'll leave your name, I'll see that the appropriate person returns your call."

The appropriate person? What happened to Chase?

On another occasion I might have given her the benefit of the doubt, but I very plainly heard Chase's voice barking orders in the background. That satisfied me that he was in fact there, but the bad girl in me couldn't help but respond, "Could you please tell Mr. Merriman that I'm calling for Sheriff Bowman Thompson, regarding—"

"Just a minute, I'll put you through immediately."

Two seconds later, I heard, "This is Chase Merriman. What does the sheriff want?"

He didn't sound happy; not at all, the poor man. Were things beginning to get to him? I bit my lip and scrambled for something to say.

"Who is this?" Chase demanded. "Say something."

My attack of laryngitis complete, I let the phone drop quickly into its cradle.

Within seconds, the phone rang.

Oh, geez, I hadn't thought about Call Return. A big, multimillion-dollar corporation no doubt had access to Caller ID at each telephone.

Chase was probably scribbling my number off a fancy display as the phone rang.

The ringing phone taunted me. Two more rings and the machine would pick up. That wouldn't work either, because Dad identifies himself on the message. If I picked it up but didn't say anything, Chase would know I was there; and if he did have Call Return, he'd have the number anyway.

Me and my brilliant ideas.

On the last available ring, I grabbed the phone and tried to answer in a deep, disguised voice which ended up sounding something like Greta Garbo with a very bad head cold. I shut my eyes and waited for Chase to reply.

"Kate, is that you? What's wrong with your voice?"

Oops. It was the other guy I was avoiding.

"John, hi. I wasn't expecting you. Sorry. I, uh, was just eating a late breakfast, you know, eating, mouth full of food and all." I rolled my eyes and contemplated sticking a loaf of bread, or anything available, in my mouth to keep me from babbling anymore.

"Oh, is that all? You sounded strange, I was worried something was wrong."

What he didn't know wouldn't hurt him.

"Look, Kate, I feel really bad about how we left things last night. I didn't sleep well. I won't go into it all again, but I'll repeat that I want you to give up this detective business. You're a reporter, not a policeman. Let them do the work. It's much safer that way."

I tried to interrupt. "But John, I don't know what you—"

He was good at interrupting too. "Kate, let's be honest with each other. You know and I know where you were yesterday afternoon. I saw you, Kate. I don't know what you were doing in Mason's bushes, but I sure would be interested in hearing what it was."

After a long, painful silence between us, John prodded, "Kate? Do you have an answer?"

I had an answer, all right, but I didn't particularly want to share it with him. Not yet, anyway. I gripped the phone a little tighter and avoided the question. "Okay, fine. What were you doing with Mason? I thought you didn't get along with each other?"

It was John's turn to be silent.

Hah, I thought triumphantly, *caught you there, didn't I?*

"Kate, that's a stupid question. Some of Mason's father's old patients just can't stand the new generation of Dr. Shelby, so they asked me to be their physician. I was merely going over to his house to get their old medical records. Are you satisfied?"

Quite simply? No.

I said, "But Mason looked like he was enjoying that little meeting. And if you were spiriting away his patients, I can't imagine him being in a good mood. John, why were you there?" I tried to sound very authoritative and was glad I wasn't looking into those big brown eyes that had the unpleasant ability to send my feminist power trips right out the window.

Given the pause over the phone line, I pictured those eyes clenched shut in exasperation with one pesky brunette reporter.

"Kate, I just told you. You've never answered me. What were you doing in Mason's bushes?"

Curses, foiled again.

"In reality, nothing," I replied. "It's not important now, anyway." I took a deep breath. "Did you tell Mason you saw me?"

John laughed unevenly. "No, of course not. I was too busy trying to figure out what on earth you were doing there. Besides, like you said, Mason was in a rare good mood. I wasn't going to spoil it by pointing out that you were building a nest in his bushes. Kate, I'll let it drop, and hope you tell me the whole story some day. But I want you to know that if you're suspicious of Mason for some reason, I think you're off base. I can't see where he would be connected to this mess. I think you might be letting the fact that he's a jerk get in the way of your deductions, or whatever you call them. I'm just afraid you're going to keep digging until you upset the wrong person. This isn't a game, remember? Trust me, okay?"

I wanted to trust him. I really, truly did. But that was the second time in less than twenty-four hours that he'd said those words, and unfortunately, all I could picture at the moment was a wide-eyed, but blatantly guilty Beaver Cleaver saying, "Honest, I didn't, honest. Trust me."

John didn't give me time to answer; he knew he wouldn't like my reply. "I hate this phone stuff, Kate. I need to see you—and not in someone's greenery. Let's meet for lunch and we can discuss this like two adults. Can you come to the hospital around noon?"

"I've already promised to meet my dad at the university for lunch."

"Fine, dinner then. I'll pick you up at your house around seven," he said. "We need to finish this once and for all. Dinner only, though—no murder scenes included."

How romantic. Dinner and a murder certainly had a different ring to it than dinner and a movie. Besides, our first date already had dinner and a murder. I couldn't imagine how we could top that.

Curiosity combined with hormones, and I agreed to the proposal, mentioning that I was looking forward to seeing him soon.

"I'm looking forward to it, too," he said softly. "Kate, stay out of trouble today, okay? Have a boring, quiet day. I'll see you at seven."

I was grinning like a 14 year old as I hung up. I knew I'd have to occupy my mind with something else before I had time to think that John might not be innocent.

I didn't have to wait long. I was hardly out of the kitchen when the phone rang again.

"Miss Kelly? Hi, uh, it's Annalee Chisolm."

She'd gotten the message after all. Apologies were in order for the Minnie Mouse sorority sister.

"Hi, Annalee," I said carefully.

"I got your message last night, but I didn't know if I should call. I think we need to meet somewhere. It's about Karen."

"What about her? Do you have new information? Did you remember her boyfriend's name?"

Annalee's voice held a noticeable jagged edge. "It's just important for me to see you, that's all I can say. I don't have a car. Can you pick me up at the SG house? Then we can, um, go somewhere out of the way to, um, talk."

I didn't like the way her voice sounded. "What's wrong, Annalee? You sound frightened."

"Look, can you meet me, please? It's important. I have an exam this morning that I can't miss, but I really, really need to see you this afternoon. Pick me up at the SG house around two, okay? I'll be waiting for you."

I was heartened by the fact that she felt the need to keep up her schoolwork, but just the same, her uneasiness was creeping through the receiver and lodging in my throat. "Where will we go, Annalee? Why can't we talk at the sorority house?"

"We'll go somewhere private, away from . . . from people. It will be better that way." The line went dead before I could ask her anything else.

I hung up the phone and stared at the floor. My calendar was filling up quickly, but I wasn't sure I should include a visit with Annalee. Why was she so anxious to go to a private place, away from people? Was it to get me away from witnesses? Would someone else—like, say, Karen's boyfriend—be waiting there as well? My stomach ached, and I didn't think it was a result of my sugared-coffee-and-chocolate-doughnut-binge breakfast.

I glanced at the clock again and realized that I'd never make any of my appointments if I didn't get moving soon. I grabbed my purse and headed out the door.

First stop, Merriman Farms. I intended to use my twenty-odd-minute drive to figure out exactly what I was going to do or say. I was breaking the rules of etiquette by not calling first, and I distinctly remembered Chase's words: "Your article is finished, Miss Kelly." I had also managed to upset Winifred with the discovery in the dumbwaiter, and who knew what condition Constance would be in. It would be a miracle if I made it into the house at all.

My drive didn't help much, because I was still trying to sort out a story to get me inside as I drove up to the gate. I'd never get past the guard once he checked his guest register and found a big blank when it came to my name. For that matter, as angry as Chase had been the day before, he probably instructed the security folk to start shooting *before* they saw the whites of my eyes.

A somewhat smaller posse of press was still camped out across the street. The satellite trucks were gone, but the collection of bored reporters and photographers remained. Heads turned slowly as I drove past, but the urge to chase me down the lane was gone for the time being.

I pulled to a stop in front of the guardhouse. "Hi," I said. "I was here yesterday—"

The guard leaned out his little window, squinted, then waved his hand dismissively. "Yeah, yeah, go ahead. As long as you're not one of those stupid reporters."

He pressed the all-important button, and the gates swung open. I chose to file my complaint about the guard's comment referring to "stupid reporters" for another day, and waved out the car window as I drove through the gates and up the hill.

I slapped on my brakes as I pulled up to the front drive. Chase's Mercedes was thankfully missing, but a large, hunter green Land Rover sat in front of the sidewalk. I parked beside it and hopped out of the car for a closer inspection.

My stomachache was returning. A shiny new grille glinted in the sunshine and didn't offer any hint of a dent from another car.

"Can I help you with something, Kate? I don't recall that you were coming out here again today."

I spun around to face Constance, who stood on the sidewalk about ten feet away. She had on a purple, pink, and white nylon jogging suit as if she were ready to work out, but her accessories of diamond solitaire earrings and multi-carat tennis bracelet begged to differ. In addition, she held a cigarette between manicured nails and carried a tumbler of ice and clear liquid that I doubted was mineral water.

"Is there a problem with my car?" she added hesitantly.

"Hi, Constance, how are you? No, no, there's no problem. I was just admiring it," I lied. "I've always wanted a Land Rover."

She tossed her hair and took a long drag on her cigarette. She squinted through the smoke as she exhaled. "Well, I guess some people like them, but I'm tired of it. I don't have a bunch of little hoodlums to drag around to soccer practice or piano lessons, so there's really no need for me to drive something so large. Chase won't give up his midlife-crisis Mercedes, so I think I'll just sell this dinosaur and drive the extra Jag."

Never in my life have I had to succumb to ditching a Land Rover for "the extra Jag." Something told me that unless one day I win the lottery or the Pulitzer Prize, that problem won't add to the wrinkles on my forehead.

I grinned politely, then nonchalantly said, "The front grille is so shiny, did you have a new one put on recently?"

She dropped the cigarette to the sidewalk and mashed it with a bright white Nike tennis shoe. Her eyes narrowed. "We've had some work done, yes. Is there something else I can help you with? I thought Chase said you finished your article."

"I still have a couple of loose ends I'd like to tie up with Mrs. Merriman. Could I visit with her for a few minutes?"

Constance sipped her drink and looked up at the house. She shrugged her shoulders. "I don't know if that's the best idea. Mother Merriman has been acting strangely since yesterday."

"In what way?" I asked slowly, as a guilty feeling crept up from my toes. She'd probably heard dozens of arguments between Chase and Constance in the past, so all I could fathom was that my discovery in the dumbwaiter was what had sent her over the edge. The creeping guilt made it up to my lungs, and I felt like someone was squeezing off my airway. "Did something upset her?" I wheezed.

Constance nodded and took another sip of her drink. "That's an understatement. I don't know what happened, but she's been awful. She's been mumbling about the past, crying like a kid all night long. I gave up and went to bed around 1:30 A.M., but Chase sat up with her until nearly three this morning."

She smiled bitterly. "I didn't know the old lady could stay up that late anymore, but something's kicked into gear, that's for sure."

I managed to find enough breath to ask, "Did she say what upset her so much?"

"No, that's what is driving Chase crazy. She just keeps mumbling that it's all her fault and why couldn't things be different. She keeps talking like Robinson is still alive. He'd know what to do, he'd have all the answers. I have no clue what she's talking about, and neither does Chase."

Constance looked up toward the second floor again. "I think she might be having another stroke. We gave her some of the tranquilizers that Mason brought over when Karen died, but they didn't faze Mother Merriman at all. I called Mason this morning and asked him to bring over something stronger because I can't bear to baby-sit her all day again. That's why I came out here. I heard the car and thought you might be Mason."

Not in your lifetime, I thought. I looked up at the second-floor windows. "Did she ever get any sleep?"

"Finally, but not a great deal. She was up again this morning and had Maria digging in the library for a bunch of old photo albums. It took everything I had to shove Chase out the door to work. I certainly didn't want to mess with both of them today."

Constance's eyes were covered in a light blue shadow, and her lashes were caked with mascara, but all the makeup on the Estée Lauder counter in Saks couldn't conceal how tired she looked. "Oh, what the hell," she said. "Why don't you go on up? See if you can get her mind on something else. If anything, it'll give me a break for a few minutes."

She flashed an anxious look my way. "But if she's sleeping, let her be. And don't plan on staying too long. Chase will be home soon and, as usual, will be an ass. I don't want you to witness that again. I'll be around." She finished her drink and sat it on the hood of the Land Rover.

I watched her disappear around the side of the house, then I gingerly made my way to the front door. "Here goes nothing," I mumbled under my breath as I went inside.

I climbed the stairs and went directly to Winifred's sitting room. The door was ajar, and I could see the back of her braided gray hair just off to the right.

I rapped gently on the door and slowly pushed it open. "Mrs. Merriman? It's Kate; may I come in?"

She was sitting on the couch, facing the window. She didn't move at first, then slowly turned her head. I was shocked to see how much older she looked. Her normally bright eyes seemed to be swimming in a cloudy blue haze. Little wisps of gray hair tumbled out of the thick braid, and her lips were pursed so tightly that they almost disappeared into the wrinkles around her mouth.

Her voice was deeper, gravelly, and strained. "Hello, Kate. Please come in. I've been thinking of you." She stretched out her hand and gestured for me to sit near her.

I sank onto the couch and shifted a couple of old, leather-bound photo albums on the glass-topped table in front of us. Another photo album sat open on her lap. I couldn't make out the pictures without being too obvious, but it was clear to see they were old, black-and-white snapshots from what was probably the thirties or forties.

"Mrs. Merriman, I'm afraid I upset you terribly yesterday," I began quietly. "I never meant to do that. Please accept my deepest apologies."

She shook her head and shut her moist eyes. "No, dear, you did nothing. Please don't think that. Many things are weighing on my old, feeble mind, but you did not put them there. The time has come to simply face some things I've had hidden deep inside me for a long time."

She opened her eyes and rested her hand on mine, and I flinched when I felt how cold and clammy it was.

"I'm old, Kate. Many things have happened in my life—some good, but many bad. I've spent a long time remembering the good and ignoring the bad; but eventually, it all comes back to reckon with you. Someday, we'll all be accountable for our actions."

She moved her gaze to the photo album and ran her hand over the pictures, almost as if she were stroking them. "When I was your age, I thought anything was possible. My husband and I had money, friends, and power. It was a grand time. . . ." Tears once again filled her eyes as her voice trailed off.

I removed my hand from hers and reached over to her thin, brittle shoulder. "Mrs. Merriman, you look very tired. Perhaps you should lie down for a little while."

She snapped her gaze to my eyes. "And what? Sleep like a crazy old lady should? Chase and Constance already tried to make me take those sleeping pills, but I won't have any of it."

She leaned over and reached toward the vanity. She tugged a drawer open and nodded toward a handkerchief sitting on top. "Look inside that tissue, dear, and you'll find all those pills. I just stuck them under my tongue, then spit them out when they turned away. I will not be put out like some toy that's had its batteries yanked out."

I didn't know what to say, so I turned my attention to the photo album. "Are you reminiscing about some of those good and bad times?"

Winifred sighed heavily and nodded again. She shut her eyes once more for such a long time that I began to worry that she was in pain, or drifting away somewhere.

"Mrs. Merriman," I began. "Are you—"

Her eyes blazed open. "You asked yesterday how Evelyn Shelby died. It's time the truth was told. Too many years and too much heartache have passed. Yes, it was a terrible, terrible accident. It never should have happened. She fell, struck her head, and never regained consciousness. She died when Mason was just a baby, and left her poor husband alone for the rest of his life."

She looked me straight in the eyes. "I killed Evelyn Shelby."

Chapter 22

I'VE ALWAYS ENJOYED the part in movies when someone confesses. The music swells eerily, there are lots of extreme close-ups, and the tension is so thick it can be sliced and diced. That's always exciting and worthy of two handfuls of popcorn, but I admit I never quite anticipated being on the receiving end of a real-life confession.

Winifred was ready to talk after all these years, and all she wanted was to tell her story. I held her trembling hands and listened.

"Like I told you, my husband and I were very good friends with Mason and Evelyn. We did everything together, from the time before we were married until several years later. We even stood up for each other at our weddings. It was the perfect friendship, but then things changed."

Her hands tightened around mine, and she looked away. "There was a very difficult time between us that I can't go into right now, but we never resolved things. The tension just grew like a bad virus. We got together one evening to try to work things out. We tried to act like old times, but Robinson and Mason began drinking, and words were exchanged and old hurts brought back to the surface. We fell into a terrible argument, and Mason and my husband began fighting."

Her eyes shut as she pictured the painful memory. Her voice was choked with tears. "Evelyn and I were arguing as well. There was so much noise and confusion, it was terrible. She tried to strike me, and I simply shoved her. That's all, I just pushed her. I didn't mean to hit her, or intentionally hurt her. I was protecting myself. We were in a room with hardwood floors, and she slipped on a throw rug. It flew out from under her feet, and she fell backwards and struck her head on the sideboard in their dining room."

Winifred's entire body shuddered. "Evelyn was unconscious before she hit the floor. Oh, it was unbearable, so awful. Mason was dumb struck with grief, and I think I was just numb. I don't remember much after that. We agreed to keep everything to ourselves and say that she fell on the steps. I remember Robinson carrying her body over to the base of the stairs, then taking her shoe off. He carried it up a few steps, ripped a snag in the carpet, and stuck the shoe's heel in the torn place."

She buried her head in her hands. "We called the sheriff, and that was that. I was terribly affected by it all. Robinson sent me to a summer home we had on the coast. I stayed there, alone, for nearly six months. All I could think of was that I had killed little Mason's mother. I knew how much I missed my darling Chase while I was gone, and I couldn't imagine what little Mason must have been going through. . . ."

Her shoulders shook gently as she cried tears bottled up for too many years. I ran my hand along her arm, and she looked at me and said, "It was an accident, Kate, a horrible accident. I've never forgiven myself."

"What happened when you came back from the coast?" I asked quietly.

"We got on with our lives, that's all, as if it had never happened. By that time, the story of Evelyn falling down the stairs was old news. Everyone believed it; there was no need to ask any questions. Mason forgave me, but I never could look him straight in the eye again. He never remarried, and I tried to help raise little Mason, but he was such a handful. He and Chase never got along. I guess I thought putting up with his tantrums was my penance for what I did to his mother."

"Did the argument have something to do with the legend?" I asked, surmising that perhaps the foursome had found the treasure and differed on how to split the winnings. If they were such close friends, it could have been a fun adventure for them to search for the treasure, and if they actually discovered it, I could see Robinson would claim it as a family heritage. That would leave the Shelbys out in the cold, with nothing. If the treasure was as large as the legend made it out to be, that could be the basis for quite an argument.

Winifred looked at me with sad, heavy eyes. "No, it had nothing to do with it, nothing at all. If only that was the true cause, but there was much more to it. I just can't tell you about it. Some things I will take to my grave."

"Have you told anyone this story?" I asked, wondering what it was that made her confess it to me.

"No, not that I can recall. We made up our minds that evening never to tell a soul. I've carried it with me for all these years. I guess I even made myself believe the story."

A troubling thought hit me. "Did you tell Karen about Evelyn's accident?"

"Why, no, I don't think. No, I didn't. I haven't told anyone. No, I . . . I'm sure I didn't tell her."

She didn't sound too sure. What if she had told it to Karen, and Karen was holding it over Chase's head? If she had been stealing antiques from the Merrimans, what's a little blackmail thrown in for good measure? I was sure that the local gossips and media would have a field day with a torrid story like that.

My eyes drifted to the framed picture of Chase as a little boy, and I recalled Constance's comment that he would do "anything" to protect his mother.

Would he kill Karen to keep her quiet?

I squirmed in my seat. What would happen if Chase found out I knew this story? Would I be next on his list? If Winifred was so relieved to confess this to me, what was to stop her from telling her beloved son, including the fact that I also knew everything?

"What made you tell me the story?" I questioned. "Was it the note we found yesterday?"

Winifred sat up straight. "No, no, it had nothing to do with that. I asked you to ignore that note. The legend has nothing to do with Evelyn's accident. With all that's been happening the last few days, I suppose the truth just resurfaced in my memory. I'm an old woman, Kate. I need to make peace with myself. It's time I did."

While I didn't doubt that, I noticed how, once again, her complexion had been altered when she thought about the note. The tears were dry and her cheeks were red. Something about the note triggered this reaction, but what?

I ran the contents of the note through my mind and tried to link it to Evelyn's accident, but nothing seemed to fit. "The fire has been put out, but for children, the history of the world will always be critical." What did that mean? I was stumped, plain and simple.

I tried to picture the obituary I saw in Mason's dining room, but like Winifred said, the story the Merrimans and Mason Sr. concocted was neat and tidy. Evelyn fell, everyone was heartbroken, and Winifred left town. Simple, effective, but obviously not true.

"What caused the argument between your husband and Dr. Shelby?"

The color grew brighter in her cheeks, and her breathing became irregular. "It's not important, not now. Those are old secrets that should remain buried. Forever." Her face twisted and she coughed violently.

I jumped to my feet. What had I done? Winifred did not look well, and her cough was growing stronger.

"Mrs. Merriman, please try to relax. I'll get you some water, something to drink." I ran to the door. "I'll be right back, I promise."

I flew through the door into the hallway, where I crashed into none other than Mason. I was surprised and relieved at the same time.

"In there! Mrs. Merriman—I think she's ill." I looked at him and took a deep breath to steady myself. "I think she needs you."

Mason didn't say a word. Roughly pushing me aside, he stalked into Winifred's room. I watched from the doorway as he knelt beside her, took her hand, and, for the first time that I had seen, acted nearly human. He spoke soothingly and tried to steady her breathing.

He truly looked like he was helping her. Maybe he really did see her as a mother figure. She was probably the only person who'd ever paid close attention to him when he was growing up.

Her coughing spell ended, and Mason glanced at his watch and fished in his pocket for something. He searched both his coat and pants pockets with no success. He told Winifred that he had to get something from his car, then he stood and turned toward the door where I was.

I smiled and was preparing to thank him for helping Winifred, when he barreled toward me, grabbed my elbow, and pushed me into the hallway. He propelled me into the wall. "Just what in the hell do you think you were doing?"

This was one man who changed his moods as fast as the stock market fluctuated. His anger startled me.

"I wasn't doing anything. We were just talking. You know something has upset her; Constance said that's why she called you out here in the first place."

His fingers dug into my arm, and his voice was a low growl. "Go home. Get out of this house and get away from this family. You have caused nothing but trouble. I'm warning you, Miss Kelly."

"Warning me about what?" I shot back.

Mason's eyes were intensely blue and, had they the power, no doubt would have shot daggers right through me. His chiseled features were rock solid, and the corner of his left eyelid twitched repeatedly. This was not hard to miss, since we were nearly nose-to-nose.

"Just do what I say," he continued. "Chase Merriman is not someone you want to mess with, and neither am I."

If Mason had overheard the confession, it would account for his anger, but why direct it at me? Why not burst in and confront Winifred? Instead, he had acted so gentle with her.

I heard someone thumping up the staircase. Chase loomed in the hallway. This was not turning out to be a pretty scene. I wasn't sure who looked angrier, Chase or Mason, but I did know one painful thing—they were both furious with me.

"What is going on?" Chase bellowed. "What are you doing? Whose house do you think this is, Mason? Did you give up on my wife?" He gestured toward me. "Get away from her."

Oh, give me a break.

If Chase thought Mason was getting frisky with me in the hallway, he was sorely mistaken. Mason looked everything except romantic. If I hadn't been so angry, I might have processed the comment about Mason and Constance.

Mason let go of my arm and backed away, and my mouth dropped open in protest. "Mr. Merriman, how could you think—"

"Miss Kelly, do I have to take out a warrant for your arrest for trespassing on my property and stalking my family? All I have to do is make one phone call and you won't be dropping in anywhere except a jail cell for some time to come."

"Stalking?" I shrieked. "Your wife and your mother invited me to come today. I'd hardly classify that as stalking."

Mason decided to add his two cents and gestured dismissively at me. "Your visit was so successful, wasn't it, that you made Mrs. Merriman ill." He turned to Chase. "Say what you want, Chase, but if I hadn't been here, your mother would be in very serious shape right now, thanks to our nosy friend here."

My grandmother used to warn me about flies taking up residence in my mouth if I let it drop open too far, and I thought that hanging a "Vacancy" sign from my teeth would attract quite a clientele. All I could do was swing mystified looks from Mason to Chase and back again.

Chase took care of things for me, no silent pauses needed. "Out!" he shouted, pointing toward the stairs.

Had everyone forgotten Winifred? Surely she could hear the commotion, and it would only upset her further.

"Mr. Merriman, your mother—" I began.

"Get out now!" he commanded.

Mason joined in the fun and reached for my elbow again. He gave me a shove. "You heard him. Go."

Absolutely seething, I stared at the two men and tried to save face. "My purse is in the other room," I grumbled and flew past both of them into Winifred's dressing room. She was still sitting on the small couch, looking out the window, but I was certain she had heard everything in the hallway.

She turned, and my eyes met her painfully sad gaze. "Kate," she said, barely above a whisper. "You are a kind girl. I know that. I'm sorry they have treated you so poorly."

I smiled weakly, but I could tell my face was burning bright red. "Thank you, Mrs. Merriman. Perhaps someday we can talk."

Someday, but not when Chase and Mason were waiting for me to leave.

Chase stood in the doorway. His voice was quieter, but the tone was still sharp. "Mother, I'll be with you in just a minute. I have something to discuss with Mason, and I need to see Miss Kelly out."

I reached for Mrs. Merriman's hand and lightly squeezed it before I brushed past Chase. Mason stood at the top of the staircase, arms crossed and scowl deepening, to ensure my hasty departure.

As I reached the bottom step, I heard Chase order him into the music room. I glanced back upstairs and saw Chase pull the door shut behind him, but given the raised voices that floated outside, Chase and Mason were not making beautiful music. If they were fighting about my presence in the house, that would be ridiculous and not worthy of eavesdropping; but as always, my curiosity meter was smoking on overload.

I knew that it was in my best interest to walk out the door and bid Merriman Farms adieu for the final time, but I just couldn't help myself. I swiveled my head around to check for Constance or any servants. Satisfied that no one was around, I crept up the staircase.

As I ascended the steps, I fished in my purse for my tape recorder. This time it fell right into my hand, and all it took was a little pressure on the RECORD button to kick the tape into gear. I reached the second floor and flattened myself against the wall.

I was only a step or two away from the stairs, but I wasn't sure how I could successfully sprint down the steps and out the door if Chase and Mason wrapped up their altercation. If one or the other flew out of the room, there would be no logical explanation for my standing there next to the door holding a tape recorder.

My reasoning skills were lacking, but there was nothing wrong with my hearing. I discovered that Chase and Mason weren't arguing about me—they were arguing about Karen. Mason was threatening Chase that Thompson was hot on his trail. He went on to remind Chase that as acting coroner, he had close contact with police sources who told him that they, in Mason's words, were "dusting off an executive jail cell just for Chase Merriman."

Chase, in no uncertain terms, told Mason he was delusional and grasping at straws to cause problems. "You've always been jealous of me," Chase ranted, "because I had everything you didn't. I had the family, the money, the job, and the wife. What do you have? A two-bit medical practice in a flea-bitten country town where everyone compares you to your father. You're so jealous of my success that you'd do anything to get to me."

I inched closer to the door. There was no telling what would come next. I grinned as I watched the little wheels of the tape turn round and round.

The gents didn't disappoint me.

"I know about you and the girl," Mason retorted. "Everyone knows that you have the libido of a 16 year old. Have you managed to use every woman in Woodbury, and now you're moving on to college campuses? Do you just kill them when you're finished with them, Chase?"

"I did not kill that girl!" Chase shouted.

Inside the room, something fell over—or was thrown. Whatever it was, it amused Mason and he laughed.

"You're pitiful, Chase. It's only a matter of time before you're arrested. That ought to give your little corporate lawyers something to do other than go after the tree huggers who don't like your precious company snuffing out the oxygen supply each time you cut down a tree."

Mason laughed again, and his voice took on a deeply sarcastic edge. "You know, once everyone finds out about the girl, that's going to seriously hurt your chances with the under-25 crowd. And I don't know what's so wrong with Constance. She still has plenty of fire left in her. After all, I know that firsthand. I may not have your money or your family, but Chase, I've had your wife."

"You son of a bitch!" Chase roared, as the sound of glass breaking and a chair or small table scooting along the hardwood floor echoed into the hall.

I figured that it was time to hightail it down the steps and out the door. I would have loved to have heard more, but with all the noise they were making, someone was sure to investigate sooner or later. My big fear was that it would be sooner.

I clicked off the tape recorder and took the steps two at a time. I sprinted out the front door and to my car with record speed, and struggled to catch my breath. Joining a gym or at least attempting to get some legitimate exercise would have to go to the top of my to-do list. Running out of a home you've broken into or fleeing a hiding place on the upper floor of a mansion probably doesn't count as a sanctioned exercise technique.

I tore out of the driveway and down the hill, pausing only to let the main gates swing open. I had a date with Dad, who no doubt was going to love this story. He'd love it, that is, once he finished yelling at me for returning to Merriman Farms and after he thought about the implications of Mason's accusations.

Dad may try his best to be indifferent and academic about dirty deeds like these, but I know deep down he thrives on this stuff as much as Mom and I do.

My little taping experiment didn't finger Karen's killer, but as I drove onto campus, I realized one advantage it gave me. I could play the tape for Annalee and see if she recognized Chase's voice as Karen's caller. That cheered me until I remembered my suspicions about Annalee. If she was either responsible for, or an accomplice to, Karen's death, my blissful rendition of all this would give her an excellent motive for making sure no one else heard my theories.

I parked in front of Dad's office. Every scenario I'd concocted lately had someone fingering me as the next victim. Maybe John was right. Maybe I was learning too much, too soon. I didn't want to cross the wrong person, but how was I to know who it was? Everyone had a pretty good motive, but all of my suspects had equally good reasons why they wouldn't commit murder.

I opened the heavy wooden door to Dad's office and found him sitting at his desk, his glasses pushed down the bridge of his nose and his fingers joined in the shape of a church steeple. I knew I was in trouble.

"Hi, Daddy," I said quickly as I flopped into an overstuffed, horribly uncomfortable chair that dated from the Roosevelt administration. Roosevelt, as in Teddy. I wriggled around and tried to get comfortable. "I have a lot to tell you."

"You're late, my child. Do you know what time it is? I was just about to call your friend Sheriff Thompson and take out a missing person's report. I don't like you missing in action when all this murder business is floating around."

I pointedly ignored his comment. "Well, I'm here now, aren't I? Don't you want to hear all my stories? I think you'll find them very interesting."

"That's what I'm afraid of," he said sternly, but despite his best efforts a smile escaped.

"First, promise me one thing," I said.

He pushed his glasses into place and leaned back in his chair. "You should know I never make promises I might not keep, especially when you begin like that. What is this request I feel I'm going to regret?"

I grinned innocently. "I'm about to tell you many things which will probably raise your blood pressure. Just remember that most of it happened yesterday, which is in the past. And I'm sitting here with you in perfectly good health, with a squeaky-clean police record. I merely seek your advice, not fatherly lectures."

The grin faded, and Dad's skin paled a shade or two. "I don't know if I want to hear this. What have you done?"

I spit it all out as quickly as possible. I filled him in on everything, including my conversations with Constance, Winifred, Annalee, and John. More reluctantly, I told him of my encounter with Chase on the dock.

That good old Kelly trait of dropping your mouth wide open kicked in with Dad on that one. "Kate, were you out of your mind?" he bellowed. "Even if he isn't the murderer, he was about to attack you. How would you have defended yourself if that caretaker hadn't been there? What were you thinking?"

It was enough to send Dad out of his chair. He paced his cramped, book-laden office with the fury of a severe storm. I was beginning to get seasick watching him.

"That's it, that's all," he ordered. "I know you are a grown woman, but I am still your father. You are not—do you hear me?—not to go back to that house. Do you understand?"

I sank a little deeper into the crumbling stuffing of the chair and picked at a rip in the red leather armrest. "Well, Dad, there's more to the story. I'm not exactly done yet," I said in a very small voice.

He tossed his glasses onto the desk, and his hands landed firmly on his hips. I hadn't seen him so upset in a long time. A very, very long time—like maybe that lost weekend in college where I substituted a visit to my Aunt Sharon's for a road trip to Virginia Beach with a carload of buddies.

"Dad, please sit down and don't say anything more until I finish this next part."

He begrudgingly obliged me, but he almost lost it completely when I got to the part about my journey into Mason's dining room and bushes. He held to my request and didn't say anything as I continued, but his face twisted into a red mass of twitching skin, and he spurted grunts and groans of disbelief. Finally, his vocal chords kicked into gear again.

"Katherine. . . ." he began, slowly drawing out each syllable.

Uh-oh, he was using my full name.

"Dad, wait, please. That was all yesterday. Let me tell you about this morning."

He rubbed his hands over his eyes. "I can hardly wait."

It was my turn to pace the floor, wearing a path in front of his desk as I told him about Winifred's confession, Constance's Land Rover, and, of course, the argument between Chase and Mason. When I finished, I flopped back into the chair with a flourish and waited for the impending explosion.

Instead, Dad finally smiled. "You have all this on tape? Good, kid, good. You're getting more and more like your mother each day. I knew it was dangerous to let you go on stories with her all those times when you were growing up."

I would no doubt hear about my reckless acts for years to come, but for the time being, Dad was melting a bit.

"So, what do you think?" I asked.

He was quiet, then leaned forward. "I'll tell you what I think. I think you've been very foolish and need to mend your ways before you get hurt or arrested. You are not invincible, my dear Katherine."

He shrugged his shoulders. "That said, I know how you think and act. You're not about to listen to one bit of my prudent advice. So, given that unfortunate fact, I'll say this: It's getting too dangerous, and too many people are upset with you."

I shook my head to protest, but he held up a finger. "I know you're trying to help, but the murderer hasn't thought twice about taking two lives. I don't think he or she will spare you just because you think you're providing some sort of community service. What you need to do is march over to Sheriff Thompson's office and deposit this in his lap. If he believes you, you've done your job. If he doesn't, at least you know you've tried."

"But, Dad, I can't tell him everything," I reminded him. "I wasn't exactly ethical in some instances."

He nodded. "At least you can admit that. I don't advocate telling the sheriff every move you made. I don't have enough bail money in my retirement fund for that. Tell him an edited but truthful version of what you've told me. What's important is content, not how you came upon it."

He stood, put on his glasses, walked to the door, and reached for his jacket. "Our next move is to go see this friend of Karen's."

I smiled. "*Our* next move?"

He pulled on the tweed blazer. "Do not take this the wrong way, dear, but I don't trust you. Immediately following our visit to the sorority, we're going into Woodbury to see Sheriff Thompson. We'll tell him everything, together. Besides, I don't want you going to see this girl by yourself. Her insistence on meeting you somewhere alone doesn't sit well with me."

He opened the door and made a face. "Well, are you coming or not?" He didn't have to ask twice.

During our quick hop across campus, Dad asked a question that I had avoided myself. "So, do you have some kind of plan of what you're going to say to this girl?"

I glanced at him. "Why, sure."

He nodded. "You haven't a clue. I figured as much."

The SG house was deserted, which wasn't a good sign. Granted, it was early afternoon, and classes didn't wrap up until 5:30, but I had hoped to see at least a handful of sorority sisters lolling around the house, doing whatever it is that sorority sisters do.

We climbed the steps, and I rapped the brass door knocker a few times. After an eternity, the door finally opened. A short, dreadfully skinny girl with a mound of black curls that looked heavier than her total body weight opened the door.

"Hi," a tiny voice squeaked out, and I realized it was Minnie Mouse. "Welcome to the SG house. Can I help you?"

"I'm here to see Annalee Chisolm," I said. "She's expecting me."

Minnie squinted and looked past me to Dad. "Aren't you a professor? Annalee isn't in trouble, is she? She's been upset, you see. Her roommate, our sister, died, and she just hasn't been the same since. I'm sure she can make up whatever she missed."

"She's not in trouble," Dad replied. "We're here on a personal visit. May we see her?"

Minnie shifted what little weight she had from foot to foot. "Well, sure, if she's expecting you. You should know she's been acting really weird today. I think this murder—I mean, unfortunate passing—has messed with her mind."

Unfortunate passing? I never realized Emily Post had euphemisms for murder. I wondered what chapter it fell under in etiquette books?

I took a step in the doorway. "What do you mean, she's been acting weird?"

Minnie frowned. "She's been upset, of course. We all have, especially since we found out that our sister didn't die, you know, naturally." She whispered the last part, nodding wisely. "Anyway, she got really excited about something this morning, then some guy came to see her just a little while ago. I don't know what that was about, but she's been up in her room ever since. I haven't heard a peep."

Dad and I exchanged looks. Some guy? Oh, like her accomplice?

I read Dad's eyes; he was ready to turn around and head straight for Thompson's office. I admit I couldn't ignore a very prominent churning in my stomach, but I wanted to hear more.

"Who was the guy who came to see her?" I asked, taking another step inside the house. I made a face at Dad, who reluctantly joined us in the hallway.

Minnie looked perplexed. "I . . . I don't know for sure. I didn't really get a good look at him." Her face brightened. "I know, I know, I think she said something about one of Karen's boyfriends coming to get some of her stuff. Karen is our sister who, you know, well, isn't here anymore."

"Kate," Dad began. I knew what was coming, and I didn't want to hear it. I had a boyfriend to meet.

I started up the stairs. "I know where her room is. I'll just run up and visit for a minute. Thanks for your help."

I flew up the stairs with Dad at my heels, hissing under his breath, "Stop, Kate. We need to leave. This isn't wise."

Our hasty ascent captured Minnie's attention, and she followed behind Dad. We arrived at Annalee's room with a screeching halt and pileup that would have made the Three Stooges proud.

I knocked on Annalee's door but heard nothing. I knocked again and called her name. Silence. Little waves of sweat broke out across my back and neck.

"Are you sure she's in here?" I asked Minnie.

Minnie sensed something was wrong. Her eyes widened considerably. "I think so," she stammered. "I guess she could have left with that guy, but I only heard one car door shut when he left. What's going on?"

There was no time for lengthy explanations. I knocked again and called out, "Annalee, it's Kate. I'm coming in, okay?"

There was no need for me to be polite. Annalee wouldn't answer, anyway.

I opened the door to her room.

Minnie Mouse let out a ferocious scream.

Chapter 23

MINNIE SCREAMED in short, nail-on-chalkboard shrieks that sounded like the soundtrack from the movie *Psycho*. Dad and I let her do the screaming while we stood there, blindsided by the scene in front of us.

Annalee was sprawled across her bed, with her right leg and arm dangling off the edge. She was lying on her back, and the peach bedspread underneath her was twisted and pulled awry, like she had thrashed about violently. Her eyes were shut, but she was obviously not indulging in a quick snooze.

I snapped out of my stupor and ran to the bed. As I stumbled over the planters sitting everywhere on the floor, I kicked an empty beer can away from the bed. Another empty beer can protruded from underneath her hip. The bedspread and Annalee's hair were soaked with beer. Her skin was pasty and cool, and her breathing was painfully slow and labored.

I shook her shoulders gently and tried to rouse her, but she didn't respond.

"Kate, over there, in the plant," Dad instructed over the clamor of Minnie's screams.

I turned and looked at the spider plant on the floor next to me. Annalee's limp hand rested between the green leaves, and I followed her fingertips to the dirt, where an empty brown prescription bottle lay surrounded by little oval pills wedged in the dirt. I scooped up the bottle and saw that the patient's name had been ripped off the label. The name of the drug was still on the bottom left corner.

"Benzodiazepine?" I asked. "What's that?"

Minnie stopped screaming and traded her shrieks for a stunned gasp. "I'm a pharmacy major," she said. "That's a kick-ass tranquilizer. What's she doing with that? And mixed with beer? Oh, man, this is serious."

"Go call 911," Dad ordered. He placed his hands on Minnie's shoulders and shoved her out the door. "Tell them to hurry."

I stared at Annalee. "Are you thinking what I'm thinking?" I asked Dad.

He joined me on the other side of the bed. "Yes, I'm thinking that someone helped her get in this condition."

I gazed at the bottle. "I don't like the fact that there's no name on this label. If this was her prescription, why would she rip her name off the bottle?"

"Because it doesn't belong to her," Dad said grimly. "If she was going to overdose on pills, she would make sure she washed everything down to get the job done. Look at her hair and all the wet sheets. Someone made her drink the beer. It's all over the place. The kid put up one hell of a fight."

"But why Annalee? Because she knew too much?" It was a rhetorical question.

"What exactly did she say to you on the phone?"

I tried to remember her exact words. "She said that she needed to talk to me about Karen. She was upset and would only say that she had to tell me in private. I thought at the time that someone was with her, because she sounded very strange."

I couldn't stand to look at Annalee any longer. "What do we do now?"

Dad smoothed a section of her hair away from her face. "There's not a lot we can do right now. At least she's still breathing. We need to wait for the ambulance, and we call the sheriff out here. This has got to stop. I'm not letting you out of my sight until the person who is doing this is caught."

I walked to the center of the room. "It couldn't have been Chase or Mason, because they were at the farm with me. Constance disappeared, but that girl who let us in said Annalee was meeting Karen's boyfriend. So who does that leave?"

The last part of my sentence caught in the back of my throat like a jagged fish bone. It left one glaring possibility—John. I felt my face flush, and a batch of angry, frustrated tears mobilized in the corners of my eyes.

Dad read my mind. "Now, don't jump to any conclusions, Kate. The killer might be someone you've never met or considered. As for the Merrimans and Dr. Shelby, you were out there almost two hours ago. Any one of them could have left the farm and come into town."

That still didn't exonerate John. I grabbed the desk chair and dragged it over to the closet. I pushed Karen's sweaters around, hoping to find her notebook that I had stashed when Annalee left me alone in the room.

"Kate, what are you doing?" Dad spurted. "Don't touch anything. You might disturb something or, worse, put your fingerprints all over the place."

"It's okay, I know what I'm doing," I replied.

Well, maybe I didn't, because Karen's all-important notebook was missing. I hoped that meant Thompson had found it, but I also wondered if Annalee had discovered it. Look where that got her.

As I stepped off the chair, the uneven legs wobbled, and I caught myself on the edge of the dresser. In the course of my less-than-graceful dismount, I knocked a couple of cosmetics and perfume bottles to the floor. I bent to pick them up and returned them to their spot on the dresser top.

I looked at the disorganized array of stuff covering every possible inch of the dresser top and realized that the majority of it was the contents of a purse: lipsticks, gum, pens, loose change, Annalee's student ID, a MasterCard, and wadded-up dollar bills. I glanced at the floor and saw a purse tossed there, with the strap caught on a knob of the dresser. It looked like someone had dumped the contents in search of something. But what?

I dropped to my knees and looked inside the purse. Empty.

"Kate, I told you not to touch anything," Dad repeated.

"I know, I know," I said and continued to study the purse.

It was a fairly large, imitation-leather shoulder bag that could be found at any discount store. It was scratched and torn near the strap and had obviously seen better days. I held it upside down and shook it, but the only things that tumbled out were little bits of lint and the corners of gum wrappers.

I dropped the purse onto the floor again, but this time I noticed a zippered back pocket. The zipper, small and black, successfully blended into the fake leather. If you were in a hurry to look inside the bag, odds were that you'd easily miss the back pocket.

I scooped up the purse again and unzipped the pocket. It was filled with folded papers and Kleenex. I quickly opened the papers and found a class schedule, a cleaning bill, and a reminder note of a fraternity party. No good. I pulled the last chunk of notebook paper out of the pocket.

It wasn't like the other sheets; it was folded into a small square and stapled together. I peeled it open and sat back on my heels to read the big, round handwriting that I recognized—from Karen's missing notebook.

"We need to talk," the note read. "I wanted to end this at the hotel last night, but you just wouldn't listen. I figure the only way I can get you to listen to me is if I write it all down, so here goes.

"I've been driving around all night, trying to figure out what to do. This has grown into something that neither of us can handle. I'm tired of doing all your dirty work, and I never meant for us to do something illegal.

"And I can't believe you don't trust me! After everything I've done! I TOLD YOU, I don't know where that money went. I didn't even open the trunk, so how could I know you put it all there? I thought you were going to hold on to it. What were you doing—trying to dump it all on me?"

All the money—Karen must have been talking about the money they received for the stolen antiques. That would account for the loose cash Thompson found in the trunk of my rental car. I hadn't been alone at the accident after all. If I had regained consciousness in the car, there was a great chance I would have seen my fellow accident partner absconding with the money. I wondered just how much cash I had been hauling around. If it was anything near the totals Karen had tabulated in her notebook, it was a sum that would plump the pockets of the holder like a turkey full of stuffing.

"Kate, what are you reading? What is that?"

I waved my hand in the air. "Shhh, wait a minute, Dad."

I continued reading. "I know you're hurt and angry with what your father did, but that's over and done with. You can't change it. And I don't see how your plan will work. You're not thinking straight, and that scares me. You don't realize how you get when you're angry. You can't hurt her. She's too sweet, and so removed from all of this. It's not worth it for just an inheritance."

The only inheritance I could figure was what would arrive following the passing of Winifred Merriman. "She" couldn't be Constance, because she would only inherit the Merriman estate if both Winifred and Chase were deceased. That left Winifred.

Why would someone want to kill her? What did Karen mean by that? And whose father had done something so awful? She had to mean Robinson Merriman, who was anything but angelic, thanks to his roving eye, ruthless business sense, and uncomfortable penchant for staging fatal accidents.

Karen's letter must have been addressed to Chase. What would upset him so much that he'd want to hurt his own beloved mother?

I had seen the results of his violent temper a couple of times. It wasn't difficult to picture Chase whacking Karen around. And hadn't Constance said that she couldn't leave him because "he'd kill me." I had let that comment slip past as just a colorful turn of phrase, but now I wondered if she meant it literally.

The part that puzzled me most was why Chase would need the extra money from the inheritance and the antique sales. He owned a multimillion dollar company. He had plenty of cash to spread around. It just didn't compute.

I clenched the paper tighter and read more. "THIS IS WRONG. I can't be a part of it anymore. I found the bookcase, what more do you want? Unless you promise not to go on with your plan, I have no choice but to tell someone about everything, including the bookcase. I just can't deal with this. I need to get out of here and go home, away from all of you."

What was the bookcase? Had Karen solved the riddle? If she had found the treasure, maybe that was the money in my trunk. If the treasure was as large as the legend promised and Chase thought that Karen had stolen it, that would be one hell of a motive for murder.

Dad walked over to me. "Kate, what is that? Read it to me."

"It's a letter from Karen, written the day after my accident. Oh, Dad, I think it's Chase. I think he's going to do something to his mother to get at his inheritance."

I read the rest of the letter aloud. "I hope you understood the message I left this morning on your office machine. Like I said, I'll be out at the lake at our usual time and at our usual spot. If you can't promise me you'll give this up, I have no choice except to tell someone. Regardless, I'm out of here, but I can't do it on my own.

"I need money to get out of the state and enroll in another school. Bring your checkbook and we'll reach an agreement, just like your father did.

"I hate to make this so hard. I truly love you, but I'm scared about the future. There's got to be a better way to deal with this. Please, please don't hurt anyone. It won't accomplish a thing."

I looked up at Dad. "Karen unwittingly set up her own death. She was blackmailing him, and she lured him out to a secluded location. She was asking for trouble."

Dad frowned. "You found that in her roommate's purse. What was she doing with it?"

"I don't know, maybe she found it. Maybe this is what she wanted to show me." I handed the letter to Dad and picked up the purse to sort through the contents of the back pocket once more.

Minnie Mouse ran breathlessly back into the room. "I called the ambulance, they'll be here any second. Oh, no, she's paler now than she was a few minutes ago. Isn't there anything we can do?" She began sobbing great geysers, so Dad slipped a comforting arm around her tiny shoulders.

I stole a look at the wad of Kleenex in the purse. The tissues didn't look used, just folded thickly. In the middle of the large wad was a small white envelope. I looked at the familiar handwriting and read the name on the front.

Then I read it again. I pulled it closer to my face, but the name didn't magically change.

Well, well. What do you know?

That churning feeling in my stomach was now a definite case of full-blown nausea. I folded the envelope and shoved it into the back pocket of my jeans.

I went over to Minnie. "The guy who visited Annalee, did you see his car?" I demanded.

"I don't know, sort of, I guess," she said between sobs. She buried her head into Dad's chest.

That was not acceptable. Why did everyone find it so difficult to talk in straightforward, black-and-white sentences?

"Well, what was it?" I shrieked to the glob of black curls. "Think, think! It's important! What kind of car?!"

She turned, her little brown eyes the only part of her face visible beneath the unruly curls. "Don't yell at me. I don't even know you."

"WHAT KIND OF CAR WAS HE DRIVING?" I shouted as I leapt to my feet.

"A Mercedes! He was driving a Mercedes! Now, quit yelling at me!" Minnie screamed back.

The wail of a siren seeped into the room and grew louder by the second. I reached into Annalee's purse and grabbed the cleaning receipt. I turned it over and scribbled a number on the back and shoved it into Dad's hand. "Here, call John. Tell him about Annalee. Then call Sheriff Thompson. Have him meet me out at Merriman Farms."

Dad forgot his manners and shifted Minnie onto Karen's old bed. The mattress coils squeaked in protest, and Minnie stared at us with wide, frightened eyes as Dad sputtered, "Have him meet you at Merriman Farms? What are you talking about? You're not going anywhere."

"I've got to warn Mrs. Merriman," I said, shocked he needed an explanation. I brushed past him and flew down the steps.

"Kate! Come back here! Don't go out there! Do you hear me?" Dad shouted as he ran to the steps.

I heard him, but I couldn't be stopped. I bumped into two EMTs rushing up the sidewalk and pointed them upstairs. Glancing back at the sorority house as I dove into my car, I saw Dad on the porch, surrounded by the ambulance workers, who jostled him around and blocked his exit.

"Call them now, Dad, please!" I shouted as I drove away.

I flew out of campus and hit the highway. It didn't matter to me if I was pulled over, because where I was going, it wouldn't hurt to have a police escort.

I slowed to a reasonable pace as I hit Woodbury and headed for Merriman Farms. As I pulled up to the guardhouse, I honked my horn repeatedly and kept the car rolling. The perplexed guard hit the button to the gates without stopping me.

My incessant honking spurred the loitering press into action, and they leapt from their perches and pounded across the pavement. The poor guard gulped and gazed at the pack of reporters like they were a swarm of killer bees. I hit the floorboard once again and flew up the curves and twists leading to the house.

Just as I had thought. The Land Rover was gone, but a Mercedes was parked in front of the sidewalk. I jumped out of my car but stopped short.

What was I going to do? I didn't have a plan, a thought, a method, a great speech, a weapon, or anything that I needed at this juncture. All I had was an overdose of adrenaline and an envelope with a name on it.

Reality slapped me with a vengeance. I stared at the mansion and felt like Fräulein Maria in *The Sound of Music* the first time she saw Baron von Trapp's immense château full of children.

She only had to face a hoard of unruly children and the Nazis.

I had to face the Merrimans.

Chapter 24

THE MORE I THOUGHT about the note and the envelope, the more the pieces of the puzzle fell into place. However, I wasn't sure what to do now that I was at Merriman Farms. Just how does one approach a murderer? Was I dressed correctly? Was I packing the correct heat? Was I versed in the proper "Stop or I'll shoot" verbiage?

I was woefully unprepared. I wasn't packing any heat except the buckets of nervous sweat erupting out of my pores, and the only thing I could shoot off was my mouth. Like a jumpy catcher in the bottom of the ninth with the bases loaded and two outs, I went through the odd motions of licking my lips, rubbing my hand under my nose, tossing my hair, clenching my fists, and taking a deep breath. I wasn't sure what that accomplished, but it bought me a couple of extra seconds to decide what to do.

One thought propelled me ahead along the sidewalk. I had bodies, and live ones at that, on my side. The whole family had been at the estate earlier, along with the staff. I wasn't used to the comings and goings of uniformed domestic servants, but in the old British movies, they were always hovering somewhere. Surely they'd be lurking in some part of the house. If need be, I reasoned, the butler could do it.

Come to my rescue, that is.

Before I reached the top step of the porch, I noticed the front door was ajar. I hesitated, then quietly eased the door open and walked inside. I waited for Maria to appear. Or Constance or Chase. Anyone.

Nothing. Just an eerie, heavy stillness that reminded me of the air before a tornado hits.

I crossed the entry hall on tiptoe and held my breath as I stuck my head into the sitting room. "Mrs. Merriman? Mr. Merriman?" I half squeaked and half whispered. The room was empty, as was the dining room just beyond the double pocket doors.

I retraced my steps back into the hall, looked around again for signs of life, then crossed over to the door on the right, which was open wide enough for me to peek inside. It was a dark, masculine library with floor-to-ceiling bookcases that circled the entire room. Could these be the bookcases that Karen mentioned in her letter? It would take a lifetime to study each shelf in this room alone, not to mention the dozens of other bookcases that surely were scattered throughout the mansion. What had she found?

I walked over to the nearest bookcase and stared at the rows of dusty, leather-bound books. I had no clue where to look or what to look for. I reached for a dog-eared copy of *Macbeth* that was slightly out of line with the other books. Even though I pulled it out slowly and carefully, the neighboring volumes fell over on their sides. I shoved both hands toward the tumbling books, but I couldn't stop them from landing with resounding thuds.

I leaned my forehead on the remaining upright books, terrified that I would turn around and find someone standing in the doorway. I counted to ten and took several deep breaths before I spun around, prepared to heave the oversized volume of *Macbeth* at the person who was in the room with me.

No one was there.

I tiptoed toward the staircase. I had come here, hadn't I, to warn Winifred that she was in danger. Why not bound upstairs like I had planned? It was one thing to surge into the house with such noble thoughts, but another thing to find the place so hushed and—dare I say it?—dead. I took a step up, then stopped, remembering that Constance and Chase had emerged from under the stairs during their rather infamous argument about me.

I backed off the step and decided to explore just to be sure no one was lurking under the stairs. I circled a tall potted tree near the banister and tripped over a small bump. I looked down, expecting to see a ripple in the Oriental rug below my feet. It was much more than that. I clapped my hands over my mouth, sucked in a scream, and flattened myself against the wall opposite the staircase.

I had tripped over a hand. Maria's hand.

She was lying facedown, her left arm outstretched and her hips twisted in a lump. Her collar was stained with splotches of bright red blood that I followed up into her dark hair, which looked sticky and matted. She wasn't moving and neither was I.

I stared at her body and struggled against waves of nausea and dizziness, then I dropped to my knees and felt for her pulse. It was there, weak and thready but chugging along. Maria had joined Annalee in the ranks of the alive-but-ailing unconscious.

I sat back on my heels and tried to stop shaking. A large brass candlestick smeared with blood caught my eye on the floor by Maria's arthritic knees. Trying to control my heaving breaths, I shut my eyes.

When I opened them, I noticed the bookcase which supported the stairs. I focused on the second shelf from the floor. I blinked a few times and leaned closer over Maria. Just above the curve of her hip was a deteriorated, aged, leather-bound book titled *The History of the World.*

"The fire has been put out, but for children, the history of the world will always be critical."

Oh, my. Just how critical was it?

I reached over Maria's hip and tried to pull the book off the shelf without bumping into her. It wouldn't budge. I tugged at the book once more, but a thunderous crash roared above my head and I jumped. I looked up at the ceiling and heard a muffled cry of "No, no!" that sounded hauntingly like Winifred.

I scrambled to my feet and took the steps two at a time, not sure what I was heading into, but knowing that Winifred sounded like she needed help in the worst way. As I bounded up the stairs, I fished in my purse for my tape recorder. I hit the RECORD button and stashed it in the pocket of the blazer I had tossed on before I left my house.

I reached the top of the stairs and saw that the door to Winifred's bedroom was open. Without thinking, I ran to her room and discovered what I had feared. She was on the losing side of a struggle with a big pillow smashed against her face, thanks to the heavy pressure of someone she had trusted for years.

I took a flying leap onto his back and wrapped my arms around his neck. "No! Leave her alone! Don't do it!"

I had taken him by surprise, but Mason recovered quickly. The "oof" that he emitted when I jumped on him was replaced with a growl that started somewhere in his toes and worked its way out of his mouth as he stood upright, with me dangling on his back like a monkey. He quickly bent over again, then snapped up straight and plowed me backwards into the doors of an antique wardrobe. I heard the wood splinter and felt the air rush out of my lungs as I slammed against the wardrobe and sank to the floor in a heap.

I tried to suck air back into my lungs and ignore the stinging sensation spreading across my back. Mason faced me. Winifred weakly pushed the pillow away from her face and pleaded, "No, Mason, don't hurt her. Calm down, you don't know what you're doing."

"Shut up!" he ordered, then he turned his attention back to me. "You. You never know when to quit, do you? You just couldn't leave well enough alone."

I was somewhat delighted that I had enough breath to make my voice work. "I didn't do a thing, Dr. Shelby. You've done it all. Your first mistake was when you ran *me* off the road instead of Karen. But then, she led you right to the lake the next day, didn't she? That probably made your day. As always, she made things easy for you."

He swept his hand across a nightstand, sending the assorted bottles, clock, and bedside lamp crashing to the floor. "You don't know what you're talking about. Shut up. I'm sick of your stories."

"They're not stories, Dr. Shelby. Karen stole the antiques and sold them for you, and you kept the cash. But then you began to trust her, and you told her about your secret. You killed Karen because she was threatening to expose your secret, and then you killed the antique store owner because he could identify you. I just happened to catch you, that's all."

I slowly rose from the floor, but Mason lurched into action and grabbed my shirt collar. He pulled me upright and once again slammed me against the wardrobe.

I tried to push him away, but he caught my left arm and twisted it around to my back. He crunched his other arm around my neck and pushed me out into the hall. I tried to kick and drag my feet, but Mason's bulk was winning, hands down. I was pressed so close to him that my cheek scraped across the stubble on his chin and his watch face dug into my neck. I was afraid to try to trip him; he had my arm twisted at such a painful angle that I felt sure it would pop out of its socket with only the slightest provocation.

We reached the staircase, and he spun me around once more, his hands digging into my shoulders as he pushed me backwards over the banister. The upside-down room below me began spinning, and I gave up clawing at Mason and, instead, desperately gripped the banister as best I could.

He leaned over the top of me and bore his narrow blue eyes into mine. "You think you're so smart, Miss Kelly, but you don't look too smart right now. You look positively frightened. As you should be, because I'm finished dealing with you. Karen learned her lesson, and you will, too."

The small of my back was screaming in pain, and I didn't know how much longer I could hold my head upright without letting it tumble back and face the ground floor. I needed to buy time. Someone had to be in the house. And where in the world was Sheriff Thompson? Surely he didn't ignore Dad's phone call.

If all else failed—a prospect I didn't want to think about—at least the tape recorder was running in my pocket.

I started talking quickly. "I know your secret. I saw the clippings in your house. It took a while, but I figured it out. Robinson Merriman is your father. He had an affair with your mother, and you were the unfortunate outcome. That makes you the oldest Merriman son and only a blood test away from Chase's money. What are you going to do? Kill Winifred and Chase? Are they next on your list?"

Mason relaxed his grip just a tiny bit. He actually seemed pleased for a split second, then his face darkened again. "How did you get in my house?"

He lifted me a couple of inches, then dropped me onto the banister again. I concentrated on holding on; I never cared for gymnastics and had no urgent desire to do a backward flip off the balcony, especially since there was no net below to catch me.

"The Merrimans have ruined my life," Mason muttered. "Robinson humiliated my father, and Winifred killed my mother in cold blood. I heard her this morning. You know it's true, and just like she said, they carried on like nothing ever happened.

"My mother was the only person who cared for me," he continued. "I never understood why my father ignored me. Nothing I did was ever good enough for him. Then I found out about Robinson. He ignored me too. I'm his son, his oldest son, and he knew it. But it was always Chase. Chase was the little treasure. I was just the poor little kid without a mother who was shipped in to play with the crown prince."

He pushed me farther over the banister, his hurt feelings turning the tide to anger again. "But now it's my turn to play. I'm tired of being compared to a man who was never a father to me, in more ways than one, and I'm tired of Chase enjoying what is rightfully mine. He's always taken things from me, including Karen. I couldn't let him have her, too, even though she was more trouble than she was worth."

"What about her roommate? Why did you have to hurt Annalee?" I demanded.

Mason actually chuckled. "The stupid little bitch was trying to blackmail me. Somehow she found out about Karen. She was all melodrama and secret meetings. Ridiculous. She was wasting my time, so I showed her what happens when you screw up a blackmail attempt—and a pathetic one at that. No one wastes my time," he menaced. "No one is going to stop me from gaining my heritage. Merriman Farms belongs to me. No worthless reporter is going to keep me from it. You, Miss Kelly, you're wasting my time."

His hands slipped from my shoulders and anchored themselves firmly on my throat. His grip was crushing, and I gasped for air with every ounce of energy I had left. I let go of the banister and flailed one hand around a small table next to us. My hand landed on a figurine that had been knocked to its side.

I grabbed it and, in one quick fling, swung my arm toward Mason. I clipped him on his jaw and heard a pop that I hoped was a bone cracking. He recoiled with a roar of pain and, in the process, pulled me up and tossed me aside as he grabbed his jaw.

Fortunately, he was no longer trying to strangle me or shove me over the balcony. Unfortunately, I landed against the end of the railing at the top of the stairs.

My already-bruised head crashed against the corner of the banister, and my ankle twisted off the edge of the top step. In a split second, I was tumbling down the staircase so quickly I didn't have time to comprehend what was happening.

I landed at the bottom, stretched out along the first three steps. I was on my stomach, and my left arm was stuck underneath me.

Every bone, muscle, and skin cell in my body ached. My hair hurt. I saw stars. I lay there quietly for a few seconds and tried to decide if I was still alive.

I figured if I were dead, I wouldn't feel like my body had been sent through a wood chipper. From all the late-night documentaries I'd seen, I thought I was supposed to be hearing beautiful music and seeing a bright white light welcoming me to the next level. I slowly lifted my head, which weighed several hundred tons, but I didn't see angels.

I saw Mason.

"You just don't give up, do you?" he said with just a little admiration. He started down the stairs, cradling one hand on his rapidly swelling chin. I couldn't fight him if I wanted to. He had won. I was a spider he was ready to squish, and there was nothing I could do to stop him.

"Freeze, Dr. Shelby! Don't take another step!"

I wasn't sure if the voice I heard behind me was real or a wishful hallucination. I couldn't turn around to look, so I watched to see if Mason had heard the same voice.

He had. He stopped on the steps and stared straight ahead. His face relaxed, his voice softened. "Sheriff Thompson, I'm so glad you're here. There's been a terrible accident. Miss Kelly tripped on a loose piece of carpet and fell down the stairs. I just came out of Mrs. Merriman's room when I heard her fall."

Thompson, thankfully, didn't buy it. He spoke in a deep, official police growl. "I said, do not move. Dr. Shelby. Stay right where you are."

Mason took another step down. "I don't know what the problem is, Sheriff, but you can see she's badly hurt. I'm a physician, she needs my assistance."

I watched as Mason reached under his suit jacket with his right hand. From my fortunate angle I saw a glint from a gun barrel.

I lifted my right arm and pointed to him. "Gun!" I squeaked out as best as I could.

Seemingly in slow motion, Mason whipped the weapon out and pointed it over my head. There was a burst of light and a deafening twin blast before he lunged backwards and slammed against the stairs. His face twisted, and a small red circle rapidly enlarged on his shirt and jacket below his collarbone. He slid down a few steps before coming to a stop, his feet just a couple of inches away from my head.

In the next few seconds, slow motion lapsed into fast motion. There was much shouting from uniformed officers, who spread out into the hallway and sprinted around me. One stopped at Mason, while another bounded on up the stairs. He paused near the top step and bent to pick up something.

"It's a tape recorder, Sheriff," he called out. My blessed little tape recorder had survived. He pushed REWIND for a second before Mason's voice cracked out from the scratchy tape, staking his claim on the Merriman fortune. I couldn't have told it better myself.

Mason even managed to moan in disgust.

Thompson, for his part, was kneeling on my right. "Don't move, Miss Kelly. It's over, everything is going to be all right."

Dad appeared on my left. I had never been happier to see him. He reached over and squeezed my right hand. "Hang in there, kid, you're gonna be okay."

He might have said more, but another set of footsteps pounded up behind me. The prettiest brown eyes I knew looked awfully worried. John stared at Mason, then dropped to his knees and purred soft promises that all was well. I wasn't too sure about that, given the way I felt, but at least I could see my two favorite guys, Dad and John.

Make that three—I never thought I'd say it, but I was pretty happy to see Sheriff Thompson and his gun, too.

Maybe all was well, after all.

I closed my eyes.

Chapter 25

REMIND ME AGAIN that vacations are supposed to be restful.

I managed to get some rest, that's for sure, but I did not rest in a fancy hotel suite, with chocolates on my pillow and little fragrant soaps in the bathroom. I wound up in yet another boring, badly decorated hospital room, thanks to my little encounter with Mason.

I woke up to find myself drugged, wrapped in bandages, and taped and wired to all sorts of nifty little machines which belched and beeped a veritable chorus of chimes every few seconds. I also woke up to find John holding my hand and staring into my bleary eyes.

A huge grin spread across his face. "Hey, soldier, welcome back."

I'd like to blame the various medications dripping into my veins, but I couldn't help but grin back. "Hiya, gorgeous."

He laughed. "It's good to hear your voice. You had us worried there for a while."

"I like to keep things interesting."

"You outdid yourself this time," John said.

I wanted him to keep holding my hand and go on to say more wonderful things about me, but unfortunately he stood and started playing doctor, poking me here and there and acting way too official for my taste. It dawned on me that I didn't feel so good. Movement of any kind was difficult, and I discovered that not only was my left arm wrapped tightly from my fingers to my elbow, but I was wearing what was probably an ugly white gauze turban around my head.

I reached up to feel it. "What is this monstrosity?"

John pulled my hand down. "Don't mess with it. It's there for a reason. You smashed your head again pretty hard, not to mention your sprained wrist and all the bruises."

"I didn't do it for fun."

"I know," he said quietly. He gently poked my side. "Do you feel any sharp pains around here?"

"I don't feel perfect, why?"

"Our friend Dr. Shelby managed to crack a couple of your ribs. It's gonna hurt for a while. Just be still. There's not a lot I can do about broken ribs; you'll have to let them heal, along with the rest of you."

"Mason. What happened to him?"

John looked away. He moved over to an enormous bunch of yellow roses sitting on the dresser. "Did you see these flowers? There's over two dozen roses here. They're from the Merrimans. I'd add to the flowers, but I've been busy with you."

That didn't sound promising for Mason, but John had brought up another point—the Merrimans.

"Is Mrs. Merriman okay?"

John looked relieved that I changed the subject. "Yeah, she's fine. We brought her in, but she was just badly shaken." He plucked a rose from the vase and brought it over to me. "Kate, you saved her life. The Merrimans are very, very grateful. Chase and Constance were here earlier, but you were still asleep."

"I'm glad I was there for Winifred, but I certainly opened a new can of worms for Chase." I sniffed the rose. "The Merrimans are aware of the whole paternity issue, aren't they?"

John nodded. "Well, yeah, it's all come out in the open, thanks to your tape. Chase came into the house just after you passed out. You can imagine how he felt when he saw you . . . and Mason . . . and his mother . . . and the maid . . . and the police. It took a while, but after all the commotion died down, the story unfolded."

"And Mason?" I tried again.

Before John could answer or avoid the question again, Dad entered the room, carrying two large coffees. He set them down next to the flowers and rushed over. "Kiddo, good to see you. Don't you ever scare me like that again, understand?"

I listened to John and Dad explain what I missed. They avoided talking about Mason, but ticked off the list of casualties. Winifred was back at Merriman Farms, resting, and Maria was in another part of the hospital, no doubt wearing a similar fashion statement like my turban. She had a concussion and a bad cut on her scalp, but she'd be back to managing the Merriman household soon enough.

Annalee was also a new occupant at Woodbury Memorial. The combination of alcohol and tranquilizers that Mason shoved down her throat nearly proved deadly, but she was on the way to recovery. The tranquilizers, as I had thought, actually belonged to Winifred. I remembered seeing Mason fish in his pocket for them before he realized they weren't there. They weren't in his pocket because the empty bottle was lying in Annalee's houseplant.

As it turned out, Karen had given Annalee the letter to drop off at Mason's house, but in her perpetual, disheveled rush, Annalee shoved it in the back pocket of her purse and promptly forgot about it. When Karen turned up dead, Annalee was so upset, she never stopped to think about the letter. She didn't even know Mason. All she had was the address on the envelope. If only she had remembered it sooner, things might have turned out much differently.

She finally rediscovered the letter, read about Karen's plan to blackmail Mason, and decided to give it a try herself. She called him, got nervous, and called me.

The story about the letter reminded me of the bookshelf. I told John and Dad about it, and Dad placed a quick call to Thompson. That was enough action for me, and I fell asleep while Dad was on the phone.

The next time I woke up, there was a new guest in my room along with Dad and John—Sheriff Bowman Thompson himself, big tan hat and all the trimmings.

"Miss Kelly," he began. "I'll forgo my lecture about interfering in police business. Just know that it will come eventually. I'm glad to see you're feeling better."

I didn't tell him, but I actually felt worse. The aches and pains John had warned me about were paying a visit. I simply nodded and asked if there was any news.

My hunch about the history book paid off. Once Thompson had read Karen's letter, he, too, figured that the bookcase comment was important, but he didn't know where to begin looking. Chase and Constance were clueless, as well.

Winifred finally broke down and admitted the key to the riddle was indeed in a book somewhere in the house. Years ago, she and Robinson discovered the book but were disappointed to learn that the "treasure" was actually several hundred dollars in Confederate money stuffed between the pages. She had forgotten the name of the book until she saw the note I found in the dumbwaiter.

What caused her to become so upset was that she realized that the book now held another treasure of sorts.

Proof that Mason Shelby Jr. was actually Mason Merriman.

When Evelyn Shelby became pregnant by Robinson, the Merrimans and Shelbys agreed to keep the child's paternity a secret. When Mason was born, his birth certificate listed Mason Sr. as his father. However, a legal document was drawn up between Mason Sr. and Robinson which admitted paternity. In addition, the men worked out a substantial payoff to keep the issue quiet, and Robinson took charge of the documents detailing paternity and the payments. He hid them in the *History of the World* book, hence the note that "for children, the history of the world will always be critical."

Mason Sr. kept hidden records, as well, and Mason Jr. eventually discovered them when he began sorting through his father's belongings. The only problem was that the records were handwritten. He had no legal proof of the paternity record that he could use to stake a legal claim to the Merriman fortune. Mason Sr.'s records noted that the two couples had used a book as the final hiding place for the documents, but he never wrote where it was. Their obvious cover-up and the lack of concrete proof stirred Mason Jr.'s deep resentment, which erupted into his murderous fury.

He was never in love with Karen, or Constance, for that matter. His affair with Constance was extra salt to rub into Chase's wounds, and Karen was merely a safe, easy way to tear the Merriman house apart in search of the documents. His fatal flaw came when his rage overtook him and he killed Karen before she told him which bookcase held the answer.

Thompson paused and chose his words carefully. "In light of all the help you, uh, actually gave my investigation, for now I'm not going to ask you how you got inside Dr. Shelby's house. I don't think I want to know. We'll just pretend it didn't happen."

John became preoccupied with the stethoscope hanging around his neck. "I had to tell him," he explained to me. "Plus you mentioned it on the tape, remember? And I did see Walenza's ledger book in Mason's house. You missed that, but I stole—um, I mean, borrowed— it when I picked up his old patient files."

I grinned at John, then glanced at the deepening frown on Thompson's face and scooted a little farther under the covers. He couldn't yell at me too much, could he? After all, I was totally defenseless, and I brought in his killer. That should make him happy.

Thompson continued, "Again, I'll ignore the fact that both you and Dr. Donovan conveniently managed to be in his house on the same day. We've now secured the scene and confiscated the old checks, photos, and files you both apparently shuffled through."

Now it was Dad's turn to waver. "I, uh, had the obligation to tell him what you told me, Kate."

"And I didn't see the dining room stuff," John defended. "I just found the ledger book and realized that Mason was involved in the shop owner's murder. I was going to tell you, Sheriff. I was afraid Kate was getting too close to the truth, and I didn't want to see her in danger. I wanted to throw her off Mason's scent before . . . well, before all this happened."

Thompson glanced to the ceiling and begged, "Lord, deliver me from the clutches of amateur sleuths."

I ignored his plea. "But why the antiques? What was the purpose behind stealing all those? Mason's a doctor, and he inherited his father's money. He couldn't be that destitute."

Thompson nodded. "Looks can be deceiving. Dr. Shelby was losing a lot of his father's old patients, and he was spending so much time trying to prove he was Robinson Merriman's son that he didn't pick up very many new ones. When I went through his credit history, I discovered he has a lot of debt, not to mention an affinity for gambling. The Merrimans' antiques were easy money, plus it was a little method of digging away at the family that had caused him so much pain.

"I thought you might be interested to know that Dr. Shelby was behind your accident," he continued. "A DMV check showed that he also owns a Ford Explorer, which is in a repair shop in Richmond."

"But Constance's Land Rover—" I began.

"Chase brought that up, himself. As you're aware, the Merrimans are experiencing marital difficulties," Thompson said delicately.

"That's an understatement," I said.

Dad frowned. "Now, Kate, that's not nice."

Thompson fought a slight grin. "As you also probably know, Constance Merriman has a bit of a drinking problem. She and Chase had a marital spat over his relationship with the college girl, and she took off in her Land Rover while she was under the influence. She didn't make it to the front gate before she ran off the road and hit a post. In the meantime, the girl was murdered, and Chase realized he was the prime suspect."

"And all the evidence," I offered, "including the wrecked car, pointed directly at him, and he didn't have an alibi to sit on. And yet he realized what could happen to his business if this tawdry story got out, so he was busy trying to cover his and Constance's tracks."

"Precisely," Thompson replied. "We're not sure why the money wound up in your trunk. The clerk at the car rental agency said he arrived earlier in the day and placed it there. Maybe he was going to double-cross her by making it look like she was holding the money from the sales of the stolen goods."

"What a guy," John mumbled.

"But how is he dealing with the news of his new big brother?" I asked.

Thompson, Dad, and John exchanged looks. "Well, he's more concerned right now with all the press attention," Thompson said. "It's quite the story at the moment. Plus, I imagine he and Constance have a lot to discuss about their future. He'll have to work through the information about Dr. Shelby eventually, but not right away."

"Mason didn't make it," John admitted quietly.

Oh. I can't say I was surprised; when I last saw Mason, he was lying on the steps and blood was charging across his shirt. I can't say I was happy, either. He had hurt so many people and tried his best to kill me, but at the same time, it was all a sad, twisted reaction to something that was beyond his control.

The secrets of families are often best kept quiet. After all, they become secrets in the first place for a reason.

I had played a part in exposing the secret, but the Merrimans didn't hold it against me. It would have come out eventually, and Mason had been on such a rampage that there was no telling what he would have done next, or who would have been hurt in his search for the truth. In fact, the Merrimans were quite happy that I'd kept

Winifred safe.

Since John held me hostage at Woodbury Memorial for several days, I had the opportunity to have a steady stream of visitors. Constance dropped by with more flowers each day, until my room looked like a florist's annex. Each time, she apologized for everything possible and even things that had nothing to do with this mess. She told me that she was going away to their beach house in St. Croix. She wasn't sure what would become of her marriage, but she thought that the time apart might clear her mind.

A subdued and jittery Chase visited me also. The first time, he came alone and stuttered and mumbled his apologies for his previous hostile behavior toward me. We avoided talking about Mason, but it was clearly on his mind. Every time we'd wander in the neighborhood of the subject, he'd turn red, stumble over his words, and promptly talk about something else. He seemed relieved to talk about his affair with Karen instead.

The second day, Winifred accompanied him, and she brought a huge bunch of multicolored day lilies to add to my floral collection. I admit, I looked less than beautiful, but I didn't expect her to start crying when she saw me. Once she composed herself, we talked for a long time, while Chase paced in the corner. Winifred informed me that her family would pick up the tab on my hospital stay and any additional medical costs.

She also asked me to return to Merriman Farms and write a new article on its many flower gardens. "We've deprived you of the chance to return to work for a while, and I think your magazine readers would prefer that story to one about a useless old legend," she summarized wisely.

So on the whole, I suppose, things worked out for the best. My editor wasn't too thrilled to learn that I'd be out of work for a couple of weeks, but he cheered up considerably when I promised the article Winifred suggested.

Mom returned from her trip before I was released from the hospital, and she and Dad promptly hustled me home, where they spoiled me rotten. I could get used to all that attention. A lot of attention also came from a certain doctor, who revived the time-honored tradition of house calls—and daily ones, at that.

I'm still pretty bruised and battered, but I am feeling much better these days. And have I mentioned how much fun it is to play doctor with a doctor?

It's not going to be easy to leave Williamsburg and go back to work. I may have to find an excuse to hang around for a while. I might come down with a cold or something.

You never know when you're going to need a doctor.